EATING PAVLOVA

EATING PAVLOVA

D.M. Thomas

Carroll & Graf Publishers, Inc.
New York

Author's Note

In 1938 Sigmund Freud was able to leave Vienna for London. With his wife Martha, youngest daughter Anna, and sister-in-law Minna Bernays, he lived first in Primrose Hill and then at Maresfield Gardens, Hampstead. Here he died on 23 September 1939. Anna Freud, whose special gift lay in the psychoanalysis of children, lived and worked in the house (now the Freud Museum) until her death in 1982.

Most of the first chapter of this novel appeared initially as chapter 11 of *Lying Together* (Victor Gollancz, London, and Viking Penguin, New York, 1990), in which it was related during a shamanistic trance by a Soviet poet.

Copyright © 1994 by D.M. Thomas

Originally published by Bloomsbury Publishing Limited, London.

First Carroll & Graf edition 1994

Carroll & Graf Publishers, Inc.
260 Fifth Avenue
New York, NY 10001

Library of Congress Cataloging-in-Publication Data

Thomas, D. M.
    Eating Pavlova / D.M. Thomas.—1st Carroll & Graf ed.
        p.   cm.
    ISBN 0-7867-0142-0 : $21.00
    1. Freud, Sigmund, 1856-1939—Fiction.   2. Fathers and daughters—England—London—Fiction.   3. Cancer—Patients—England—London—Fiction.   4. Psychoanalysts—England—London—Fiction.   5. Freud, Anna, 1895–   —Fiction.   6. London (England)—Fiction.   I. Title.
PR6070.H58E23   1994
823'.914—dc20   94-19644
                                                                              CIP

Manufactured in the United States of America

For Andrew and Margaret Hewson

I dream, as I have often done, that he is here again. The main role is played not by my longing for him but rather by his longing for me. In the first dream of this kind he openly said: I have always longed for you so.

The main feeling is that he is wandering about (on top of mountains, hills) while I am doing other things. Eventually he calls me to him. I am very relieved and lean myself against him, crying in a way that is very familiar to us both. Tenderness. My thoughts are troubled.

ANNA FREUD

ONE

l

Existence almost unbearable. Fortunately Schur promises to
keep his promise.

'Is this the war to end all wars?' he asks. 'For me at any
rate,' I reply.

There will be a measure of relief even in Anna's sorrow.

I dream that we live in a mare's field. It must relate to my
first sight of my mother's genitals – but not the last, for we
lived in just one room.

I could never see her thick black tuft of pubic hair without
longing to go with my father into that dark Moravian pine
forest, stretching all the way from the Carpathians, which
surrounded our home. The constant view of so much hair
excited in me a love of nature, wild nature, that has never
waned. The hairs prickle on my nape whenever I see a picture
representing a deep, dark forest. I must go there.

If my past work has any value at all, it lies in my
having exhorted my readers to love the forest depths; to feel
the enchantment of their vast silences, their cunning hidden
flowers; their murky scents; the sighing of their leaves; the
teasing hints of sunlight or moonlight through the tree tops.

Happy is the infant whose father fills him with a passion
for forests by coupling with his bride in full view.

My mother was a woman of great piety and orthodoxy;
and when she allowed me to look into her forest depths I found
them good. Our room was an ark; and I had no wish for the
dove to bring home a green leaf. I hated the dove; I preferred
the raven, that black leaf torn from the dark forest.

The other children, my playmates, meant little to me; so little that one day they all rose from the field and vanished, like angels.

Like my patient the Wolf Man, I was fortunate or unfortunate enough to be lying awake in the night when the five candles of my destiny glimmered on the tree outside. The candles glimmered on the moon-blanched tree like Christmas candles. I have heard it denied that the candles – different candles – glimmer for every child when he or she reaches the age of three or four; but of course that denial is nonsense; simply, most children are asleep in the depths of the night when the candles shine out.

They represent the hand we have been dealt in life, for life. In my case, the first and most important candle stood for the dark forest. Ever and ever, as I have said, I return to it. Another candle stood for the trivium, the place where three roads meet. I know beyond question that I am Oedipus and he is I. I should make it clear that I hold no truck with the theory of reincarnation; it is just as clear to me that I am Marie Romanov, whose life overlapped with mine. But that past tense, 'overlapped', is simply a necessary fiction. All life is contemporaneous, is now. At this very moment, Oedipus stands at the crossroads, killing the testy man, his father. I am at that crossroads.

As with Oedipus, often we are compelled to relight the candle against our will. It was the case with my first sexual experience. The young woman in question, a casual acquaintance of my family in Vienna, had inflamed me with cunning caresses. She was the type of young woman who loves danger; and she insisted that we lie down in the entranceway to a park. At night, carriages containing prostitutes and their clients would come hurtling out of the park towards the entrance, and they could come from two directions. Because the drives curved, it was impossible to see the carriages before they were almost on top of you. We lay down and made love, in extreme danger.

Since I was unprepared, lacking a condom, she and I

4

were endangered from two directions in another sense also: from disease (for we were strangers to each other) and from a pregnancy desired by neither of us.

It would have been so easy and commonplace to move into some bushes; but my partner insisted that I light my second candle.

A third candle was ambivalence, and usually takes the form of two women who are close allies and rivals. The woman Rebecca, my father's childless and rejected wife, haunts my early years. I would often see her watching me as I played in the fields. She was close at hand at my birth as well as at my conception; and she and my mother were often together. What my father felt about this conjunction I can only guess. When we moved from Freiberg, Rebecca followed us at a distance. I don't know where she lived, but years later, as I walked to the *gymnasium*, I would often turn a corner and see Rebecca's burning eyes.

I hated Vienna, because we now had several rooms and so I was further from the forest.

Days and nights merge in a common pain, relieved scarcely at all by Schur's drugs.

I dream that I am visited by a poet called T.S. Eliot. This is surely a babyhood memory, slightly corrupted, of seeing the word 'toilets' reflected fleetingly in my nurse's spectacles, when we travelled from London to Dover to sail for the Continent. A great fuss was made of us on that trip, according to my mother. As well as our maid, Martha, we had her sister Minna with us. I was very upset, I have been told, because we had to leave our chow, Lün, behind, owing to quarantine restrictions.

En route for Austria, we stayed overnight in Paris. For many years I was convinced we stayed with a lady by the name of Marie Bonaparte. I think it likely that some enthusiastic exponent of Paris's history must have spoken the names Marie Antoinette and Napoleon Bonaparte in my hearing.

It would be extremely tedious to go through my life chronologically; therefore I shall break off, from time to time. 'From time to time' is a meaningless phrase, all time

5

is instant. The fly, which has settled on my forehead and reads to me from the Sixth Book of the *Aeneid*, is the same fly which buzzes round the head of Vergil in Mantua. Man is more individuated than the fly – but not by a great margin. I know, for instance, that I am Marie Romanov, struggling through snowdrifts in the Winter Palace in Petersburg, and finding the gold clock still ticking at her bedside. I have even dreamed as Marie Romanov: a nightmare in which I and all my family were taken down into a cellar and shot.

They say the child is father to the man; yet looking back, across those immensities, those aeons, separating myself now from myself then, I can see almost nothing that I owe to him, almost nothing we have in common. Yet also, at the same time, I smile with his smile, weep with his tears.

And my beloved mother – can it be that she ever existed? The years without her stretch away; years in which I have done without her well enough, have been sometimes happy, sometimes sad for other reasons than her eternal absence.

And yet the years have lessened the gap in age between us: she is more like a sister to me now. Sometimes I find myself calling her, in my thoughts, 'Anna', as a brother would, or even a father. When I am being helped into a bath of hot water, however, I draw in my breath and cry out for her: 'Mama! Mama!'

To tell you something very strange, there are times when she returns, and fusses over me as before.

I said to Schur, after reminding him of his promise, 'Tell Anna.' Isn't that odd?

I understand life, and the family ties that make up almost all of it, much less than I ever did. Families are like constellations of stars: we see each one as an entity, because they make some recognisable design, yet the individual stars are scattered all over the universe, apart.

And marriage? It is like an endless, exhausting game of tennis, deuce after deuce. No wonder its most common term is love.

Anna, my mother, is standing beside me now, I sense it. She has returned again, and feels lost, unable to do anything for me.

A dream I had not so long ago took me back to my first years in Vienna. I am waiting for my mama, and neither Martha nor Minna can comfort me. She is away for hours; perhaps a whole day. I think she has left me for ever. She went away with some men in brown uniforms, and will not come back to her little boy.

I do not understand the memory. I scarcely know which is memory and which the recent dream. The men in brown uniforms must belong to the dream: an image of defecation. My mother would never have left me without telling me when she would be back. She was not the kind of mother who by carelessness would make her child feel insecure.

I was quite sick at the time. I was a very sickly child, and so my memories of those first years are dark. I was in bed almost continuously.

There was something wrong with my mouth, which stopped me from talking properly.

I remember I had a dream, when I was five or six, of all the books in my mother's library being thrown on to a bonfire with piles of other books and burnt. I must have been jealous of her life away from me, and wished to have her entirely to myself.

Ah! a very early memory . . . Just a flash. An autumnal garden bordered by shrubs . . . A maid, Paula, trimming them. I am in a swing-couch. The garden resembles what I have been told of Primrose Hill.

Nothing connects. Nothing explains why we are here. A banshee wails. Anna, sitting near me embroidering, rises and goes out. She comes back carrying a shaman's mask. She asks me to reconsider my decision never to wear one; I shake my head. She bends over me, her bright beads swinging, and kisses me tenderly.

Dreams, dreams . . . Often, though, with a most vivid

7

reality. Anna as shamaness! I'm handing the mask over to her; I'm leaving her to fight the banshees and all the dark forces.

2

I am giving up my kingdom, like Lear. To my three daughters. Their names are Mathilde, Sophie and Anna. Woman is always threefold. The three Fates, three Furies. Mother, wife and daughter. Midwife, mistress and layer-out.

I rest in my hanging shroud in the sun-drenched garden. There has never been such a September, Jones says. Two wasps buzz around a sticky lemonade glass. Martha brought me the lemonade; also a photograph album. I must take farewell of the living and the dead.

Here are Sophie and Anna, children, muffed and muffled as snow falls round them, as if preserved in crystal. Their coats, ribboned bonnets, thick black stockings and stout shoes are identical; they are so clearly sisters. Sophie's warm, smiling, generous face gazes fearlessly at the camera, at life; Anna, the younger, smiles too but with a downward glance, gazing at the flakes dancing, falling: enchanted.

Photographs have a way of changing over time; or it may be that they only reveal themselves fully with the passing years. This photograph changed, or revealed more of its secret, the year Sophie left for Hamburg with her husband; yet still the photographer's art, magical as Leonardo's, kept the full secret back. Not *all* was revealed on that day the telephone rang so innocently, and we heard that Sophie was dead – but enough.

And clearly it was there all the time, in her bright bold gaze and in the dots of snow – her early death. And still it is changing; in many ways now she is closer to me than Anna.

I remember how, after the shutter had clicked, Sophie laughed, pushed little Anna away from her, and then the two girls ran off shrieking and giggling, sliding and slipping.

Those fearless eyes! Generous mischievously curling lips!

While I am gazing at these two daughters my eldest daughter Mathilde arrives. She is wearing a most elegant blue dress, the skirt of it so tightly sheathing her thighs that one can clearly see the shape of her suspenders, almost as though they were being worn externally. This sexual overtness is so unlike Mathilde that I comment on it. She explains that she is on her way to have tea at the Savoy with an English friend. Pauli brings out a glass of lemonade for her into the garden. A white-gloved hand lifts the glass delicately. She tells me that on her way here in a taxi she has seen a column of children being led into a station for evacuation; also that she has learnt that at London Zoo all the poisonous snakes are being destroyed, for fear of bombing. The news from Poland is very bad, she says; the Polish cavalry is being cut to ribbons. I can't recall anything else of her conversation. After finishing her drink she stands, bends forward to kiss me gently on the cheek, and leaves. I watch her vaguely, moving slowly, gracefully in her high heels across the lawn and into the house.

I don't know what to make of this dream. Dreams no longer slide easily into their interpretation as once they did. Now it takes an age for meaning to begin to dawn. I interpret Mathilde, my eldest, as the oldest of the Fates, the one who brings death. Death is older than anything on earth. She comes clad in blue, the merciful illusion of the heavens; yet her bones are, as it were, visible beneath the comforting externals. As she sits bolt-upright sipping the drink brought by a maid she takes on the appearance of a hieratic Egyptian goddess. She is forewarning me that I have drunk my life almost to its dregs.

And the horsemen, those riders of the libido, are extinguished. Poland bears little meaning, except that I have always admired the fiery Polish spirit. The column of children is following a Hamelin piper. Then there is the mysterious killing of the poisonous snakes. I have an image of Behemoth, and the fiery serpents threatening God's realm in the Kabbala. They need more thinking about.

So does Mathilde's sexual overtness. The visible corsetry is not merely an external skeleton; there is still – God help me – an ember of the former flames. That old dyad of sex and death.

Savoy. She was going to the Savoy . . . Puzzling. Yet a shrivelled kingdom, an icy Alpine territory. Yes. An uncertain border.

Anna appears, her bare feet rustling across the grass, her hands thrust in the pockets of her loose brown swinging skirt. Comfortable unattractive Anna! She fluffs up a pillow. I ask her to wind up my watch. I no longer have the strength for it. I have wound it up every day of my adult life. Now this may be the last winding. She and I exchange a painful, tender glance.

I am preparing for death. I shall fall into the hands of the living God. Maimonides, I remember, somewhere disputes that phrase. It is a diminution of God, he says, to represent him as living. Why should not God have the experience of being dead? Of course in Christianity he does. Strange, but I still can't comprehend the reality of what it will mean to be dead. Most of my friends and enemies – and Sophie, and my father and mother – have stolen a march on me. How briefly are body and its life united. This must be why the sexual act is of such paramount importance to us. We find in the brief mutual surrender a symbol of our tenuous hold on life.

I recollect that heretical book by the author of the Zohar in which he gives the creation of numbers, and of multiplicity, a sexual basis. In the beginning, he wrote, was a God without attributes, living only for and in himself. He was driven by boredom to masturbate continually. Thence he called up the Shekhinah, his female companion, his wife, the God who is imminent in the universe. Duality sprang into existence: sun and moon, spirit and nature, day and night. Also time,

11

driving between two points. Also good and evil, eternity and mortality. There were, suddenly, shadows, as well as delight.

One lover was not enough for the Shekhinah. She gave birth to a son, and loved him. They both loved him, and he loved them. They might have enjoyed this spiritual synthesis for ever, but they had grown curious. From their triple union a fourth was born, a bride for the son. This gave us the four seasons, four directions, and everything orthodox. Soon there were five beings, copulating together in a tangle. Hence our five senses. Five was a good number. Six less so – it could be split into two threes or three twos. Quarrels ensued, division, infidelity, ambivalence. Seven brought another possibility of perfection, symbolised by the basic scale in music. The square and the triangle were reconciled in those heaving, sweating bodies, in that cornucopia of sucking, copulation and anal intercourse. But with eight, the interlacing serpents of the Greek caduceus, everything went haywire.

We Jews wanted to stop at nine which, when it multiplies itself, reproduces itself by simple addition: 18, 27, 36, and so on. But God and the Shekhinah made the mistake of not listening to his chosen people. Ten was bearable in the eyes of zealots, since one equalled God and nought equalled the Shekhinah. But on and on rolled the numbers, into increasing chaos and evil. Now no one can begin to measure the number of vigorously sexual shapes which we term, inadequately, the Holy One. If just for a single moment, said the author of the Zohar, one shape withdrew himself or herself from union, the world would collapse into nothingness.

Moses, I believe, caught a glimpse of God's sexuality, the only human to do so; but the Shekhinah bribed him to silence by lying with him. This was when Moses gave up having sexual relations with his wife. He can hardly be blamed for that decision.

I would have liked to study this.

12

I confess to many lies and half-truths. I said of one book someone had sent to me that I assumed it was in Hebrew – so claiming ignorance of the language. Yet I learnt it thoroughly in my youth, and my father, Joseph, wrote me a touching dedication in Hebrew on my thirtieth birthday.

My mother, Amalie, spoke in a coarse mixture of Yiddish and German. Both she and my father were coarse Jews from Galicia, Eastern Jews, and I find it hard to forgive them for it.

When I am dead, shall I be any different from those who have never existed? Will it mean anything to have once lived? I think not.

I can't remember leaving the garden. I'm in my study, surrounded by glimmering Classical and Egyptian figures under lamplight. Anna enters in her dressing-gown, comes to my bed and holds the chamber for me to urinate. It is very painful and embarrassing. I sometimes confuse dream and reality now but I am only too conscious of this sordid reality.

She asks me about the pain. The pain.

She removes her dressing-gown and climbs into her bed. The lamp is out. I wonder how this darkness differs from that other.

I still feel her eyes watching over me. Mother-Anna. Anna-Antigone. A woman in her forties, with no life but mine. Poor little Anna! I warned her about Jones, that he was a womaniser, when she visited England, and worried myself silly about the picnic trips they shared. But she came back in love with Jones's mistress, Loe Kann! My God! And I, who had analysed both, was in love with Loe too! She was a lively spirited, ravishing creature. I travelled somewhere – Prague? Budapest? – to attend her wedding to an American, and wrote to tell Jones all about it. I said I liked him, the American. He too, I remember, was called Jones.

The frothing champagne as we toasted the bride, Jones and I. She was out of the hands of Jones. The compulsion to repeat.

Is Lou Salomé's friend, Nietzsche, right, that we repeat endlessly? Shall I start again in Moravia?

My God! All that pain and joy! In that Eden. It means joy in Hebrew. Like Freud.

3

And again it's Anna, bending over me in the dark. It seems
I've been moaning. She bathes my forehead with a flannel.
Her touch so gentle. I grasp her other hand. 'Tomorrow,' I
say thickly. 'It's become pointless, my dear.'

'No, Papa, please. Not tomorrow. The day after.'

'Well, we'll see. Perhaps I can bear one more day.'

She lays her face against my hand and I feel her tears.

In the morning light, when Schur comes, I tell him Not
yet; and he nods. As he prepares the injection I whisper, 'Not
too much.'

With him is the woman called Martha. Her sad eyes, the
grey hair and sunken features. I can recognise Anna in her,
only Anna's hair is black and her eyes still glow with a fire
that might have appealed to men. I have wronged Martha.
I called her our maid, but that is incorrect; she is of course
my wife. Once upon a time I wrote passionate letters to her,
pleaded with her to be faithful.

Mistakes will inevitably creep into this memoir. I believe
I called my father Joseph, whereas his real name was Jacob. It
is I who always, as his eldest son by Amalie, have identified
with Joseph. Perhaps I find it hard to see my mild father, who
once stepped into the gutter to retrieve his hat after a Gentile
had insulted him, wrestling with an angel.

A more extraordinary error in this narrative was my
changing our faithful maid Paula to Pauli. Though Pauli
was born in Vienna in the same year as my *Intrepretation of
Dreams*, the year 1900, I am not aware of ever having met

him; but Einstein recommended to me an essay of his, for an encyclopedia, as the clearest explanation for a layman of the Theory of Relativity. I made a small effort to get hold of the encyclopedia, however it proved difficult and life rolled on. But his name has occurred several times since. I recall being told about Pauli's conflict with Bohr at a public lecture in Denmark. Pauli had expounded some new idea in quantum physics – I believe in fact it was the concept of multiple, universal coitus first touched upon by the Kabbalists – and Bohr leapt to his feet exclaiming: 'It's not crazy enough! It can't be right!' And Pauli snarled in reply: 'It *is* crazy enough!'

And surely he was right. The imagination faints before the concept of millions of godlike creatures wrestling sexually together, sustaining life thereby. It is a crazy idea, yet also with a certain aesthetic grandeur and simplicity.

It may have been the association with dreams, my book of dreaming, that sent Paulo across the mare's field to bring my daughter Francesca a glass of cool lemonade in this Indian summer.

I am fondling Venus. A gift from my Parisian friend Marie Bonaparte on her last visit, she is nude to her hips, where drapery hides her sex; she is holding a mirror.

The sudden wail of a banshee, her shrill note rising and falling. Anna, who has been squatting at my feet reading, rises in a panic and runs into the house. She returns with two Egyptian masks in her arms and makes to put one on me; but I wave it away. What more should I have to do with masks? She concedes, bowing her head; lays both masks on the ground. She sits on the grass, drawing her broad brown skirt around her legs, and resumes her reading.

Let the banshees wail, let the demons appear in the cloudlessly blue sky.

The wailing stops. Silence falls. Only the humming of insects. Ants scurry along the arm of a garden seat. They too have their Adam and Eve, their Moses, their Jacob, their sacred book, their exile, their Red Sea, their literature, their Shakespeare. Their Freud.

16

The banshee wails again, but this time on a prolonged monotonous note. Anna relaxes. 'Another false alarm,' she says. 'You were right, Papa. You are always right.' Her words, half respectful half annoyed, remind me of one of my sisters left behind. The aunts are attracted by a speck of jam. '*Stwawbewy jam! Stwawbewy jam!*' Anna pipes up, an infant; her first dream.

My father came to Freiberg in the middle of the last century to join his grandfather, a merchant. After a while his two sons, Emanuel and Philipp, came to Freiberg also; and with them was my father's second wife, Rebecca of the burning eyes. They lived in one second-storey room of a house of a street whose name escapes me. My father was then about forty. Within three years he had married my mother Amalie, aged nineteen. She was of an age with my half-brothers. When I was born I was cauled and covered in black hairs from head to toe. Julius, who came next, fortunately died within a few months. Then followed five girls, Anna, Rosa, Mitzi, Dolfi and Pauline; finally a second brother, Alexander. In my infancy my two playmates were my nephew and niece, children of Emanuel and his bride Marie; their names were John and Pauline. One day, playing in a meadow, John and I fell upon Pauline and robbed her of her golden flowers.

My half-brothers could have been my fathers; my father could have been my grandfather; my nephew and niece could have been my brother and sister; my mother could have been my wife as my shaggy-haired face buried into her oily, sweating teats. I also had another mother, an old and ugly maid called Monika. Although she could not have been so very old, since one day her bath water became the Red Sea. She allowed my chubby little hairy hands to explore its source. She laughed as I urinated into the Red Sea.

We could have been Germans or we could have been Jews. My father, an unbeliever, studied the Talmud constantly, and my mother was all-Jewish. It did not matter who we were: the Czechs not much caring for either Germans or Jews.

We shared the one big room. And my mother, my mothers,

17

my sisters, showed me the forest. They led me into its depths, where I smelled the divinely secret fragrances of flowers.

I recall an afforested *cabinet* in a train. My mother let go of my hand and I saw the white flanks of the Carpathians, and a golden hissing cascade that went on and on. The train rumbles and jerks; I don't know where we are going.

Amalie, I think her name was. Or was it Anna. Anna baths me now; Anna at night lifts up her nightdress, crouching, unashamed. She holds the chamber for me; her head turns aside, but at the end she sees it, unashamed, the organ that conceived her. Shrunken now. Anna is Mama. Well, it's natural. I'm her helpless child, and the forests spin around us. Forests of wolves and banshees, spirits and flowers. I have swallowed my Mama, I wear her nightcap. Anna enters with her basket of strawberries. *Stwawbewies!*

The world only exists because of seemingly trivial, random rules. I know little of physics but I know that two electrons cannot occupy the same position. If they share the same position momentarily, one will have a different velocity; if they share the same velocity they will not be together in space. It's as arbitrary and crazy as the rules of chess, yet otherwise the universe would collapse into a soup. This, as I understand it, is the law Paula discovered.

A dream that my daughter Anna brings a letter. It is from France, and enclosed is a photo of Eva. Eva is my favourite grand-daughter. What lovely eyes she has, and what a fresh look of hope for the miserable world! How it stretches out – life – beyond me. She will marry and have children, and be a little old lady receiving photos of her grandson; who will marry, have children, etc. . . . It stretches out further than the line of stars from the Hunter to Andromeda. I should see the stars for the last time; and yet it doesn't seem necessary. As we were born from the stars, so we carry them with us, on into death. In the dust of my body the constellations will glow.

But I would like to have seen Eva one more time. We don't carry young children on into death. Eva is fifteen, I think. She means more to me than Oliver her father. My sons have become very vague creatures. Martin fancies himself as a bit of a Romeo, but his wife dies at least every day. My third son is called . . . I have forgotten for the moment. In dull middle age. Mediocrities, I fear.

Ernst!

It's very easy to forget the name of one's son, not the eldest.

I named them after heroes. Cromwell. Luther. My old teacher. But alas . . . *Martin* Luther would not have allowed his wife to find a photograph album of his girlfriends, standing on street corners. And Martin a banker! *This* apple hasn't fallen under the tree. Ah, well . . .

Late in the morning, cumulus builds up on the horizon; yet most of the sky remains bright blue. The cumulus is pure white, and looks in contrast as the first sight of Antarctica must appear to the southward-sailing mariner. There is a hint of chill in the air today, and I sit hunched in overcoat and cap. When our chow Lün appears and rushes up to me, I bend to stroke her but she retreats, she cowers. Only Anna now, and Schur, steadfastly come close without betraying their disgust at the smell coming from my jaw.

Faithful Schur arrives again to give me a top-up injection. The pain eases slightly.

The long, quiet afternoon is made eventful by the appearance of three guests – Lou Andreas-Salomé, Isaac Newton and Charles Darwin. Stout, bosomy Lou is particularly welcome, since I had thought she was dead. No one could be more alive than Lou, her clear blue eyes sparkling, her generous mouth curved in a smile, the sunlight glinting on her rich wheaten hair. Her radiant personality completely outshines that of the dour Englishmen, in their dark frock-coats. Her fur coat, glistening, seems to embody all Russia's forests; the philosopher Plato and the poet Goethe loved to vanish into their depths. She visited her native land with Goethe after the Revolution – which paled in face of Lou.

I am at first embarrassed because Darwin, Newton and I are all Fellows of the Royal Society, whereas Lou is not.

However, she quickly makes us feel at ease. Conversation flows among us all; for a while I feel free of the years and of pain. Darwin discourses on his great discovery that Love binds together everything in the universe. I ask him how he made the discovery and he tells me it was when a sparrow fell into his lap.

'For us women', Lou reflects, 'love and existence are one. We have no need of a seam – ' she lifts her fur coat slightly, turning on her chair to show the back of a leg – 'we are all of a piece. Similarly with our bodies: the cloaca is only taken from our vagina on lease.'

'My friend Darwin', Newton murmurs, 'was referring to spiritual love.'

'Yes, but for a woman there is no difference. The spiritual and the erotic are one and the same. That's why we women make such good analysts – am I right?' She glances at me for confirmation, and I nod. 'We don't find anything shocking, you see. For example, masturbation . . .'

She slips out of her fur. Soon she is stark naked. She squats, one heel digging into the region of her anus. Her face wears a seraphic look, the eyes closed. After a few minutes she starts to shiver, to shudder; throws her head back in a scream.

She lifts her heavy, white buttocks from her heel; lies on the lawn, an arm flung out. And slowly from her anus emerges a green snake. When its tail appears I see the snake is about five feet long. A green mamba. It winds itself around Darwin's dark-trousered leg and continues up. Its head enters his long white beard; eventually the whole mamba disappears into it.

'Don't worry, it's poisonous,' I say. 'It's because they're killing the snakes.'

At this moment I have an impression of Anna bending over me tenderly, asking if I want anything. I shake my head.

Lou quotes a line from a book of Russian poetry she gave me once. '*When Psyche-Life descends into the shadows . . .*' we hear, in her resonant, husky tones. A Russian poem by the geneticist

Mendel. She bought the book on a return visit to Petersburg after the Revolution. She was with her husband Andreas and her lover Rilke.

I speak of the difficulty of finding a safe haven in the tall unbroken white cliffs. With the seas mountainous. 'But you will make it; you were always a conquistador, Freud,' says the sombre-eyed Newton.

'Yes.' I sigh.

Monika, hobbling, ungainly, brings us tea. We sprawl, Lou naked, like that famous picture by Manet. Perfectly at ease.

My vigorous mood ebbing fast, I drowse; and dream of pain, and of Paula and Ernst carrying me into the house. Paula echoes Paul, the Jewish Gentile; and Ernst brings back my good-hearted teacher, Brücke. A bridge between two worlds.

I drowse on the threshold of waking, and half-see, half-create, newspaper comments adrift between sense and absurdity. One of them is 'A common interest in the meat haulage industry links Mussolini and Mrs Virginia Woolf.'

I remember the Woolfs visited me. He with the face of an English garden, she with the face of a constipated horse.

When I force myself to go over the threshold, I find Anna making me comfortable. 'Sophie called in to see how you were,' she says.

A confused joy overcomes me. 'Sophie!' So radiant on her wedding day; though it was taking her away from us.

She nods. 'She's growing into a lovely girl. In her teens she's becoming much more like Martin.'

'Ah! Yes. Sophie.' Martin's daughter.

There's still that slight resentment about the living, on Sophie's behalf, on Heinele's, her dear son.

Picnics in the Woods, as Mathilde and Anna tried to make him forget the loss of his Mama . . . 'Picnic on the Grass.' Or it may have been Renoir. Anyway, the exhibition I saw with the Charcots. Jean-Martin: '*Mon cher*, these so-called painters are crazier than our patients!' His bright, laughing eyes; hand on my shoulder.

Life resplendently open to me. No Sophie yet, even as a dream; no Heinele, playing with flowers or closing his eyes in death.

4

I *ought* to have attended Mama's funeral. Sickness was no excuse.

I would love a cigar.

I don't grieve for the men I smoked with; Federn, for instance, who shot himself in his analyst's chair; or Silberer, who hanged himself outside a window with a flashlight aimed at him so his wife would see him when she came home. I grieved much more over cigars. The grief never ends. One can say death is necessary in order to put a stop to addictions.

I shall become disputed memories and anecdotes, and then only – biographies. They will speak of Amalie and Martha and Anna, and not know that these were all the same woman; a woman who also called herself Elizabeth and Irma, Gradiva and Lou, Helene and Psyche – indeed her names are legion. This woman, the important woman of my life, or rather my life itself, will not be mentioned by biographers. Possibly because she was a prostitute. *Die Freude* means prostitutes, and my life has been bound up with them. It was not for nothing that always, when visiting a new city, my footsteps turned instinctively towards the area of prostitutes.

I feel still a vague guilt because I fought my way up my mother's birth channel ahead of those millions of other Freuds who did not quite make it. I had no compunction: it had to be me. Had I come all that immense way from Palestine to Munich to Galicia to Moravia, only to be vanquished at this stage? It was unthinkable.

This was just a few nights after my parents' wedding.

It's a life-and-death struggle from the first. And then that nestling-home, the sense of arrival, of burrowing into the soft feminine nest. And this is me, too: the welcoming ovum!

Pierce me! the egg cries, and Hold me! cries the sperm.

I have said that we all lived in one room. Myself and Jacob and Amalie and Rebecca and Philipp and Emanuel and Marie his wife and John and Pauline and Julius – until he conveniently died – and my hated sister Anna; and Monika. And that is how the flickering film shows it, one large and loaded bed. Outside was the sloping meadow dotted with yellow flowers and lined by little cottages. Couched in Amalie's strong arms I looked down at it from the first-floor window. I don't think I could see the steeple of the Catholic church in the broad square. Only the woods, the forest. Always the forest.

Yet, besides the dense bodies in the one room I can recall a separation: it seems to me that we shared the house with the Zajícs, who were locksmiths. They had one bedroom while my parents and I had the other. Philipp lived across the cobbled street, while Emanuel and his family lodged not far away. Downstairs at our house was my father's shop and Mr Zajíc's workshop. I'd go in there to breathe its stuffy, acrid smells and hammer toys out of metal. Johann – yes, that was his name. The locksmith.

And if I shared my parents' bedroom why do I remember straying into it to urinate, and my father's angry rebuke?

Memories are not, you see, simple; even from infancy, when you would imagine everything would be sharp in one's recall. What is unmistakable is my mother's soft white breast, lightly aureoled around the jutting nipple, milk-oozing. Philipp eyed it thirstily as I sucked. He and I shared that bedroom with the young bride and her aged husband.

Joseph looked elderly and separated beside Mary in the Philippson Bible I pored over. I knew them because Monika took us secretly to church. Monika was dismissed, with much sobbing, because she had stolen something from my mother. Philipp betrayed her. My mother disappeared at the same time as Monika was boxed into a police cell. My mother

24

was fat-stomached when she disappeared and thin when she returned: carrying a baby called Anna. I looked for my mother in a cupboard because Philipp said she was 'boxed in', meaning Monika.

It may be I'd told my mother Monika had bathed me in the Red Sea. She had stolen my innocence.

And always there was Rebecca looking on, with red eyes; she had led Philipp and Emanuel, and Emanuel's family, out of the land of Galicia. Rebecca, I believe, was the younger sister of my father's first wife Sally. The two sisters made him drunk and lay with him; though I don't know if the resulting child was Philipp or Emanuel. I wanted to ask them when I visited them in Manchester in my youth, but they were wearing smart waistcoats and I didn't think they wished to remember Galicia.

There was a lot of plunging into the soft white breast, to the engorged nipple; and a lot of being torn from it.

When Julius died, that waxen baby, my mother cried, and I and Jacob and Philipp had to relieve her swollen breasts.

Once I sat on Monika's lap in church as she talked, in a space no bigger than a cupboard, seemingly to herself, and in Czech. She babbled, and sounded upset. Then I heard a man's voice, scaring me. He spoke in the tone of voice my father used when I wandered into their bedroom and urinated in their chamberpot.

It may be, of course, that there are always at least two versions of reality, at every moment, for every individual; and so the confusion that we think memory creates actually belongs to events and incidents. We possess, perhaps, some faculty which brings the twofold event into one, as the brain focuses the separate images from our eyes. It may be that a dream, seemingly so vague and unclear and uncertain, is every bit as clearcut as a waking event – or rather the opposite, that the waking event is as unclear and ambiguous as the dream, if we only saw the former correctly.

Or is the *dream* reality? A dense poem, part of the universal stream: and what we consider reality is a weakening, a thinning-out, a turning into separate prose fragments, even contradictory ones?

Thus, I recall endless journeys by cart or by train across Germany, until we eventually settled in Vienna. I am not aware of separations. It is not until much later that I am conscious my half-brothers and my nephew and niece have vanished.

On the other hand, I recall the wrench of leaving them. Tears running down my father's cheeks into his long greying beard.

But did that separation happen in Freiberg? Did my parents and I and Anna the baby travel direct to Vienna?

All of these versions of the truth seem probable, valid, remembered.

I recollect my first sight of a train, after we descended from the horse-drawn carriage. It frightened me. I never lost my fear of trains.

A dream: Schur speaks to Anna and me of seeing a train filled to the brim with white-faced, hollow-cheeked children from the East End. Nothing could more clearly evoke that childhood journey of mine, in which I was not one child but a host. The East End is a reference to the ghettoised Jews of the East. Schur, my present kindly doctor and bringer of death, is reminiscent of Joseph Pur – the name leaps into my mind across a century – our kindly one-eyed doctor in Freiberg. Pur brought me into the world and Schur will send me out of it.

Joseph, interpreter of dreams. ('Where do you think of settling, Jacob? Is it wise to move on, my friend? Especially with two small children? We'll miss you here. I will, at least. The natives are not that unfriendly, are they?' – It comes back, word perfect; the good doctor drinking a glass of beer on a hot summer's day. Amalie had eaten some poisonous berries. Was I echoing that, last year, when saying to Schur: 'We had to move on for Anna's sake. And the English are very friendly and helpful.')

I seem to be standing outside the door of our shop, reaching up to turn the handle, but I'm stayed by a conversation inside. Philipp is saying, in a broken voice, 'It's best if I go to England with Emanuel,' and my father, his voice shaky too, replying, 'Yes, you're right, you're right.' My mother is sobbing.

She got very angry with me on the journey to Vienna: shouting at and slapping me. Actually Mama shouted at and spanked me quite a lot, all the time. I see her face as red and angry as the sun, looming above me, and that massive hand descending. My God, and they think we should love our mothers! She was always quite a bitch. I pity poor Dolfi, who has to look after her.

Has? Had. Mama is dead. With an immensely old person, the gulf between living and being dead is not so great. Oh, I visit her faithfully every Sunday but in between I forget her.

A chink of light shines between the curtains. It falls softly on the figure of the Buddha. Anna is snoring lightly.

> *What seas what shores what granite islands towards my timbers*
> *And woodthrush calling through the fog*
> *My daughter.*

I speak the lines to myself. A poet who visited us gave me the signed book in which they appeared. I found them moving.

Almost unbearable pain.

A louder snore wakes her with a jump. She rises on her elbow, looking across at me. I breathe more deeply to show her I am alive; she relaxes.

After a few moments I hear her sofa-springs recoil. My eyes closed, I feel her gentle hand stroking my brow; her kiss. The rustle of her dressing-gown and the door opening, closing.

> *What seas what shores . . .*

Yes. Memories are more or less faithful accounts of acutely ambiguous and confused events.

For instance. I'm standing among many colleagues, relatives and friends in our drawing room at 19 Berggasse. It's Martha's birthday. She has missed a period and is pregnant with our sixth child. I'm annoyed about that: is there no end to responsibility? The woman who is of supreme importance in my life arrives; at the present time she calls herself Irma. I go up to her and say, 'If you've still got pains, it's your own fault, Irma.'

A maid offers her a glass of wine but she brushes it aside, saying to me, 'Oh, Doctor Freud, if you only knew how I am suffering! My throat, my stomach! I'm choking!'

Alarmed, I take her face between my hands. Her face is pale and puffy. 'Come over to the window,' I say. I lead her to the window. Our flat is on the first floor, looking down on to a small garden. 'Open your mouth.' She seems reluctant, like someone embarrassed about wearing dentures. Irritated, I gently force her mouth open.

I see a big white patch; also extensive whitish grey scabs. I signal with my hand to two or three colleagues; they break off from their pleasant, joky conversations to hurry across. 'Take a look at this.'

Otto peers down her throat while Leopold starts percussing her through her bodice. She has a dull area around the left shoulder, he says; and in spite of her dress I can see he is right. Otto moves back from her, looking puzzled; 'Her throat', he murmurs, 'shows every characteristic of the nose.'

Others come up to us, including Martha and her sister Minna. 'Is anything the matter? What's wrong with her?'

'She has an infection,' Leopold says. 'But there's no need for undue alarm. She'll have an attack of dysentery and that will get rid of the poison.'

Both he and I glance at Otto then immediately avert our gaze. Otto is flushed. He has been treating Irma recently, gave her an injection of trimethylamin, and probably the syringe was not clean. But at least *I* am not to blame; that is some consolation.

Martha and Minna take her away to sit down and rest. I have my glass refilled, accept a savoury from a tray, and the party goes on without further untoward event.

A simple enough occurrence, you will think. Yet in my memory it has appeared much more complex; and this, now I realise, is because it *was* more complex. It is not, for example, Irma whom I lead to the window, but Martha. I don't examine her throat but lift up her dress – newly bought for the birthday – and examine her vagina, with the aid of my colleagues. One of whom is not Otto but my great friend from Berlin, Fliess, an expert on the nose. We see the relics of my ejaculation, and I curse the failure of contraception.

'It was you, Fliess,' I say accusingly, 'who told me those days were safe in a woman's cycle!'

He gives a shrug. His wife is pregnant too.

Hopelessly I stare down at the sloping meadow dotted with yellow flowers. Forty years fly away, I'm witnessing my conception.

In this event too there is no Leopold but instead my old friend Fleischl, whom I killed with an injection of cocaine. Ernst is looking at me sorrowfully, reproachfully. Irma, an observer of the gynaecological examination, meets my eyes for an instant before glancing away. She loves me. What might have been, in another life!

For all that, I'm feeling a great relief. Martha's genital infection will surely lead to a miscarriage.

A wrong guess, as it turned out.

I accept an Ananas. If she goes, regrettably, to full term the child shall be called Anna.

A third version of this complex memory: Fliess has operated on Irma's nose in order to try to cure her tendency to masturbation. After the operation she became very ill, and my colleague Rosanes was called in. He finds to my horror that Fliess left half a metre of gauze in her nose. Pulling out the gauze leads Irma to suffer a massive haemorrhage; Rosanes and I work frantically to stanch it; her blood is all over us; she is close to death. At last we succeed in stopping the flow; I rush to the next room and vomit.

When I return, Irma (her real name is Emma Eckstein) smiles faintly at me and whispers, 'So you see I wasn't imagining I felt ill! But don't worry, this was an amazing experience – I had an orgasm as I felt myself slipping into death.'

I don't doubt the truth of her statement. She glories in her menstruation. When she was thirteen, her parents had part of her labia minor circumcised and she was given the labial skin to eat. It's not surprising if dark, smouldering Irma has become a witch, able to make me have doubts about Fliess's competence.

I have no doubt this summary far from deals adequately with those concurrent events of my thirty-ninth year; events which, perhaps, were simply paraphrases of the central reality – my seminal 'Dream of Irma's Injection'.

Perhaps the whole course of a human life is merely a narrative created to make sense, to our weak intellects, of a dozen or so really powerful dreams.

I try to get outside my pain. I wonder what Pauli says about the electron-whirl in an idea, an emotion, a memory, a dream?

The study door opens again; I hear Anna's rustling steps. The light is a little brighter. I watch her, murkily, remove her dressing-gown and then, after a slight hesitation, looking in my direction, pull her nightdress off over her head. I dimly view the forest and her breasts. Does she know I'm awake? Is this her gift to me, in thanks for staying alive one more night? Even in hope that I'll want to be alive at tomorrow's dawn? Who can say; but she is observant, a good analyst; I think she knows I'm aware of her.

Usually she dresses and undresses in the bathroom.

Her corset snakes around her. Its suspenders dance and clink together metallically. My Anna hates the restrictions of womanhood. She'd be happier as a peasant in a free-flowing skirt and blouse.

When she is fully dressed she comes and kneels beside me. 'Are you awake, Papa?'

I open my eyes. She smiles tenderly, squeezes my hand. 'How are you feeling?'

'Pain.'

She nods; blinks tears back. 'Is it unbearable?'

'Bearable,' I lie. Her face radiates happiness. 'The doctor will be here in a little while.'

When Pur comes, his glass eye glinting, I grunt in relief, the morphine flowing through my veins.

Ernst, I'm sorry. I thought cocaine was a wonder drug. I didn't know I was killing you.

I was trying to help. You were already in a bad way, my friend. It didn't seem such a bad injury at the time; just a cut, in a laboratory experiment. But then I remember the day you told me shakily your fingers would have to go. The addiction to morphine followed the infection. I told you to take the cocaine by mouth, to overcome the morphine addiction; I had no idea you were going to inject the stuff.

What agony you suffered! Well, you're paying me back now.

All the same, I would not have changed places with you in your coffin.

It was always Cain and Abel with me. He who is my beloved brother or friend is my hated enemy. It's quite possible I strangled Julius in his cradle. I was his Brutus. Girls are not such a threat. With my sister Anna I could simply tell my parents her piano-playing was interfering with my studies, and the piano went out of the window.

Girls with that wound under their skirts.

Yet in the end, in the end . . . My mother, in the kitchen making dumplings; rubbing her palms together and creating dirt, dust. 'Dust to dust, Sigi.' From flesh. Fleisch, Ernst. The vigorous rubbing of the penis in order to shrivel it. In the end, they bury you. Woman is cocaine.

Ernst – we had some good times, sucking at the breasts of wisdom and science, didn't we?

Did I tell you that story of my patient who was talking about her marriage? In case I didn't, let me tell you now. 'If one of us dies,' she said, 'I shall move to Paris.'

5

I first became intrigued by dreams because of another great
city – Manchester.

I visited it during my undergraduate years, in the summer
of 1875. Emanuel and Philipp met me off the boat; they were
affluent, solid men, already in middle age. On the train journey
I dipped into English newspapers, and saw that the last queen
of the Australian Aborigines had died in Tasmania. I think her
name was Trucaneli, or some such. She was only four foot tall;
had seen her mother stabbed to death by white convicts, and
she herself was raped; afterwards she would sell her body for
a handful of tea or sugar. Now, crying out 'Rowra catch me'
(Rowra being an evil spirit), she had fallen down dead.

An unhappy and sordid life; but what intrigued me were
the accounts of the Aboriginal Dreamtime which two of the
better journalists had provided.

'Are we Jews cleverer than the Aborigines?' Philipp asked
in the stuffy compartment, as rainy fields chugged by.

'I suppose we must be,' Emanuel said.

I subsequently spent two days in the Manchester City
Library reading all I could find about the Dreamtime. I came
away with a sneaking feeling that Emanuel was wrong. How,
I wondered, could a primitive race invent a *Weltanschauung* as
elaborate and poetically beautiful as the Dreaming? I imagined
myself as an explorer of those hot red desert wastes, coming
across the Dreaming's mythic gods and creatures; those beings
who lived for ever in their own sacred time, divorced from
death. Manchester became for me, in my memory, not the

city of beautiful parks and splendid buildings, such as the Royal Exchange, the assize courts and Chetham's Hospital and Library, but the place of the Dreaming, where night after night I dreamed events in the Dreaming; where began, at nineteen, a fascination with dreams that bore fruit twenty-five years later.

Speak the word 'Manchester' and I am likely to think of the Yulungi Snake (I rely on an uncertain memory) devouring the Two Sisters.

During that summer an Englishman called, I think, Webb swam across the Channel. My half-brothers rejoiced patriotically. The English are great athletes and swimmers: Byron, the Hellespont; Webb, the Channel.

I liked my English relatives. Emanuel and Marie remembered me as a baby born in a caul. Their son John had become quite the elegant, sophisticated young Englishman. Pauline seemed nervous of me; perhaps she remembered how John and I had ravished her flowers in the Freiberg meadow. Bloomah, Philipp's English-born wife, was a jolly soul, big with child. She had a good singing voice, so far as I could judge. She was sad to read of the death of Bizet in Paris, his health destroyed by the venomous reception of *Carmen*, which the critics had characterised as obscene, pornographic and tuneless. Tuneless!

It would become the only opera after Mozart's I could sit through with enjoyment.

Of course the bull ring has something in common with the analytical encounter. The huge, muscular energy of a neurosis, charging again and again. The gradual weakening with darts, then the thrust home.

Alas, poor Bizet!

I also, while I was there, had an encounter with a black prostitute.

By contrast to the richness of Manchester, Paris, where I spent several months a decade later as a student of the great, bull-like, clean-shaven Charcot, made little impression.

Oh, I loved the Egyptian and Assyrian statues in the

Louvre; but I was haunted too much by Martha to breathe in the full romance of the city. I saw everywhere the sweet, pure, unperfumed form of my delightfully provincial Martha. I had been staying with her family in Hamburg; for six whole weeks had been tormented by the closeness and unavailability of that Notre Dame beneath a tight-fitting skirt. She and her family thought I was devilishly anti-religious; they had no idea of my state of adoration.

'Could you tell me how to find *la rue Richelieu?*' I asked a passer-by. 'A Jew shouldn't need to be told how to find the *riche lieu,*' he responded, his accent mocking my Yiddish problem with French vowel sounds. He stalked by.

Others didn't care for me because I was German. The Franco-Prussian War was still fresh in their memories and cemeteries.

Whenever I could take a break from analysing the pathology of diseased children's brains, I strode the corridors of the Salpêtrière to visit some of those poor tormented women, each in her own world within the humane regime of Charcot's kingdom. These women, at least the hysterical ones, made me decide to abandon the laboratory for the living psyche. 'At the root of all their problems', Charcot insisted, 'is sex.'

Eight thousand fluttering female arms, reaching out greedily to try and touch us as we passed; their pleading cries: '*Mon cher Jacques!*' . . . '*Mon pauvre petit fils!*' . . . '*Baisez-moi! Baisez-moi!*' . . . They were ready to explode; not for nothing had the Salpêtrière once been an arsenal for saltpetre.

Hamburg again, *en route.* Martha's chaste kisses.

She exploded, just once, in late middle age. Amazing . . . Apart from that brief explosion . . . But sex isn't everything.

There's a hole right through to my cheek.

Ah, it's my good, faithful Schur.

'A little help, my old friend?' he whispers.

'A little, yes, thank you.'

I am quite conscious of Papa's presence. He wants to talk . . .

Schlomo, I want you to know I'm proud of you, my boy.

You were always top in school. You have more brains in your little toe than I in my whole body. As I wrote to you on your thirty-fifth birthday, in Hebrew, in the illustrated Bible you loved so much as a child: *At the age of seven the spirit of the Lord began to move you/And spoke to you: Go read the books I have written/And there will break open to you the fountains of wisdom . . ./'Spring up, O well – sing ye unto it'* . . . You're a good scientist, my boy; you didn't boast to us about your discovery concerning the eel, but your friends told me it was an original contribution to knowledge. Cocaine too; your name should have gone alongside that other scientist as responsible for discovering its anaesthetic effect on the eye. You should have complained. But never mind you will do other things, greater things.

I'm troubled, though, to hear what you say about Rebecca. She wasn't Sally's sister, and they didn't lie with me when I was drunk. Sometimes you let your imagination run away with you. And your mother and Philipp had nothing to do with each other. Not in that way. All right, you guessed that Monika wasn't guilty of theft. It was awkward. She was related to our landlord, you understand. I didn't like getting her jailed. I felt like Abraham sending Hagar out into the desert with just one bottle of water. But it was necessary. You don't want to bother your head over why. It doesn't concern you. We can't know what's going on in the lives of our parents. And what did you say about the unconscious? – that it's hard to separate fact, in the unconscious, from emotionally intense fiction? Have I misquoted you? You're too clever for me. You'll write books one day.

You think I'm weak. You didn't like that story I told you about the Gentile who cursed me for walking on the pavement, and knocked off my fur hat. You pursed your rather prim lips when I said all I did was go into the road and pick up my hat. But this is the way of the Jew, my son; we obey what has been ordained by the Lord. One day you'll know what I'm talking about.

Look after your mother, your sisters. I don't have to say

that. And one other thing – don't take life too seriously! There is 'a time to weep, and a time to laugh; a time to mourn, and a time to dance'.

My time for laughing and dancing is over. It's not so easy, dying in Baden, far away from you all. I'd like to have said goodbye to my grandchildren. I'd like to have seen them grow up; but I am old; one event happens to us all; I can truly say, The spirit of the Lord God is upon me. I have made my peace with Him.

– By the way: poor Tilgner. I was sorry to hear that.

6

I had almost totally forgotten Tilgner's fate, until my father reminded me. Tilgner was a fine Viennese sculptor who had forged his way up from a poor background. Yet he had never quite made the highest rank. In the year of Papa's death, the year when I was starting my self-analysis, he won a commission to sculpt a large statue of Mozart. It would be the triumphant culmination of his career, and would not be before time, since he was past fifty. The statue was made; all that awaited was its public unveiling.

I happened to meet him in a coffee-house, just a few days before the ceremony was due. I was shocked to see him look gaunt and distressed. 'Victor, good to see you! But what on earth's the matter?' I exclaimed. 'You look awful!'

'I think I need your help,' he replied. 'Please join me; let me buy you a drink. It's totally irrational, but I've convinced myself I won't live to see my statue unveiled.'

'But that's rubbish! You're in good health, aren't you?'

'Yes, so far as I'm aware. Of course, at fifty-two . . . Who can say?'

I reassured him; though it's true that fifty-two is a particularly dangerous age. He relaxed a shade; over pastries we were able to discuss a last-minute engraving he intended for the base of his statue: a few bars from *Don Giovanni*, the appearance of the Commendatore's ghost. He hummed the sinister music. He made reference to Mozart's unfinished *Requiem*, reverting to his own obsession. I told him there were simple psychological reasons for his fear; we are all afraid of being cut down before we can enjoy triumph and fame. Parting, I said with a twinkle there was more chance of Mozart stepping off his plinth than of his dropping dead. He gave a weak answering smile.

That same night, I learned later, he played taroc with some friends (or, in another version, consulted the Tarot). In the morning he suffered a heart attack, caused by a coronary thrombosis, and was dead within twenty-four hours.

The shock and sadness I felt for Tilgner was soon overwhelmed by news of my father's dying.

And here he is, forty-three years later, in Hampstead England, speaking to me. An illusion, of course. But a comforting one. His voice hasn't changed. Still equable, moderate, conciliatory, indulgent. My grandfatherly father.

It is the day of his funeral. I have arranged for it to be simple, irreligious; I have not even announced his death in the papers. My barber, trimming my beard, doesn't know I am bereaved. By a morbid coincidence he tells me an anti-Jewish joke as he snips away. (He is a Jew himself, of course.) Abram Goldstein has died. Frau Goldstein is inconsolable. Her daughters tell her she should announce his death in the newspaper. She goes to the newspaper office, and is told that death notices are a schilling a word. She suggests 'Goldstein – dead.' However, she's told there's a minimum of five words. She thinks, and then adds: 'Suit for sale.'

And I chuckle, matching my barber's grin in the mirror.

I should not be having my beard trimmed in this time of mourning.

Suddenly I look up at the clock and see that I'm already late. How horrifying! My mother and sisters and brothers will never forgive me. Above all my father will never forgive me. He's lying in his coffin thinking, Where is he? I fling some money at the barber and rush out.

It's as if I have lost all sense of direction; I find myself, for no good reason, in a railway station. And here is where, again, the event splits into two or three alternatives. I see, in the waiting room, a notice saying NO SMOKING. It bothers me, since I'm having trouble with my heart; I should give up smoking; my friend Fliess is urging me to.

At the same time the poster is saying, YOU ARE REQUESTED TO SHUT THE EYES.

And also: YOU ARE REQUESTED TO SHUT THE EYE.

I must shut his eyes, perform my filial duty. I rush from the station. I must also, secretly, wink at the attractive widows, some of whom are patients of mine, who will be present. For I'm alive, and death has brought a rush of libido. I realise this is why I am at the station. I want a journey, an adventure.

I run through the streets, and arrive at last, dishevelled, agitated. Martha opens the door to me; she holds baby Anna in her arms. She looks at me murderously.

'I'm sorry. I got held up.'

In yet another version of that incident I arrive dutifully, well before time.

I meditate on my father's visit, wondering why he thought Abraham and not Sarah had cast Hagar out. I think it's because Father was a woman masquerading as a man. So warm, so weak, so milky kind and passive. Mama was the man in that family.

I drowse, half-wake, drink a little, am injected, drowse again, dream. In one of my dreams Jones comes and announces that, sadly, the British government has declined with regrets to rush through a bill giving me citizenship. It might, they say, open the floodgates. Jones is appalled by the decision; apologises to me profusely for having built up my hopes after instigating the whole thing. I tell him it doesn't matter. He takes my hands between his before leaving, and looks deeply into my eyes.

I assume the significance of this dream is that a part of me has always wished I had left the Continent with my half-brothers when they emigrated to Manchester. It would have been good to have lived my life in such a pleasant, liberal country, almost devoid of anti-semitism. The dream is saying, Now it would take an act of parliament to grant you your wish – and what would be the point anyway? Since Austria is finished, you are stateless; you live in the state of Freud.

The fact that the dapper, kindly, but rather deceitful Welshman tried to help me gain my wish and announced the failure of his efforts, is a confirmation that I have been right never to trust fully anyone in the movement except Anna. Well, and a few other women – Lou, for instance. But the men . . . They all think they are my sons and so have wanted to kill me. Jones, in my dream, gazed deeply into my eyes. He wishes to have the honour of shutting my eyes. He has another think coming.

Terrible pain during this dream, as if my whole body and soul were one intense, searing toothache. Now, in I think early afternoon – at least the sun is almost overhead, making the autumnal flowers blaze with colour – the pain has eased considerably. I rest in my hanging-shroud.

Anna, in her comfortable loose brown skirt and white smock, ghosts barefoot across the lawn and tells me I have another visitor: Emanuel's younger son Samuel, who took over his father's business. I grunt with pleasure at Anna's news; I have always liked Sam – named, not after the prophet, but after a character in Trollop's *Mr Pickwick*; he's sharp and he's deep – a rare combination. He shuffles towards me on a walking-stick, portly, dark-suited, spectacled, grey-bearded. We greet each other warmly, speaking in English.

It soon becomes clear that he is embarrassed. Not because I am about to join our ancestors but because he has something to say that he thinks will upset me.

'I've been reading over your letters to my father,' he says. 'They were marvellous letters. Do you remember, in one of them – it's dated 1897 – you asked him a painful question. You yourself said it was painful: did he have any knowledge of sexual abuse or seduction on the part of your father?'

'Yes, I remember that. He replied that he had no knowledge of any such behaviour.'

'That's true. He told me. Just at the onset of the Great War. He had a premonition of death; he was old, of course, and if an accident hadn't killed him he probably still wouldn't have survived the war. It upset him greatly that you and he were officially enemies. He also told me that – ' He stops; Pauli has stolen up, bearing a jug of lemonade. He thanks her, saying how warm it is for September.

'– That he hadn't precisely lied to you, uncle, but also kept certain things hidden. And now he was beginning to regret it. You were making a name for confronting the truth, however painful, and here he was, not trusting you with important family matters. They would be painful for me too, he said; and my mother must never know any of these things; but perhaps some day I could find the right moment to tell you. I've waited a long time, but I think the moment has come.'

He sips the lemonade and looks away, towards the house with its brightly painted white small-paned windows. 'We should all know where we come from before we die.'

'Then tell me,' I say. 'Don't be afraid.'

There is silence. A brief, cool breeze, making the leaves tremble.

'When they settled in Freiberg, Father was only twenty. Already married. You know Grandfather had come first, and Papa and Mama joined him later, with Rebecca, Grandfather's second wife. You know about Rebecca?'

'Of course.'

'I'm sorry, of course you do. Only no one has ever mentioned her. This is excellent lemonade, I must ask Martha for the recipe. Well, Papa felt restless. In such a small town. In between helping Grandfather with the business he made trips to Vienna. There was a contact with a businessman called Nathanson. Very orthodox. Their family had migrated from Galicia too, and still spoke quite broad Yiddish. Papa dined with them a couple of times. And, to cut a long story short, he fell in love with a daughter called Amalie.'

'Mama!'

'Yes, your mother. And she responded. Papa didn't at first tell her he had a wife and child – my brother John was a year old, and my mother was carrying Pauline.'

'Is there any news of John?' I ask.

'No,' he says sadly. 'Not a word. He just vanished.'

'Ah!' The green and sloping meadow; John and I pulling the yellow flowers out of Pauline's hands. Pauline wailing and running off. 'Maybe he died somehow, somewhere, in the war.'

'Maybe. Who knows? . . . But I was saying, they fell in love. They both felt very passionate. They met at his lodgings while he was in Vienna. She got pregnant. It all came out – a terrible scandal.'

'My God! I always wondered if Philipp . . . But *Emanuel!* Your sober papa! – that I never dreamt of.'

'Well, who would? Grandfather was summoned to Vienna; a Nathanson family conference. Everyone was crying. It was a situation, Papa said, without a solution. He loved my mother, but it just couldn't compare with how he felt about Amalie Nathanson. He'd married too young.'

He asks if I'd mind him smoking. I wave my hand permissively. His silver cigarette case glints in the sun. I sigh, breathing in the fume.

After his second deep intake and long exhalation, he continues: 'They worked out an arrangement. Grandfather wasn't especially happy with Rebecca. She had not borne him children, so she could be renounced. The Nathansons were fairly well off, and promised to look after Rebecca if he divorced her and married their daughter. Your family were struggling to survive – Grandfather wasn't very good at his business, was he? They would help him too. Within reason. Papa and your mother were willing to go along with it provided they could still be lovers. On the quiet. They were amazingly unconventional; but Papa said it was not under their control, so strong was their passion for each other.'

'*Vénus à sa proie tout attachée,*' I quote.

'I'm sorry? I knew it would upset you. Rebecca was put aside, and Grandfather came home from Vienna with his beautiful young bride. Papa performed his husbandly and fatherly duties at home; and met Amalie privately a couple

42

of times a week. In the forest, mostly. Occasionally in the shop, at night. And then – you were born.'

I stifle a cry; and for something to do I take out my watch. I see it has stopped. I ask Sam to wind it for me; he does so.

'So my mother and father didn't –?'

He shakes his head. 'Apparently not. But at forty a man is – well, less in need.'

'Yes, I know. But still . . .'

'You had a servant, about Grandfather's age.'

'Ah!'

He nods. 'Once in a while.'

'I see, I see . . .' More light, more light. Everything clear.

'So you and I are actually – brothers, Sam.'

'That's correct; but I'm used to thinking of you as uncle, Uncle Sigi.'

'Well, it's late to – '

'Yes. My father said you mustn't think too badly of your father. Of Jacob. He did what he thought was best in an awful situation. He loved his son, and was sentimental; saw that he was deeply in love. He himself had had to give up his real love for an arranged first marriage. And then when he was widowed, he married someone who was good and kind with children rather than someone whom he could love deeply. Papa and Philipp liked Rebecca; but she was not good-looking or clever.'

'I remember her eyes,' I say. 'They burned into one.'

I feel a weight fall from my shoulders. Jacob was not my father.

'Well, then your mother became pregnant again, and gave birth to your brother Julius.'

I nod. Blind rage. Wanting to smash his face in the crib.

'He died after only a few months; and that was the turning point. Papa and Amalie felt it as a divine punishment for their horrific sin, and decided to stop sleeping with each other.'

'You mean they were falling out of love?' I suggest tartly.

'Well, it may be. I don't know. But after that, Grandfather and your mother started having normal relations at last.'

43

'So you mean my sister Anna – '

'Auntie Anna was their first child. Correct.'

'It's not surprising I've always disliked her.'

He takes his gold watch from his waistcoat pocket. 'I should go. I have a little business and must catch the early evening train back to Manchester.'

'What I find hardest to take, strangely,' I say slowly, 'is that Papa – Jacob – slept with my nurse, Monika. I thought I had her to myself, I suppose.'

'He had to dismiss her, after their marriage became normalised. She had become emotionally attached to him, you see. Regrettably. She became hysterical, Papa said, when Grandfather didn't want her any more. She threatened to tell my mother what had been going on. They had to get her out of the way. She'd stolen some trifling bit of jewellery, and they threatened to go to the police unless she left quietly.'

My cancerous mouth gapes in a silent, mirthless chuckle.

'Business got worse, and they went seeking somewhere better all over Germany. Then – well, I think Grandfather caught them making love again; and it seemed better if the family split.'

'I thought that was Philipp,' I murmur. 'I heard them whispering, crying.'

'No, it was my father. Although – your mother was very beautiful, wasn't she? It wouldn't have been surprising if Uncle Philipp too became disturbed by her presence. Now you mention it . . .' He gnaws at his thumb . . . 'Papa hinted as much.'

'And we finally settled in Vienna.'

'And had a rough time at first, I believe.'

'It was terrible! In the slums. We moved four or five times in as many years. Prostitutes leaning against our wall! I have no memory of those years!'

Only of my mother, rubbing her hands vigorously together, and showing me the dirt that resulted; saying we came from the earth and to earth would return.

We sit in silence; I'm hunched forward. 'I'm sorry, Uncle Sigi,' he says, leaning and touching my arm.

'Why didn't my mother's family help us?'

'They did. Who do you think paid for your education?'

7

When Anna is washing me, as if for burial, with Lün cowering in the corner away from the overpowering odour, I whisper: 'Sam.'

'Sam? My cousin? What about him?'

It has been in my mind to pass my knowledge on to Anna; but I realise I have not the energy and say merely: 'Good. Good man.'

Anna, puzzled, murmurs, 'Yes. I like Sam.'

Her touch, flecking the sponge over my body, is infinitely gentle and tender; yet the pain is so great again that she might as well have been scraping off my skin with a razor. Fear is in her eyes, fear that I'll ask to die today.

'Schur,' I whisper.

'Yes. He's coming.'

'Anna, don't let on that I took morphine. Or only at the very end.'

I try to make my consciousness seal itself off from the pain centres, like a foetus in the womb, so that I can begin to think about the scandalous things I have heard from Samuel. I imagine that marriage ceremony eighty-three years ago. Presumably in Vienna. I look at the joyous celebration from the viewpoint of Marie, Emanuel's wife. Just nineteen, already a mother and pregnant with the second child. She sees the blushing, sparkling bride in white silk, a net over her hair; sees her father-in-law, dressed in a white robe to remind him of death and judgement, go under the canopy held up by four men. Marie is enjoying the occasion, a rare change from the dull atmosphere of Freiberg and the daily grind. She glances aside at Emanuel, and he smiles back at her, raising an eyebrow in good-humoured amusement. She grips his hand.

The Rabbi says the blessing over a wine cup, which he then gives to Jacob and Amalie. The mature but still handsome bridegroom slips the ring on Amalie's finger, saying, 'Behold, thou art consecrated.' The old Rabbi reads the marriage contract. Marie glances at the bride's parents; they look solemn yet happy.

And it's all false; a perversion, a terrible sin. The father marrying, as it were, his daughter; his son's concubine, at least. The son sleeping with his father's wife. Why did I never sense anything? Why has all the family always denied Rebecca's existence? Nor was Sally, his first wife, ever talked of. I don't know when she died, or of what. None of us ever bothered. I recall an uncle, proposing a toast to my parents (my parents!) on some anniversary, quoting with a smile the Talmudic saying that a man's second wife is the one he has deserved – and that Jacob has deserved the best!

And now I begin to recall something even more disturbing. Breuer has told me excitedly about his patient Bertha Pappenheim, paralysed in three limbs and with other dreadful incapacities when she came to him. It seems she has talked herself into a cure. Fresh from the good meal, the hot bath, the clean underclothes provided by the divine Mathilde Breuer – after whom I would name my first daughter – I rush home and straight upstairs. I find my father, as usual, in his study, poring over the Talmud. I quickly explain what I want; that he will let me hypnotise him. A scientific experiment that may help my career. He is eager, as ever, to help; my monograph on aphasia has pride of place on his holy bookshelves. The amenable man is soon under.

We sit facing each other. He is soon talking volubly, confessing his sins. One great sin in particular. I sit frozen to the chair. Then unleash a torrent of deserved accusation.

'Yes, you're right, Schlomo,' he responds, almost whimpering; 'I am weak. I was always weak. I shouldn't have gone into the gutter to retrieve my hat. I shouldn't have married your mother in those circumstances. But what else could I have done? Could anyone have done? Made her have an abortion? Perish the thought. Or should we have ruined poor Marie's life? And my little grandchildren!' A heavy sigh, a sob. 'You can't imagine what a state Emanuel was in. He loved his wife, in a way, and he loved your mother. Loved her? He was besotted with her. This way, I thought I could keep everybody happy.'

'Rebecca.'

Another deep sigh, and he waves his arms helplessly.

Her burning eyes. I don't believe I ever saw them. I think I've seen them *since* that evening in my father's study. What does one remember from the first three years of life?

And Monika. It was my mother, I realise, who told me she was old and ugly: a belated jealousy.

I do remember the Red Sea. I've thought it was her menstruation, her uncleanness. Suddenly I'm convinced I walked in on her, naked in the tin bath, and the blood flowing from her wrists. I ran out, calling Mama. It saved Monika's life.

Exodus.

'Emanuel couldn't help it, he was crazed,' he pleads.

'Crazed! Then why didn't he kiss the hot stove?'

His lips twitch humorously, but he quickly realises smiling is inappropriate, and gives a doleful grimace. 'I knew their passion wouldn't last, Schlomo. I knew he'd tire of her eventually and go back to being a faithful husband.'

(For Gentiles: a husband returns home to find his supper cooking and his wife being kissed and mauled by the young lodger, who dashes off. The wife says to her husband, 'He couldn't help it, he's crazy,' and the husband replies, 'Crazy? Then why didn't he kiss the hot stove?')

My father loves Jewish jokes.

'What I think really motivated you', I say with brutal directness, 'were greed and lust.'

'No, Schlomo!'

'Yes! You were incapable of supporting your family by your own miserable efforts. And you had this beautiful, passionate girl in your bed suddenly. All right, you couldn't have her at once; but it excited you to have her warm body pressed against yours, and to think she'd made love to one of your sons, a few hours earlier.'

'No! No!'

'That his sperm was inside her, still wet! His child was growing in her womb! No doubt she let you stroke her, while showing her distaste. Why don't you admit it? – you were excited by it; because you're spineless; it gives you pleasure to be hurt, humiliated and insulted.'

His head is sunk in his hands.

'All right,' I say, more gently, 'you're going to wake up when I click my fingers three times; you will remember nothing of our conversation; you will think we were recalling our walks together in the Viennese woods when you helped me with my school-work. You will be feeling quite calm and relaxed.'

When my fingers click and he awakes, he is indeed calm looking and wearing a cheerful smile. It is I who am an inferno of painful emotion, but I do my best to disguise it. It helps that his sight is deteriorating. 'I'm sorry it didn't work,' he says; 'but we had a nice talk about your school-days, didn't we? I knew then you were destined for something great, my boy.'

'You helped a lot.'

He beams his childlike pleasure.

I too must try to forget this conversation. I'll go out, though it's late; the long-lasting twilight of a hot July day has settled to almost dark. Mother is still up, sewing in the kitchen. I kiss her on the cheek and tell her I'm going out. I'm going back to the Institute to see how an experiment is going, and I'll probably stay there all night. Before she can express her fear that I'm working too hard, I'm out of the door.

I should be writing to Martha.

The friend at whose door I knock is already wild with cocaine. He is pleased to see me. With coca, with alcohol, even with an experiment in self-hypnosis, I attempt to bury tonight's knowledge deeper than Pompeii.

When I drift into parched and stupefied wakefulness, the

sun is already burning through the window. I'm on a sofa and my friend is stretched out, as white as a wedding robe, on the carpet. A wine glass has tilted out of his hand, staining the dirty-grey carpet red. I don't know why I didn't go straight home after the Breuers, I curse my unwonted dissipation. Luckily, I recall, Brücke told me to take the morning off as he feels I'm over-working. I declined his kind offer, but he will think I've changed my mind.

After cleaning myself up, I decide to walk to Breuer's house. I find Joseph in a terrible state, and Mathilde not much better. In the midst of his session with Bertha at her home this morning, she suddenly pulled up her skirts, screaming 'Your child is coming!', opened her legs wide, and gave birth.

The child didn't live.

Breuer, in a panic, left mother and dead baby there, amid blood and afterbirth. Her parlourmaid would clean up. 'Of course it *wasn't* mine.'

He and Mathilde have decided to take a second honeymoon in Venice.

'That's a good idea, Joseph. But still, the talking cure works.'

'Oh, yes, it works. There was no sign of paralysis during parturition. She's well.'

Several years later, when I persuaded him to write up the case, he asked me what we should call her to disguise her identity. Instantly I moved the initial letters of her name one space back. 'Anna O.', I said.

I knew it was perfection. 'In the year nought.'

She became a very good social worker.

Until today I have never recalled my father's confession. For every individual, history begins with his birth; all that has gone before is myth. They came out of the East, from Galicia, Rebecca and Philipp and Emanuel and Marie: following Jacob. The men (for who else mattered in that primitive world?) came in superstition, out of nowhere, like the Three Wise Men. From the long gabardine coats and skullcaps, long sidelocks, phylacteries, ritual baths, *dybbuks*.

I am writing my diary like Captain Scott, and reading Darwin, while all around me the mad, cold blizzard rages.

'I am going outside,' I whisper to Anna as she dries me. 'I may be some time.'

8

I am not sure where I had reached in this memoir. I think it was the birth of Anna and the arrival of my sister-in-law Minna in our new apartment at 19 Berggasse – events which were almost simultaneous.

Minna is, or used to be, a highly intelligent and well-read woman; the sort of woman who would wander around a kitchen with a ladle in one hand and a serious book in the other. She was not conventionally pretty, but had a certain sexual appeal arising from a great deal of repression.

During the time of my passionate engagement to Martha, Minna became engaged to a close friend of mine, Ignaz Schönberg. One day a tuberculosis bacillus, unsure whether to choose Schönberg or me, luckily chose my friend. When he realised he was terminally ill, he nobly broke off his engagement. Minna's sense of betrayal was scarcely eased by her former fiancé's subsequent death. She closed her libidinal life.

She came to us for a few months' vacation, and stayed for the next forty years. I did not at first know if I welcomed a companion for Martha, or begrudged an extra mouth to feed, on top of little Anna. It was a weird stage in my life. I had at times almost no patients, then occasionally too many, filling my days and draining the energy that should have gone into my dreambook. At times I was able to live in a creative trance like that of a poet; at times I was sunk in paralysis and depression. I was plunging into my own underworld. I should make it clear that no paralysis, depression, castration complex, matricidal or patricidal urge, hysteria, neurasthenia,

sexual perversion, suffered by any of my patients could begin
to rival the equivalent mental state or perverse desire in my own
psyche. Besides all these I was suffering from a heart condition
that I thought likely to kill me at any moment.

And here was a new arrival, a second wife as it were,
who appeared to be the incarnation of the death goddess. In
mourning for her libido, she seemed like one of those hapless
spirits in Vergil who are dead but unburied, and so haunt the
banks of the Styx, unable to cross. Schönberg had let her down
dreadfully by dying, and so, like Dido's, her face had become
'unmoving granite or Marpesian stone'.

One day I missed some belladonna from my consulting
room. Alarmed, I made enquiries of Martha and others,
and came at last to the conclusion – which I kept secret –
that only Minna could have been responsible for taking the
deadly drug from my room. I asked her to come to my study,
under the guise of wanting to show her some old letters from
Schönberg.

I confronted her with my suspicions, and she broke down
and wept. She had intended ending her life, which was pointless. Her life should have ended with the death of her beloved
Ignaz. Theirs had been the perfect love. She was too old and
plain ever to attract another man.

Casting around for some consolation, I mentioned that my
friend Fliess, a Berlin rhinologist, had found her charming and
intelligent on meeting her during his recent visit to Vienna. It
was true he had said she was intelligent; I had added the other
epithet as a well-intentioned white lie. Minna immediately
brightened – though it perhaps needed someone experienced
in the psyche to detect the slight change. She confessed that
she had liked Fliess.

Two years younger than I, Wilhelm had become almost a
brother to me: perhaps the brother who had been lost, Julius.
My Anna would have been named Wilhelm if she had been
born a male. We exchanged a passionate correspondence on
our discoveries. Fliess was subject to sudden all-engulfing
enthusiasms. He was convinced, for example, that our lives

are controlled by a female periodicity of twenty-eight days, and a male one of twenty-three. He believed the nose, his specialism, and the sexual organs were intimately linked. He believed that everyone is bisexual. With this last concept I whole-heartedly concurred.

Clearly Minna had also responded to him, even in the depths of her despair. Extreme measures, I felt, were required to bring her back from the gates of death. I plunged in, with a reckless disregard for truth: 'He told me, in complete confidence, he would welcome the chance to correspond with you. His wife, you see, is brainless; you must have noticed that. He desperately needs an intelligent, sensitive, open-minded woman on whom he could try out his ideas.'

Minna looked stunned by this; yet naturally flattered. How would Frau Fliess react to this, she wondered? Very badly, I replied; and therefore she should not know about it. There would be absolutely no harm in a platonic correspondence, surely? Minna looked dubious, but finally said she supposed not. If it really would help him . . . It would help him greatly, I urged. Every man in our profession, studying the relationship of the sexes, needed a sensitive female listener.

The deal was struck. I said I would let Fliess know of her consent in my next letter to him. He could enclose his sealed letter to her when writing to me, and I could send on her sealed response with mine.

When she had gone, promising not do anything stupid, I paced up and down, agitated. I wondered if I should take Wilhelm into my confidence, and ask him to write a few flattering letters to my desperate sister-in-law. But I soon saw it was unthinkable; he had too much rectitude.

Over the next few days I could see Minna was pleasantly on edge, waiting for his letter. When I duly wrote his letter to her, I made sure it was full of compliments. She took the envelope from me with a show of indifference, and went straight to her room.

The next day she gave me her reply. I opened it in my work room late at night, my mind full of the day's dreams. How articulately and how warmly she responded! A correspondence with him would give her great pleasure; so long as he was sure of the ethics of a private exchange.

Fliess replied with due assurances. With even more fulsome compliments on her prose style and substantial intellect. Over the next weeks and months their letters became more relaxed and more intimate. He asked her to recount her dreams, and she provided him with some amazing ones. Whereupon, with great delicacy, Fliess hinted at sexual meanings underlying the mundane domestic detail. Far from being shocked, she assented eagerly; offered additional information and interpretation. I learned of her first, incomplete sexual activity with Schönberg; her temptation to masturbate – which Fliess in response assured her was harmless and natural.

Whenever I asked Minna how her correspondence was going, she pretended it was agreeable but wholly formal.

Gradually, though I have never been a seducer, I did my best to seduce Minna with words: for her sake, since everyone remarked how much more blooming and vital she was, how the air of Vienna suited her. The day came when Fliess begged her to masturbate while thinking of him. She fought shy of it for two letters, then yielded.

Fliess and his wife were due to visit Vienna again. He told Minna that seeing her again would be both ecstasy and torment. He could not betray his wife Ida by attempting to arrange a private meeting; and of course, in our company, neither of them must give the slightest hint they had been in communication. Freud, he said, would be devastated if he knew how the correspondence had moved on.

They came. It was always wonderful to see Fliess. He was his usual charming self to Martha and Minna. The latter held herself painfully under control. I knew she suffered when Fliess and I withdrew to my room for cigars and discussion – leaving her to Ida Fliess's talk about her baby. (She and Martha had 'shared' a pregnancy; I had fantasised her child as mine, and ours, Anna, as Fliess's, thus drawing us even closer.)

I was on the verge of discovering the Oedipus Complex.

Chaos churned in my skull, though with hints of form and light, as he and I talked excitedly until dawn.

After their return to Berlin, Minna looked pale and agitated. I invited her to tell me what was wrong. She confessed her involvement with Fliess. I expressed surprise, yet understanding. In his next letter he begged her to try to arrange to have herself photographed in the nude. He was suffering the most intense frustration; to be able to see her naked would be some small consolation. Minna's bosom rose and fell tumultuously as she told me of his outrageous request. Yet she loved him; wanted to please him. Was she very wicked?

'You're not at all wicked; neither is he,' I said gravely. 'Think how appalling it must be to live with a woman like Ida Fliess. A lesser man would visit prostitutes. All Wilhelm wants is an image.'

'It's such a relief to hear you say that! You're a dear, good man!'

'Nonsense! You and I have passionate natures. Martha is a wonderful wife and mother, but of a calmer temperament. One of my former patients is a photographer; and I know he sometimes takes so-called artistic photographs. He's very discreet, very professional. I could make enquiries.'

It cost Minna a great deal of shame to visit the artistic photographer; yet it further liberated her libido. From that moment, almost nothing requested by Fliess was denied him. And since 'the appetite grows by what it feeds on', he began to pour out the most flagrant and perverse fantasies. Taking me into her confidence, Minna increasingly told me about them, asking my opinion. I was able to explain their possible origin, and encouraged her to try and satisfy him.

Fliess, to my surprise, turned out to be a closet transvestite, desiring some of Minna's clothes. Nor were urolagnia, coprophilia and zoophilia alien to his secret nature. Whatever man can imagine, sexually, Fliess imagined it and wanted to experience it. And Minna either helped him achieve it, or sympathised and listened avidly to his accounts of experiments. She admitted to me that some of his perversions gave her a peculiar excitement.

56

Their mutual lust permeated my life, and poured into my dreambook. The enigma of the dream was opening to me like a woman's lips. In fact dream, I found, was the mother. In his letters to Minna, Fliess was expressing greater and greater ambivalence towards me; he urged her to – not exactly seduce me but find out if I were seducible. Minna resisted this strongly, saying it would be a treachery to her sister; but Fliess persisted, pleading that my apparent ethical and moral strength was a constant reproach to him, made him feel weak and unworthy.

Our first kiss, manoeuvred by Minna, occurred while she and I shared a walking holiday in northern Italy. Fliess should have joined us; both he and Minna were tremulous with expectation. However, I wrote to Fliess telling him a meeting would be inconvenient. Subsequently both Minna and I received letters from him excusing himself from the 'congress' – our whimsical term for our holiday meetings. Minna was desperately disappointed, but had to accept his explanation that the temptation would be too great. So, after dinner one night in our *pensione*, taking the air on my balcony, she inveigled me into an embrace. For Fliess. She wrote an account of it for him. She had found it not unpleasant: shutting her eyes and imagining I was he. The stern Freud, after all, she assured him, was not made of marble.

She really was good company. Unlike Martha she had by now an intense interest in and understanding of psychoanalysis. We exchanged dreams. When she related the very same dreams to Fliess, they changed, became more overtly sexual.

I was appalled when Minna confessed that she'd confided in her friend Emma Eckstein ('Irma'). She'd been desperate for a confidante, Minna explained somewhat tearfully. Emma, of course, had had her own 'affair' with Fliess – his gauze left to create infection in her vagina. (Or nose, but Fliess scarcely distinguished between them.) Though she later became puritanical and neurasthenic, Emma at that time still greatly enjoyed the exotic in Eros, and so had encouraged her friend's flowering freedom and liberality. Since Minna had never quite overcome a squeamishness about menstruation, she admitted that Emma, who adored it, had actually provided certain items. Fliess, I said to her with a smile, had presumably adored them as if they had come from his beloved. I forgave Minna her breach of confidence, insisting it should go no further.

Fliess's actual references to my sister-in-law's existence, in his letters to me, never went beyond a cursory request to pass on his and his wife's respects. Our correspondence in general was becoming more cursory; our intimacy was dying. I found the Berlin Fliess a rather dull creator of absurd theories, compared with the 'golden fleece' (Minna's joke) of his letters to her. This golden Fliess, despite his almost dwarfish stature, was a man worthy of Minna's passion; his letters to her moved me, astonished me sometimes, and often filled me with aching desire. He was the only man she had ever encountered, she said, who was as intellectually gifted as I, and with – she hesitated to say it – the additional appeal of possessing a fantastic, if somewhat disturbing, sexual imagination.

On the date I knew to be Schönberg's birthday, I referred to our poor dead friend, once her beloved. Minna gave a shrug. 'We wouldn't have been right for each other,' she said.

Writing feverishly the last chapters of my dream, I decided to put a stop to all the correspondence with Fliess. I had outlived him. He and I had one final acrimonious congress at Achensee where, during a rather perilous ascent, I stumbled against him and almost sent his puny body tumbling into a chasm – it would have been little loss. Writing to Minna subsequently, regretting his rupture with me (but I was an odious plagiarist, stealing his bisexuality theory), saying also he could no longer bear the force of his passion for her, never to be consummated, he bade her farewell. Minna withdrew for a couple of days. When I sought her out, I found her weeping into her handkerchief. I consoled her to the best of my powers; assured her that she, too, meant as much to me as my wife – if not more.

A splendour inevitably went out of her life, with the cessation of the letters from Fliess; yet she never again froze into Marpesian stone. She remained alert, lively, intellectual, occasionally impassioned, and invariably a good companion.

When word came in 1927 of Fliess's death, Minna withdrew into herself for several days. She re-read, for the hundredth time, all his letters, reliving that overwhelming passion of the last years of the nineteenth century. I, too, at that time re-read all of her letters to him. No doubt one day, long after Anna's death, some scholar will find the double *cache*, and will know he has a fortune on his hands. The Fliess–Minna Bernays correspondence will cause a great stir. My letters to him, which have come into the hands of Marie Bonaparte, will never leave her custody; but some of his letters to me will surface, and will be endlessly compared with his secret and salacious letters to my sister-in-law. However damaging they might be to his personal reputation, he will gain immense and undeserved credit for his superb style and his brilliant flashes of psychoanalytical insight. They will say, Freud stole shamelessly from Fliess. So be it. They will wonder also if Freud knew of his sister-in-law's secret passion, her masochistic personality. They will say, she at least kissed him once, on a balcony overlooking an Italian lake; but deceived him even in the act of attempted seduction. Did it go further?

Then there will be the usual maverick scholar, noting shades of difference in the Fliess handwriting of the correspondence with Minna as compared with letters to others, who will claim that they are forgeries. He will be shouted down, since Minna's letters are so clearly authentic. This, it will be said, is the real, unrepressed Fliess, so small wonder if his hand flowed slightly differently.

9

A drowsy kind of semi-dream, in which I have to choose which of the 'wolves' of my life shall be allowed to rape me. They are: the Wolf Man; Wolf our lovely Alsatian, so infallible in judging when the fifty minutes were over, bounding in at the door; Antonia Wolff, Jung's patient and long-enduring mistress; and the mad Mrs Virginia Woolf, who won't be analysed in case she loses her (by my judgement slender) gift for writing . . .

All seem equally unpleasant. I've no wish to be raped by a large dog or a mad Bloomsbury horse or my poor old Russian friend. Toni Wolff was attractive, but I've no desire to have intercourse with a woman who has chosen to entertain Jung's uncircumcised penis hundreds of times.

This threat of rape would seem to be a punishment for my sin against Minna and Fliess. You will already have guessed, from my somewhat over-jocular account, that I have a guilty conscience. All I can say in expiation is that it didn't seem, at the time, as if I was playing games at their expense. I was, as I say, disturbed during those years. Their correspondence became a pulsating drama and a drug. Sometimes, when Minna had started to confide in me, I felt genuinely upset on her behalf that Fliess had written something tart or off-hand.

When I 'yielded' to her flirtatious smiles and hand-touches on the balcony that night I knew I was Fliess to her eyes, and that thought added to my pleasure. That I was being simultaneously seduced and betrayed. And I kissed, not Minna especially, but Wilhelm – possibly; and certainly my new patient of that year, 1900, Ida Bauer; my 'Dora'. She had come to me, as a failed suicide, yet with so much youthful charm and spontaneity. My God, how they all came, all those women! Letting me strip them and seduce them into opening up – raping them, indeed, since the resistance is most of the pleasure. And paying me too, as if I were a prostitute!

I thought of Dora too, as Minna's older, drier lips pressed against mine, because the lake was glimmering in the moonlight beneath us, and Dora had told me how the husband of her father's mistress had pressed himself against her by a lake. It was irritating me that I couldn't get her to admit the obvious – that her disgust concealed desire. She claimed she preferred the company of his wife, 'Frau K.', even though she was her father's mistress.

Yet, for all my irritation, her warm fresh lips clove to mine as Minna kissed me that night by the lake.

Minna and I have only very infrequently slept together. The betrayal of Martha? Sisters know about such things; Martha never liked to be away from Vienna for long; she was often grateful to pack me off with Minna. Our experiences of coitus were never earth-shaking, for either of us; her most rapturous explorations of Eros were all with 'Fliess'. He never suggested to her that actual sex was a possibility; and even had she hoped for it some day, perhaps through the death of his wife, she would have discovered the negative side of love that Sabina Spielrein has described so beautifully. I quote from memory: 'One feels the enemy inside oneself, in one's own glowing love which forces one, from sheer necessity, to do what one doesn't want to do: one feels the end, the fleetingness, from which one vainly seeks to escape. "Is that all?" lovers ask themselves. "Is this the climax, and nothing further, nothing beyond?" . . .'

I am thinking of Spielrein because of an association of ideas with my Dora. Dora's father was a charming syphilitic. Spielrein, at the end of her nightmarish love for Jung, had a dream in which he appeared as a 'syphilitic Don Juan' . . .

Martha and Minna loom briefly at my bedside, in their dressing-gowns and nightcaps. We exchange a few meaningless words and they kiss my forehead. Poor dear Martha – is this the girl I so tormented myself about as I wandered the Parisian streets, hungry in every sense? To whom I wrote that we were certain to achieve our dream of a little home into which sorrow might find its way but never privation? A closeness through all life's vicissitudes, a quiet contentment, a little world of happiness full of beds and mirrors and linen tied with pretty ribbons? My God! *That* Freud is more fictional than my Fliess was.

When the old ladies drift off, Anna comes and wipes away my sweat tenderly. The pain surges; I am 'bound upon a wheel of fire'.

Anna says she must talk to me about something painful but necessary. The biography. She is much too close to write it. What about Jones? On the other hand, since our movement has welcomed women into its ranks so generously, perhaps it should be Tod? She was moving to this country, so would be conveniently close to Anna and archives.

'Jung,' I whisper hoarsely.

She frowns. 'To write your biography? Impossible!'

'Liked you a lot.'

'Oh, I see. Well, it wasn't mutual.'

'He'd have wanted to marry you, Anna, if he'd been free.'

To become truly my son. And at the time (my God! Jesus Christ!) I'd have welcomed it.

She stands, shadowy in her white nightdress, lifting her arms to loosen her hair. She reminds me in that pose of the caryatids on the Acropolis. I see the white marble and the dazzling blue sky over Athens for the last time. Recall my peculiar 'absences' and memory loss as I stood there, the first time. Realised later it was because of poor Papa. He had never come here nor wished to, not being educated. I had gone beyond him. It made me sad.

Anna Jung. No, thank God.

That was when, knowing Anna was impossible, he'd turned to a fourteen-year-old psychotic patient at the Burghölzli Hospital in Zurich. I have known several significant analysts who have gone mad; but fewer lunatics who have become significant

62

analysts. But this is what happened to Sabina Spielrein. Few of us, who saw the petite, dark-haired newcomer command her professional audience in Vienna, would have dreamt the truth, which was that she had great difficulty not believing that we were all defecating. From the age of three, this was her torturing obsession. She could not look at people, since they all insisted in carrying out that private function in public.

Jung wrote to me about her in, I think, 1906. It was our first communication. She was fourteen, from Rostov on Don in Russia. She had been beaten by her father ('A child is being beaten') and watched her brother likewise being thrashed. Consequently she developed an anal eroticism, holding back her stools – once for two weeks – in order to produce a more intense masturbatory pleasure.

It was, I have to say, brave of Jung to analyse a sufferer from psychotic hysteria; yet also doomed to failure and highly dangerous. She did not even know the facts of life – and remained ignorant of them throughout the first year of analysis! When he said to her, 'Well, you must obey me,' she orgasmed violently on the couch, he informed me. For the adolescent girl, Jung was not merely her father but her father when she was three – actual, living, present. I am forced to believe they told me the truth in insisting their love was beyond anything earthly: it is all too likely to happen in such circumstances. Sabina, when she came to me at last to cure herself of Jung, described the trance they would be in, gazing at each other, for an hour, two hours, three hours. 'We became each other,' she said; 'he even menstruated.'

Jung behaved abominably when someone (no doubt Emma Jung) reported him to her parents; but I do believe he was justified in saying that sometimes one must behave unworthily simply in order to live.

Gazing into his eyes; seeing her reflection there; Jung's solid Germanic skull, neat moustache and spectacles replacing – or probably superimposed on – shit.

Well, as dear H. D. would say, that figures!

She taught Lou Salomé the trick of squatting so that her heel pressed against her anus; keeping it back, keeping it in; the eyes raised in ecstasy. Spielrein was a noble woman; her heart was of the purest. Truly in sex the highest and the lowest are in touch. I said to her once, when she was in tears, 'Those who don't see the shit, Fräulein Sabina, don't see the stars.'

I too gazed into her sombre, spiritual eyes and felt love for her. She wanted that scoundrel's child. Siegfried, he would have been called. Instead, she got her doctorate in the field of schizophrenia, and went on to psychoanalyse Pasteur. No, Piaget.

When he realised he was seeing his mother in this slight Russian brunette he said, '*Je comprends tout*,' and walked out.

I don't suppose he realised she was watching him defecating on the couch, constantly.

Well, usually they give us a load of shit. Patients.

I urged her to marry and have a normal child. She did; in fact I think she had two daughters. Her husband unfortunately died after a long illness, in which she nursed him devotedly. We kept in touch. She communicated to me, together with several exclamation marks, Jung's 'last words' on me. They went something like this: 'A sinful rapist of all that is holy. He spreads darkness rather than light. New light is born out of deepest darkness, and our Siegfried will be that spark. I lit in you a new light. Nourish and protect it devotedly . . .'

Well, she knew by then what trust to put in the Aryan gods of light.

I was able to help her with a little money. After her husband's death she chose to return to her native land. I heard from her twice. The first time, she was involved in child analysis and working with Luria, of whom she spoke warmly. Her elder daughter was studying the cello at the Moscow Conservatoire. Music meant a lot to Spielrein. Minna saw her once at a symphony concert, and told me she sat throughout with her eyes shut, a rapturous expression on her face. I didn't tell Minna her eyes were probably closed because she didn't want to see the members of the orchestra and the conductor defecating . . .

Her last letter came on the very day the Gestapo paid us

a visit; the time they asked me to write a note saying we'd been correctly treated and I duly noted that I could recommend them to anyone. Sabina had written to say she was spending a few days in Kiev; I was in her thoughts especially because she had met another former patient of mine at some function to do with the Kiev Opera, with which this woman was connected. Sabina thought my ears would have burned. She sounded quite cheerful but there was a possibly macabre note towards the end, when she said her three brothers were working in a factory making ice cream. It seemed innocent, and I know the Russians love ice cream; but it was an unlikely occupation for educated men, and I recalled a dream of Sabina's in which ice cream was a deathly image. Her youngest brother had once dropped his ice-cream cornet in the snow, and their father had thrashed him into unconsciousness.

It's likely, however, that our sinister visitors made me take a casual remark too seriously and morbidly. Probably her brothers are indeed happily making ice cream.

— No, of course I didn't write Fliess's letters to Minna for him! When their letters are published, you can rest assured they are authentic. A Jewish joke. I merely read them in transit, out of familial responsibility.

— Or not. Who can tell what happened in the past? Those events are happening somewhere else, in a land where there's strict censorship.

10

I've mentioned, I believe, the prostitute who lay with me in the entrance to a park. Years later I discovered she was no prostitute but none other than the Empress Elizabeth. Nor was I her only 'client'. Touched by family madness (but all Bavarians are mad), she had taken to wandering out on her own, clad only in a dress – no underclothes or stockings. When the Emperor asked her what gift she would like for her name day, she replied, 'A fully equipped insane asylum'.

But she already had that. The Empire was full of death and madness. Franz Joseph's coat of many colours was gradually torn apart. First his richest provinces, in Italy and Germany; then his beloved Elizabeth, the most beautiful woman in Europe, goes mad and is rarely at home. Then his only son and heir, Rudolf, kills himself and his mistress in a suicide pact, after one last act of love, at his hunting lodge at Mayerling in the Vienna woods.

'Well, what could you expect?' says my Mama in frenetic Yiddish, drying her eyes and sniffing back her tears. 'With a father who spends eighteen hours a day working at his desk like some clerk, and a mother who's crazy? She should have pulled herself together for her son's sake. *Now* she has the right to go crazy.'

Some madman or other set fire to the Ring Theatre in 1881, while the *Tales of Hoffmann* was being performed, killing four hundred people. My fiancée Martha and I, and my sister Anna and Martha's brother, had been due to attend, but something prevented us. The opera house was rebuilt as an opulent apartment building, called the Sühnhaus or 'House of Atonement', and Martha and I moved into it after our marriage. The rent was far higher than I could afford, but I wished to show that I wasn't superstitious. For the same reason I forbade Martha to light the Sabbath candles on our first marital Friday.

I have never been afraid of the dead. When my rather repulsive friend Nathan Weiss, a young neurologist, hanged himself after a brief honeymoon, I immediately took up residence in his apartment. No ghost appeared then, and none later in the House of Atonement.

My few, early clients sometimes nervously sniffed the air, smelling smoke. But it was only my cigar. Not that I dismiss experiences of the uncanny, I've had too many of them.

A terracotta figurine of Nefertiti came apart in my hands on a day in 1898, in the midst of my self-analysis. This death of the most beautiful woman of ancient Egypt made me, incomprehensibly, think that the most beautiful woman of modern Europe was dead. Elizabeth was on one of her interminable and aimless travels. The next day we learned she had been shot by an anarchist in Geneva.

But still, the more death's cancer ate into Vienna, the more fiercely she danced, the more fiercely she fucked. (Poor Schreber, who wanted to insert a ravenous rat up his father's arse, yet thought he adored him – his publishers excised 'fuck' and 'arse' from his memoirs, with great cowardice.) The louder the band played Strauss in the Prater for the late-night schnapps drinkers under the gas lamps. It wasn't difficult, in a city whose Empress was a full-blown hysteric, narcissist and anorexic, to decide to become a psychoanalyst.

If I try to find an image for the dying Empire, I see a worm, dropped from a bird's beak, writhing in grass. The image is associated with Emma Eckstein. One day, while strolling in the Prater, I saw her coming towards me. Her slightly misshapen features, a consequence of Fliess's bungling, were a reproach to me. She was with her sister Therese, a socialist politician, one of the first women members of parliament. Fraülein Eckstein, after our greetings, said she would like a private word with me about a patient. (She had just made the change from lying on my couch to sitting behind her own.) Her sister strolled on, leaving us together.

Emma spoke about the patient cursorily, then moved to her real reason for wishing to talk to me: Minna, whose relationship with Fliess was nearing its culmination. Minna was suffering acutely, Emma said; I should use my influence with Doctor Fliess to persuade him to divorce his wife and acknowledge Minna. At the very least, *meet* with her. 'He has corrupted her innocence,' she said.

'Innocence? At thirty-four!' A woman (I did not add) who had masturbated Schönberg almost nightly for a year.

'Innocence, certainly, when faced with such depravity. He is more sick than I ever was. He *must* divorce his wife.'

'One doesn't say *must* to such a proud and honourable family man.'

Though, in truth, I was becoming a shade jaundiced with him. I did not think our friendship would survive much longer.

She looked at me intently through her small but fiery eyes, and her narrow lips tightened. 'She has strong feelings for someone else too,' she said. 'It might be better for the Frau Professor if her sister went away.'

Our path had taken us into a secluded spot. She stopped, came up very close and murmured, 'I want to kiss you, Professor.' It was very clear why she wished to get Minna out of the way, and I have already implied I wasn't indifferent to my former patient. In face of my polite rejection of an urge born of transference, Emma bent down, scooped up a worm that had been writhing in the short grass, and held it in her palm. 'You swallow us alive!' she said bitterly: and plunged it into her mouth.

Well, after having been forced, at thirteen, to eat part of her own labia, a worm was nothing.

I lie unable to sleep. Anna is restless too. I hear her tossing and turning and sighing. I love her less than Sophie and more than

Mathilde, though I love all three. And certainly with none but Anna have I felt a telepathic connection. We proved it with experiments, and I wrote a paper on it, which my colleagues dissuaded me from publishing.

Now, lying both sleepless, there is an invisible bridge between us.

Mathilde was the first baby born in the Sühnhaus. The Emperor, ignorant of my adolescent intercourse with his wife, sent me a congratulatory letter.

One of our neighbours was an early patient, whom I cured of migraine. He became Director of the Linz Technical School. Though we'd moved to Berggasse he kept in touch and showed sympathy for my battles with outraged citizens by inviting me to present diplomas in 1904. The diploma for junior engineering, I recall, went to a young lad called L. Wittgenstein and that for senior art to a rather truculent-looking youth called A. Hitler.

Now this is more like it, this is more like a traditional memoir. You're learning some *facts* at last; you're sitting back in your armchair more comfortably.

Berggasse was a much more nondescript street than the Ringstrasse. Our apartment was about half-way between the Fleamarket at the bottom and the smart middle-class residences and University at the top of the hill. And that's where we are – half-way up. I'm too good to sell old clothes and not good enough to be a full professor. I know my place. I'm not in the brains of Vienna nor at its stinking feet. Half-way up.

Here I encounter young poets with no illness except poverty and starvation, whom I send away with money to buy a few steak dinners; and Russian aristocrats, who confess to wishing to bugger me and shit on my head, and who require more complicated treatment.

Around us stand or sit the imperturbable, unshockable gods and goddesses.

They made no murmur when Anna said quietly to me one day, 'Doctor Schur has given me a way out in case of . . . you know. But is it worth waiting? Shall we die together, Papa?'

We might have been found lying together, like Prince Rudolf and his mistress at Mayerling. Such deaths were no longer an exception; hundreds were taking Rudolf's way.

An elderly Jew unfortunate enough to be called Freud had been beaten up in the street and left for dead. Anna didn't want it to happen to me.

But it's the survivors who do the dying. I thought of Tausk, that unusual double-suicide – shot himself and hanged himself. With a letter to me saying it's been an honour to have known me, and please look after his sons from time to time! That's what I call aggression! Tried to reach me through Frau Lou's bed and Frau Deutsch's couch; didn't succeed. I didn't reward his final act of aggression with grief or even regret. Let him rot, I thought.

On her way back from visiting the bathroom Anna comes to me, wondering if I am awake or asleep or dead. My eyes opening, she smiles tenderly and kneels. She wipes the sweat from my face with a handkerchief.

'You're not sleeping too well, either,' I murmur.

'I'm being woken by my dreams.'

'Are they so upsetting?'

'They're very stupid. I think I'm back home, in 1914, and taking my teacher's examination. Every paper is simple but I'm paralysed mentally, I can't put my thoughts together. I've failed, and I don't know how I'm going to tell you. But then I'm given a second chance, in middle life – now – and the very same thing is happening!'

I rest my hand on hers. 'It's a strange phenomenon,' I say, 'examination dreams. We only ever dream of failing exams that we've already passed.'

'Really?'

'Yes. We always think we didn't deserve to pass. We're conscious of our ignorance even if the examiners were not. But I think in this case you're afraid of letting me down, Anna;

that you won't be able to rise to the occasion for much longer. You're wondering how long you'll be able to go on enduring the stench from my cancer.'

'That's not true!' she exclaims, agitated.

'Well . . . probably not. I've not often been right in my interpretations, so why should I expect to do better in this last one?'

I twist my mouth into a glimmer of a smile – and in so doing can't help grunting from the pain of it.

After enabling me to urinate, she kisses me on the brow and returns to bed.

I watched Martha, a couple of times, teaching her to sit on the little chamberpot.

Whether or not her dream is the instigator, at the end of this night – or rather in the early morning, since I go on sleeping fitfully between brief encounters with Anna, Minna, Martha and Schur – I dream vividly though inactively. Schur tells me that a ship called the *Courageous* has been torpedoed; five hundred men have been lost. The Russians have crossed the border. In America a former ace-flier called Lindbergh has made a powerful speech proclaiming the need for his country to remain neutral, and praising Hitler. Martha and Minna tell me there is to be a census in a week's time to decide how many in each house are entitled to identity cards and ration books. I upset them by saying I shan't need a card as by then I shall have no identity.

Martha upsets *me* by replying, 'You'll live for ever; I have no identity; you made me disappear. Since my marriage I had one year – *one* – when I was somebody; and you ground it out of me, Sigi. You probably don't even remember.' Dabbing her eyes with her lace handkerchief, she hobbles out of the room. Minna gazes at me open-mouthed, and I shrug. Minna starts to cry too; she says, 'I shall miss you more than anyone; more even than Anna.'

Anna brings me a letter with a Hungarian postmark. The letter is signed 'Gisela Ferenczi'. Gisela writes that she wishes me well in my new abode.

I lie reflecting on this last dream (perhaps) before death. Anna, Minna and Martha represent the three Fates. Schur is the shaman figure who must provide the ritual of easing my way into an unconsciousness deeper than the unconscious. The lost ship calls to mind the Egyptian funerary barges that stand on my shelves; I fear that not only Anna will lose courage. Five hundred, in Roman numerology, is D, the initial letter of the English word for death. Schur's face was suitably grief-stricken as he related it.

'Crossing the border' is obvious too; and the Russians are themselves a borderland people, hybrid of Europe and Asia. It would be pleasant to have an identity card and ration book: they would guarantee that I still had an identity – and moreover one which was able to eat.

I have long felt that America was the enemy – no, the antithesis – of psychoanalysis. It has no buried layers. Neutrality would therefore be some gain, from our point of view. But Lindbergh . . . flew the Atlantic, as our movement tried to do. 'Hitler' refers to the German megalomaniac responsible for burning my books. The fact that he is praised by Lindbergh ends that part of the dream on a note of pessimism, despite his promotion of a neutral view of our science. They may become neutral but they will never understand.

Lindbergh is *Linden*, lime trees, and *lind*, gentle, plus Freiberg. I have the scent of the gentle lime in my head – strengthened by the first line of a love poem by Friedrich Rückert, orientalist as well as poet: *Ich atmet' einen linden Duft*. It links me with the real subject of the last part of my dream: an adolescent infatuation.

The letter from Gisela Ferenczi is the most personal part of the dream. The name has a direct meaning – Gisela Ferenczi is the widow of a man who was a good and loyal analyst until he went mad late in his life. But why should I imagine that she, of all people, should wish me well? No reason – except that a different Gisela, Gisela Flüss, was the first love of my life. She lived in Freiberg; I stayed with her family during my one and only return to my birthplace, when I was sixteen. I walked with her, hand in hand, in that sloping green meadow, dotted with dandelions, I remembered (very imperfectly) from my infancy. The touch of her hand, the first touch of a woman's hand not my mother's, induced a sentimental and erotic delight greater than any much more intimate act since. First love – the love that, Turgenev wrote, cannot and perhaps should not be repeated.

I quoted to her the Rückert love lyric, striving to impress. I had just learnt it at school. In general our conversations were stumbling and inarticulate. We spoke mainly through our shy eyes, our fingertips, the silences as the hem of her long blue skirt rustled through the long grass. Or when, scarcely able to eat her mother's tasty food, I raised my eyes from my plate and met hers, fleetingly, before she glanced blushing away. Gisela!

I developed a raging toothache while I was staying with them, and her kindly mother gave me some spirits to drink. It was my first experience of alcohol and I sank into a drunken stupor. The next day I could not recall climbing the stairs to bed. Gisela's mother, with a merry smile, said she had been worried about me, and had come to my room twice during the night. Instantly, with that remark, my erotic feelings redoubled; to the daughter I added the mother. She was indeed a beautiful lady, with long sable locks, intense black eyes, an aquiline nose and firm lips; but above all she was highly intelligent and well read – a contrast to most Jewish mothers, who are content to give birth to male geniuses.

I wanted to stay in Freiberg; I regretted ever having left that paradise. *There* was where the deep forests were.

And so I had the illusion that Gisela – both the daughter and the mother – was wishing me well.

The mother, of course, must be long since dead; so may the daughter be.

And Ferenczi?

It echoes Firenze (Florence), where I saw the Gates of Paradise, at the entrance to the great breast of the Duomo, at the time when I was writing my *Interpretation of Dreams*. I am reminded also of another breast, across water in a city of shimmering, liquid reflections – its name escapes me for the moment; and of the great city, Amor, where day by day

I contemplated the disturbed and angry Moses. There, too, I entered the vast vagina of the universal Church.

'I am going outside. I may be some time.'

Anna blanches with terror.

'It must be today,' I say, touching her arm gently. 'I can't stand it any more.'

She pleads, but I remain firm. She weeps, but eventually dries her tears. There is the sound of a motor car drawing up; it signals Schur, my redeemer.

He enters, brisk and cheerful. 'Good morning, my friend,' I murmur. 'You know what you have to do. Anna concurs.' His face becomes grave.

'Are you sure?'

'Yes.'

He unfastens and opens his Gladstone bag.

'I'll fetch Mama and Auntie,' Anna says in a choking voice.

'There's no need. Why worry them? I won't die for a day or two. They can say goodbye while I'm unconscious. Anna, my darling, don't forget you are an analyst. Study your own mourning. Expect to feel that I am lost in some deep forest or on some high and freezing mountain. That I'm unhappy. It won't be so: it is you who will feel lost and unhappy. But that will pass.'

There is also *Berg*, mountain. I feel as I have felt in the icy eternal shadow of some overhanging mountain in the Dolomites or Alps.

She flings herself into my arms, sobbing. Salt water against my cheek. Schur gently removes her. The needle pricks.

'Thank you,' I say to him. 'You've been good to me always.'

He too is blinking back tears; rests a hand on my shoulder. 'Goodbye, old friend.'

The pain is already easing a little.

His voice comes as it were from a distance. 'Don't you think you should say goodbye to them?'

I open my eyes and glance around at the indifferent observers. I lift my hand. 'Goodbye.'

I I

A dream: I have to undertake a test about something called the black-out. I fail at it. Feel deeply ashamed.

12

Since time does not exist in the unconscious, it's a few years
after the Great War, in the early years of my war with cancer;
I am sitting in the Ronacher Café with Lou Andreas-Salomé.
(Though I don't know why one should have to bother with
her husband's name, since they have never slept together.) It's
the first time she has seen me with the prosthesis and she is
naturally shocked by my appearance and speech. But she says
my eyes are as bright as ever. I tell her it's a great tonic to see
her. Though she is over sixty, her hair is still luxuriant, her blue
eyes still profoundly erotic. She is indeed a 'fortunate animal'.

It grows late but I have no wish to leave. She speaks about
female narcissism, the ability of certain women to rest content
in passivity, in their attractiveness, loved rather than loving,
being rather than doing. I agree with her as vigorously as I
am able. She is supremely such a type, yet combines it with a
masculine forcefulness and intellect. She talks of how appealing
the narcissistic personality is to many men, and how it enables
women to be undivided in their spirit and their flesh. 'The
flesh, our desires, are perfectly at home in our spirituality,'
she reflects; 'whereas men's are always divided.'

My gaze drinking her in, I relate with difficulty how a
white cat climbed in through my window, becoming a regular
guest – yet totally, narcissistically indifferent to my feelings and
attentions. 'She enters the room because she feels comfortable
there! She doesn't do it for me, even though I enjoy her
presence. A woman ought to be like my beautiful white
cat. Though of course when such a cool woman becomes

impassioned by a man and sets out to seduce him, she can be utterly devastating.'

'You're thinking of Martha with Philipp Bauer,' she says.

'Yes.'

Bauer. There will be plenty about *Breuer* in the biographies, but nothing about Bauer; except in relation to my case study of his daughter Ida ('Dora'). Even though Bauer caused me infinitely more trouble.

'According to Felix Deutsch, who performed my operation,' I say, 'Ida Bauer is teaching bridge to aristocratic ladies and gentlemen! And her partner is – guess who? – Frau Zellenka! "Frau K.!" Her father's former mistress!'

Frau Lou throws back her head in a gay laugh, making her hair shimmer in the light of the candelabras. 'Good heavens!'

'So the two homoerotic women have got together at last! Frau Zellenka's husband has conveniently died, and Ida's husband is brain-damaged from a war wound. Deutsch treated her for tinnitus and dizziness for a short while: she feels guilty because she's burdened with unwanted responsibility for her husband.'

Her laughter composes itself into a serious, compassionate expression. 'Yes, it must be hard for her. What pain comes from love; and yet who can do without it?' She quotes her own translation of a poem by Mandelstam, a poet she met during her recent visit to her birthplace, Petersburg – now Leningrad – with her lover Rilke and her husband Andreas. They talked with the poet one whole night, she says, while the distant Civil War explosions rattled the windows of his apartment. 'His poem breathed a longing for Eros rather than Thanatos. One line especially stirs me and makes me sad: "*The sea, and Homer – everything's moved by love.*"'

Her mind leaping from idea to idea, Frau Lou speaks next about the closeness of the anus and the genitals. The waste products from the first conjure death, and the genitals, life. She likes to think life and death themselves are as close: their separation merely an illusion. I start to frown, then remember this is Lou speaking and smile instead.

We are the last ones in the restaurant; the waiters stand close, polite yet anxious that we should go. After summoning the bill, I ask Lou how she has been getting on with Anna. At my request she has taken over her analysis. 'She's an extraordinary young woman,' she replies. 'She's doing fine.'

'Is she irremediably homosexual?'

'What did you think?'

A waiter brings her her sable coat, and she drapes it loosely about her shoulders without standing up.

'It's difficult when it's your own daughter.'

Absently she takes a cigarette from her gold case; a waiter springs to light it for her. 'Thank you so much. Well, she seems extremely fond of this Eva Rosenfeld. Extremely. But, you see, she is *you*, my dear. Since the objects of your desire are almost invariably women, it's natural she should follow suit. Ah, a bridge metaphor! Nevertheless, she's shown me a story she wrote during your trip to Rome. Did you know she was writing?'

I shake my head.

'When she'd helped you to bed after dinner and was back in her room. It's much like the masturbatory fairy tales of her youth, only much more powerfully sexual, and again she assumes the male persona: but this time it's very direct, very *you*! And she's actually your wife! Your daughter-wife! However, there are hopeful signs too. To answer your question – I don't know!'

The waiter collects the plate of notes, bowing slightly. It's an enormous amount of currency for pathetically little food; still, the situation has improved since the armistice. I wave away the change; Frau Lou and I rise. At full height, giving proportion to her stately opera–diva girth, her magnificence is apparent. 'I'm very grateful to you,' I say, helping her slip on her coat.

'Oh, it's a great pleasure! She's delightful. We get on like a house on fire.'

It's a warm, pleasant night and we decide to walk. She slips an arm into mine, supporting me as we make our way slowly.

'How's Martha?' she enquires.

'Very well.'

'And Minna?'

'Quite well too.'

'What a beautiful moon! . . . I don't know what I'd have done if you'd not come through the operation. Or what Anna would have done. Her fantasy expresses not merely love but devotion, passion. She's based it on episodes during the first period of the war, when she says both you and her mother seemed disturbed.'

I point out that our beloved Sophie had left (though not so irredeemably as she has left us now), Mathilde had married too and gone from the nest; and above all our sons were in the Army. Naturally we had been disturbed. Just three old people and Anna.

'Of course, but she felt there were other influences. She's terribly sensitive to atmosphere.'

I stop to rest. The click of her high-heeled shoes ceases too; I breathe the warm scent of her fur.

'But it's none of my business,' she concludes.

We walk on again, in silence.

'Of course I remember how deeply in *love* with Martha you were, all of a sudden; and it seemed strange. Anna, in the story, has a character called Kofman or Kaufman . . .'

'The name doesn't ring a bell.'

Aha! The Cough-Man! I smile to myself. Little minx!

'Ah, well, I expect he's fictional. Fiction's a wonderful release. I always love to get back to it. One can say the most awful things about people, and when they object you pretend to be horrified they imagined they could be *that* idiot, or *that* whore!' She laughs delightedly, and tightens my arm closer to her.

We have reached Berggasse. Fumbling for my key, I ask her if she'd like to come in.

'No, I'd better not.' – Kissing my cheek. 'It's very late.'

Our maid Martha is up still, writing a letter at the kitchen table. She greets me as a mildly annoying disturbance, glancing

79

up over her spectacles, muttering a word or two, then concentrating once more on our son-in-law Max. A warm impulse to show affection, born of the memories conjured up by the conversation about Anna, dies on me. But I lay a hand on her shoulder and overlook her letter: 'Anna, too, grieves deeply for Heinele; on top of which she still hasn't got over the shock of her cousin Mausi's suicide . . .' Death. Death. The erotic impulse withers.

I must read Anna's story.

I say 'Good night', and Martha mechanically echoes it.

Minna's door opens as I walk by. She is dressed still – still with that little white cap on that characterises Minna-Martha. 'Sigi,' she whispers, 'would you come in for a moment, please?'

I enter, and sit on a cane chair. With a creaking of whalebone she sits on her bed. I can see she has been crying.

'Do you know what anniversary this is?' she asks.

I answer, with only a momentary pause for thought, 'The assassination of Julius Caesar.'

She makes an impatient gesture. 'Fliess wrote me his last letter.' She glances aside at his framed photograph, a smaller version of one I still have in my study. She keeps his portrait in a drawer usually; apart from myself only Emma Eckstein and – years after the 'affair' was over – Martha have seen it. Those eyes are rather weak, in contrast to the stiff Prussian bearing and manly black beard; yet they bore into one.

She picks up his letter from the bed – I recognise the script. 'What did I write, in my letter, that made him decide to finish it? Did I hold back too long when he asked me for – for certain things? Or was I too ready to please? Was he appalled by the obscenity of my imagination? It's all right for men to have certain desires and urges, but not women. What do you think, my dear? I was wondering if – this' – she picks up a copy of her own letter – 'might have put him off me . . .' She reads me the passage. I assure her there was nothing he could have taken amiss, and that the reasons he gave (mainly his hostility to me) were the real ones.

If only, she laments, I'd allowed her one direct communication, one embrace, one kiss, that time in my study! She is referring to Fliess's last visit, not long before our 'divorce'. Minna had burst into the study on some pretext, and hoped I'd find an excuse to leave them on their own for a few minutes.

'You know I couldn't have done that, my dear: not with his wife in the house.'

'I know, I know!' She sniffs back her tears. 'It would have been wrong. But he looked so sad, so – yearning.'

Women are more noble in love than men. Such loyalty! Such enduring devotion! I was tempted to tell her the Fliess she loved, the golden fleece, did not exist; but it would have been pointlessly cruel.

Anyway – Anna's story went completely out of my mind. Not until 1934, another decade, did I read it, or part of it, when something or other brought it back to consciousness. I wonder if I can remember it. It may be a useful exercise; memory will vanish soon, taking with it *Hamlet*, *The Punic Wars*, *The Trojans*, *Rosmersholm*, sections of *Brothers Karamazov*, medical textbooks, Anna's poem *Dichter*, read to me in analysis, in which she longs to be David to my Saul. Everything I know by heart will go, wiped out.

I'm sure I shall badly misquote her; her prose is not elegant but simple and direct.

13

On hotel notepaper in a smart grey Italian folder bearing the title, **Strictly Private** . . .

1

I have fallen in love with my wife Anna.

The strangest thing about that is that I am sixty, Anna is forty-three; we have been married for twenty-five years and have several children. Also, as a result of various negative factors, we have slept in separate rooms for almost half our married life.

The night when everything began to change started with a routine meeting at a colleague's house. We had a fairly stimulating discussion. I walked home with a sense of satisfaction but also undercurrents of sadness. Our house, when I arrived, was silent. I climbed the stairs to bed, removing my collar as I did so. There was a light under my eldest son's bedroom door; in his first year at the University, he would be studying, I hoped. Or would he be exploring forbidden literature? There was a light too under my wife's door; she would be reading some romance or detective story; I did not bother to say good night. I undressed and got into bed.

I do not have a natural gift for accepting the death of the libido. Anna has never completely lost her attraction in my sight. For a long time I had tried to stir a response in her, though by now I had given it up as a useless exercise. Partly I sublimated, partly I clung to memories of our passionate youth. I had a very small artistic talent in my schooldays; in our romantic years she allowed me to resurrect my gift, making some extremely erotic sketches of her. I still cherished them; and used them. I planned to use them that night. I was opening a cabinet when the door opened and Anna appeared, smiling, clad in a gauzy dressing-robe.

'I'm feeling better!' she said blithely. She climbed into my bed, removing her robe.

When I climbed in beside her she embraced me, pulling me to her and pressing her lips to mine. This woman – growing wrinkled, her bosom less firm, her waist thickening – was unfamiliar to me. Where was the slim form of my erotic drawings? I didn't want her; felt hatred for all the years of denial, of punishing me for my commitment to work; felt anger that she should so coolly assume I'd want her. Well, I didn't; she repelled me like a succubus, writhing under me. Her vagina was slack; where I wanted to be gripped, I was not. I craved the drawings. Just leave me to my memories of you, I wanted to snarl.

Though she was so much younger, a woman ages less well than a man. Yet this was not the reason for my revulsion: it was a raging resentment. The sex that night was more like death.

I was happy to turn to my interesting patients, next morning. Yet something had stirred in me; and that night I did not stay up so late, working, writing up the case notes of a male homosexual. I was happy to watch Anna undress before me. As we embraced I started to find newly remembered sensations from long ago. Her infinitely subtle kisses, for instance, that suddenly became lost to everything except the need to explore me with her tongue, teeth, gums – her entire soul concentrated in her mouth. And how wonderful it was to hold so much flesh! Such mature amplitude! This was better than slimness. And I liked the slack, cavernous vagina: it told us that she had lived, loved, given birth many times.

She, the reader of detective stories, surprised me by quoting a lyric by Hölderlin. My God, I thought, she's intelligent! 'It's just that you didn't notice,' she said. 'I've been reading a lot, thinking a lot.'

We wanted each other again, and took each other. I groaned: 'I feel happy!'

She murmured, laughing, that I made it sound like a complaint. 'I thought the most one can expect is normal human unhappiness!' she teased.

'But why this change, Anna? What's happened to you?'
'Don't ask. Be grateful.'

The early, spring dawn was already breaking; birds had started tentatively to chirp. I felt a great liberation of body and spirit. Soon I heard her breathing gently in sleep, but I lay wakeful, too tranquilly happy to waste this moment in oblivion.

14

2

I have lived most of my married life with the helpless feeling that I could do nothing to rescue a bad situation; even though I loved Anna and felt, deep down, that she loved me.

I believed I had allowed myself to be led astray by the romance of her family background. Anna is from my own native town Freiberg (following the war, Pribor), the youngest child by far of a textile merchant called Flüss. He and his wife were friends of my parents before my family's departure for Vienna. When I was sixteen my mother took me for a return visit, and I was dazzled by the Moravian countryside and, even more, by a beautiful girl, Gisela Flüss. Her mother also evoked my heartfelt admiration and gratitude. When I suffered from excruciating toothache during my stay, and Herr Flüss plied me with spirits, Frau Flüss visited me twice in the night to make sure I was all right.

I became engaged in my twenties to a young woman called Martha. We were separated by my going to Paris, to work under the great Charcot; I grew jealous of Martha's friends, and broke the engagement. I assumed I would be a lifelong bachelor.

However, some ten years later I chanced to meet and recognise Frau Flüss in a street. The family had followed our example in moving to Vienna. The much-aged lady invited me to her home, half-expecting I think that I would still be charmed by Gisela. But her bloom, of course, was gone. Instead, I was dazzled by the rather boyish charm and intelligence of her sixteen-year-old 'baby' sister: Anna.

After a whirlwind courtship we married, much to the distress —

indeed, anguish – of her mother. Her protestations, however, were quelled by the enthusiastic support of Anna's father.

Many have been the times when I wished her mother had got her way; when I lamented the loss of Martha; regretted I had not married my niece Pauline in Manchester, as was mooted during my visit there as a young man. I felt I would even have preferred Gisela.

Gisela lives with us, helping her sister with the house and the children. She has been a good companion and comforter.

But now – no more regrets! To whom can I give thanks for this miracle?

After the relief, and the joy of a second passionate night, a day dawns when I realise I am in love with my wife. Is there any other sixty-year-old man in Austria in love with his wife of a quarter-century? I doubt it.

The discovery occurs in an antiquarian bookshop. It's a glorious May afternoon as I enter the dark shop smelling deliciously of old leather bindings. Among the half-dozen browsers, I see – after my eyes have adjusted – my wife! She notices me at the same time and we move towards one another, smiling. 'You had the same idea!' I say with a chuckle.

'A present for Herr Kofman!'

'Yes! How extraordinary!'

She holds a book up for me to read the title. It's a biography of Rothschild. 'But that's just what I'd have chosen for him, darling!' I say. 'It's perfect!'

'You can pay for it, then!'

I take the book from her. We separate, drifting around. I'm conscious of her presence, her beauty. Well, perhaps not her beauty exactly; her sexual charm, her new vitality – which was once her natural condition. She has on a lovely, form-fitting blue gown and a coquettish bonnet. She looks like a Renoir cocotte; her generous lips are exaggerated by a dashing scarlet lipstick; when she moves close again, to show me a book she would like to read sometime, her eyes sparkle, and I catch a trace of some delicate scent. It lingers as she turns away. But not for long. She calls my name softly: 'Sigi!' Another book she would quite like to read sometime, though in a cheaper edition than this. Both of the books she has shown me I *also would quite like to read sometime. Our tastes are so alike; we are really so well suited!*

She hasn't called my name so softly, so intimately, for years.

I am conscious of her genitals beneath the blue hobble-skirt; I feel that she is too. No, let me call a spade a spade: her cunt. It's the obscene word we used to employ in the most passionate moments, and have begun to use again.

She swirls out of the shop; I see admiring eyes follow her.

How can she have shed ten years in a few days?

Because she is in love with me again. She has experienced passion again.

I know, suddenly, without question, I am in love with her. Helplessly adoring, like an adolescent.

Dreamily I pay for the book, then forget to pick it up and have to be called back. As the warmth and the light strike me, I reflect that we'll get a little drunk tonight, as I don't normally drink wine; and I hope our guests the Kofmans will leave early.

The Kofmans have been our neighbours for the past four years. Martha Kofman is my former fiancée. It was a shock for both of us when we met on the stairs on the day they moved in. Her husband, a factory-owner, is wealthy. He is also ill educated and rather coarse. Their apartment, luxuriously furnished, has a cold air.

We meet them socially perhaps twice a year. That is quite enough. Today it is Kofman's birthday and they are to join us for supper. I was somewhat surprised when Anna suggested inviting them to celebrate his birthday and buying him a small gift; but she reminded me that they presented me with a gardenia, my favourite flower, on my birthday.

Arriving home in the late afternoon, I find Anna getting ready. I steal up behind her and put my arms about her, half-dressed. She leans back her cheek to touch my beard. 'That's a wonderful perfume!' I cup her breast.

'Not now! Later. Do you like it? I think it's rather nice. Do you think Herr Kofman will like the book?'

'I'm sure he will. It's bound well. He likes expensive bindings.' Her nipple erects under my stroke.

After our maid Josefine has poured me tea in the kitchen, I go to my consulting room. The room is on the mezzanine, isolated from the rest of the apartment; it is cool and numinous; full of antique statuary; I stroke the 'Gradiva' plaster cast. The graceful gliding woman has become Anna. All the goddesses, the Venus and Athena and Isis, have become Anna. I rejoice that my sole early-evening patient due today has a cold and will not be coming. I open my notebook to write; I pick up my pen and lay it down; I wish only to think of Anna. To dream of what will come later. I can still feel the twitch of her nipple, the brief tingle of her lips against mine.

The Kofmans arrive. His beady, avaricious eyes above a hooked nose glint with pleasure as Anna gives him a colourful package. He purrs at sight of the biography, his smooth, plump hand caressing the leather binding.

My sister-in-law Gisela appears. She is rather over-dressed for an elderly lady. Hard to believe she was my 'first love'.

Wine and joy at our renewed erotic life have stimulated Anna into flirtatiousness, and I am happy to go along with her mood. Our hands make contact. I am aware of Gisela's surprise – even slight displeasure. No one likes to see unhappy people suddenly become happy. She is used to us quarrelling, or staying at an aloof distance.

Now, in her happiness, Anna radiates charm and seductiveness. Max Kofman's beady eyes drink her in as he hunches towards her across the table. She was unconventional and madcap in youth, I used to call her my Schwarzer Teufel, my black devil. It is wonderful to see that playful streak in her, buried for so long, reasserting itself.

We discuss the war situation, of course. I should explain we are in the year 1914. We expect a triumphant conclusion soon.

Mars yields to Venus as Anna steers the conversation towards the subject that is on both our minds: first asking them if they saw the recent production of Carmen, then moving us into love and passion generally. What is life without a little passion and danger, she asks? – Whatever age one is. The Kofmans are seeing a new Anna too, and are taken aback. Martha's elderly face, which resembles a camel's, grows longer and longer; she is all at sea with this topic. Even in her youth she was cool, and I cannot imagine that she and Max have slept together for many years. Previously, when my situation was no better than Kofman's in that respect, I have envied him his wife's mild domestic virtues and calm temperament; but no longer. Glancing from her to my radiant, sparkling, flirtatious Anna, I exult in my good fortune.

And clearly Kofman envies me, of a sudden. In his late forties – several years younger than Martha – he has a certain coarse attractiveness to women, I should imagine.

When at last they are gone, we go at once to our bedroom, our arms linked. Undressing first, I lie on the bed smoking a cigar and watching her. Like Lou Salomé, she is a magnificent animal. So boyish when young, there is, in her full-bodied maturity, still a distinctly masculine element: wide shoulders and heavy upper arms. Below the waist, though, she is all woman, broad in the thighs, plump in the buttocks.

We make love, at first energetically, with long, varied kisses; then, tired, gently, our torsos apart on the pillow. Her eyes are closed, her face turned from me; her lower lip protrudes, and her small pearly teeth are bared. An animal, being satisfied, and she emits soft grunts of pleasure. Her matted hair is drawn back at the brow, leaving a widow's peak; she looks suddenly vulnerable, innocent, and young again.

As vulnerable, innocent and young as she was in her mid-twenties, when I took her on a holiday to Siena. What a boyish beauty she had! And it blossomed in the Mediterranean sunlight. I had forgotten how wonderfully we could make love. 'I'll love you like this,' I had cried, 'until my dying day!' 'No, longer, longer!' she cried, pulling me in tighter.

It faded, after that time in Italy. Anna was subject to black, black spells. She said they happened because I was too set in my ways when she came into my life; she wished she had been there from the beginning. There were long months of pure hatred from her, when she had fantasies of knifing me or castrating me at least. She suffered also from the suicide of her father: driven to it by malicious rumours that I had slept with her mother – and even worse.

I found what consolation I could in my daughters Mathilde and Sophie – and in the erotic drawings. Years went by – I vaguely remember a Russian poem Lou Salomé spoke to me once; years without life or inspiration or love; but now it returns, taking everyone by surprise, as Odysseus to Penelope.

Anna slides from me and climbs on top. Her breasts, slightly *wrinkled, swing; her skin is livid under her right ear; veined and creased; her jowl seems to puff out, from the pressure of bearing down on me, thrusting, yet making sure she keeps me in. Once, indeed, I lose her and she feels me and moves me about till I am in again. Red-faced, creased, she is suddenly old. It does not matter. I only regret I shall be no longer alive when she is truly old, so that I can show her I am still in love with her . . .*

Life, a matter of indifference to me before, suddenly seems infinitely precious. What if I should die tomorrow, before I have had a chance to explore this joy? I cannot bear the thought of Anna remarrying – probably someone of her own age or younger – someone like Kofman perhaps – and giving him all this; driving him mad with her kisses, enfolding his penis with her lush lips, sucking him into her: and with even greater passion since he will be younger and more virile . . .

15

What I read of *Strictly Private* disturbed yet impressed me. How cunningly she had taken Martha's role! How adroitly she had taken my adolescent excitement in Freiberg to suggest I might have married my own daughter. I remembered telling her about Gisela while resting at a café near the Trevi fountain after a too arduous expedition in stupefying heat. She had drunk my words in eagerly. My wistful eyes must have gladdened her by revealing I had yearnings far beyond her mother's capacity to satisfy. That was the day I haemorrhaged, spattering Anna's white dress with blood. I suppose it made her feel her time with me might be short.

I even, I think – but probably only in retrospect – sensed her feelings after I had finished my romantic reverie. I see her hands poised at her chin, her elbows resting on the table, her eyes absorbed in mine, tender, compassionate, black as her boyishly styled hair; the figures slowly drifting past us, the wisps of cloud in the heat haze: a tremulous, becalmed moment in our relationship, much as I had experienced on the Acropolis about my father.

I stopped reading her fantasy, from a sense of guilt at treading where she had not invited; it was really quite pornographic. From where, I wondered, had she drawn her vivid and realistic account of an older woman squatting on someone, making love? From her adored and adoring teacher, Else? From Frau Zellenka? Or had she added it later, after she'd met her close friends Mrs Rosenfeld and Mrs Burlingham? The question troubled me; but I think also I was afraid – afraid of what I might discover concerning her knowledge of my actual marriage. One's children know nothing, and yet also everything. She might even know more than I knew.

If I probe beyond guilt and fear, I touch a sense of betrayal. Here was Anna, my nurse and loving companion in Rome, pretending to total concentration on the present reality (that's to say, our exploration of Roman antiquities) while her mind was really engaged with fiction; a fiction based, all too clearly, on events she had witnessed or suspected from the early war years in our apartment. She couldn't wait to escape from me to her hotel bedroom. And there she would seek to *be* me. I felt betrayed by her attempt to 'take me over'.

So I stopped reading, after skimming through the remaining fifty or so pages. Kofman, I could see, was a central character. Anna took the Freuds and Kofmans on a holiday visit to Naples. It emerges that Anna and Kofman had already been engaged in a light, secret affair before his birthday. There are hints of *She* in a scene in which Vesuvius is erupting and I have grandiose visions of renewing my youthful vigour in its flames. But there are also dreams (typical of her) of murdering and dying and beating. I read these fragments with half-averted eyes; they flashed by as a landscape flickers, half-seen from a speeding train while one daydreams. By 1934 when I guiltily stow the story back in Anna's file I am old and sick and the libido has long since died.

Martha too is old. Actually she has been old for most of our life together. I rage at the wasted years of our youth when we were mostly apart. The young should be allowed to copulate freely. But she was very strict; a kiss, no more. It seems absurd now that I was monstrously jealous; almost had a duel with a certain musician; hated even her brother Eli getting too close to her. I undoubtedly loved her more than she loved me. It should have warned me, probably.

At twenty-five, when we married, her bloom was still there – just. By thirty, when she bore our third child, Ernst, she was already deep into middle age; and quite happy to be so. I don't think it was only child-bearing and rearing: she always *wanted* to be middle aged or old. Minna didn't have children to age her, yet the same thing happened to her. Minna was really plain. The idea that Fliess, who was quite handsome in a weak and stunted way, could have desired her! . . . And Martha became plain, very quickly. Plain and staid. She thought my work was pornography. If I hadn't had Fliess as my soul mate, my sole mate, during my difficult, four-year-long pregnancy with psychoanalysis, I would have gone mad.

Not Ernst: Oliver was our third, I remember.

Just for one year, when past fifty, Martha recovered miraculously some of her youthful bloom – as Anna guessed. If I've time, I'll tell you what *really* happened. But now, it's 1934, my cancerous jaw makes life scarcely bearable; I've just read as much of Anna's fantasy as I can take; and I'm disturbed – by sex! By the memories of desire. And Kat is due; I can smell the strong Egyptian cigarettes she smokes: Kat, my American poetess.

She's in Vienna for the second time to consult me. She walks to Berggasse through streets bloodstained with unrest. It doesn't put her off coming. I liked her from the first. She is not much older than Sophie would have been. I showed her Sophie, my favourite daughter, in the locket attached to my watch-chain. Kat's daughter is called Perdita, and Kat is a Perdita to me, this shy, pale, whimsical woman with American phrases but almost English accent. She brings me, like Shakespeare's maiden, 'flowers o' the spring'.

Kat is tall – it was disconcerting, on first meeting, to find this classical beauty towering over me. Her dreamy grey eyes gaze always from some rocky Greek shore – knowing that those ships on the blue horizon will find only Helen's shadow in Troy.

Slightly masculine, of course. Strong mouth and nose, short bobbed hair. A blend of Hermes and Aphrodite. Her clothes seem to be thrown together from some jumble sale, yet are strikingly apt. Today she wears a baggy white smock over a tweed skirt. I've pleased her over something; we're at ease with each other.

'You know who you remind me of?' she says.

'No.'

'Jesus. But after he was resurrected.'

'You mean I'm not a man to you. I'm too old.' I thump the sofa arm.

'No, I didn't mean that. There's just something eastern about you; you've been through death and come out the other side.'

'We Jews are survivors, Kat.' I tell her the joke about the Jew, emerging shakily from a train crash, who makes the sign of the cross. A Catholic priest asks him if he's a convert and he says no he was just checking: spectacles, testicles, wallet and watch. Kat laughs. I add that, with the hint of rhyme, the joke seems to go even better in the language we are using, English, than in Yiddish or German.

'You should move to America,' she says. 'They'd think you were wonderful, fantastic. Actually you resemble one of our baseball coaches. You could get a job as analyst to one of our baseball teams! And they have these young girls who act as cheer-leaders, jumping up and down, chanting. They'd be screaming out *Sigmund's our guy!*'

'He's no goy but he's some guy!'

'That's right! You've got it, Professor!' Grinning, she slides a large white hand under the neck of her smock, to scratch. I go with her hand. 'I wish I'd met you when you came over. When was it – 1909?'

'Yes.'

'That year I was wavering between Frances and Ezra. I guess I've never stopped – ' she removes her hand to make a seesawing movement ' – wavering.'

'From what you've told me about Frances, I don't think she would have been right for you.'

She is silent, purse-lipped, displeased.

'But you like Bryher,' she says uncertainly.

'Yes, I like her, I like her.'

'So, that's all right . . . She named herself after an island, you know.'

94

'She told me.'

Rather sleepily: 'I love islands, I love islands.'

Pre-Oedipal, she longs to find her mother.

I add: 'And she's rich!'

She chuckles. 'Yes, that helps. She's generous to me and my lovers.'

'And to me.'

'True . . . So did you like America?'

'I fear not. I couldn't take waking up every morning to face so much paranoia, hysteria, greed, lust, vanity, selfishness . . .'

'My God! You really hated it!'

'No, I was talking about Jung.'

My lips crack into a smile, though with the prosthesis it's painful. Her rich laugh rolls out. 'You're in a droll mood, Professor!'

'You make me feel cheerful, Kat.'

'Good!'

'But I'm pretty fed up with being your mother.'

'Ah, well . . . I saw her breast last night, in my hotel room.'

Kat suffers from hallucinations.

'The mother's breast.'

When she pushes down her smock collar to scratch again, she reveals a mole on the first soft slope of her bosom.

'Bet you've never seen your mother's breast floating in front of you, Professor!'

'That's very true.'

'Do you miss her?'

I reflect on her question. 'No. I'm grateful she's dead at last. She couldn't have stood my dying before her.'

'I told you, you've died already. But if you have to die again, like Lazarus, promise me you'll appear to me.'

'All right. *OK*.'

Her head on the cushion nods. 'I think you'll find you're surrounded by dusky Egyptian maidens. You're a serpent of old Nile.'

'Ah! *Antony and Cleopatra*! "As soft as air, as sweet as balm, as gentle – "'

She completes it: 'O Antony!'

'"Dost thou not see the baby at my breast / That sucks the nurse asleep?"'

Her hand slides under, to cup her breast.

'You *can* feel that with a man, Kat.'

'I know.'

The smock ripples above her gently moving fingers. I utter an involuntary sigh. She hears it, interprets it, gives a soft chuckling purr. 'You could, you know. You could,' she murmurs.

It is my last stirring. I know her offer is genuine. A woman who urinated on Havelock Ellis out of simple generosity and gratitude would let Freud stroke her breast.

She senses my discomfort as I recross my legs, and moves easily into the subject of her loving but remote father. His thoughts on some stellar object; her mother silencing the dinner-table conversation by saying, Your father is about to speak. Kat can talk about him now with greater balance. When her talk drifts to an end, she asks, 'How do you define love?'

'It's beyond me, Kat.'

'Well, it's here, you know that? It's here.'

She is right; it has stolen into the room, another mysterious presence among my odd assortment of antiques. More powerful than any of them. For a timeless period we are silent, like lovers on a calm summer lake, absorbed in each other, the oars at rest, the water lapping.

Now an almost inaudible, pulsating sound; it grows and, without ever becoming other than distant, can be distinguished as the relentless, hate-filled chanting of a mob. It is all too familiar these days.

'He will win in the end,' Kat murmurs. 'I'm sure of it.'

Her remark surprises me. She's totally uninterested in any politics later than the Trojan War.

'Who, Dollfuss? Probably. In a way I hope so; anything is better than anarchy. – Or do you mean Hitler?'

A slight shake of her bobbed hair. 'Immortal Eros.'

TWO

16

It is dusk outside, muting the pleasant English garden. Birds are tiredly singing. Anna sits at my desk writing, under lamplight, though it is not yet dark enough for her to pull down the thick, black blinds that Minna has had made.

Anna is in black – black dress, black stockings, flat black shoes. Only the pearl earrings I gave her add a livelier touch. She looks so sad, writing, blotting, sealing an envelope, that I murmur: 'My *sorgenkind!*'

She looks up, across at me – startled, stunned even. Those dark deep brooding eyes widen. 'Papa!' She pushes my chair back and rushes to me. She kneels and smooths my brow with her hand, and smiles with a mournful love. 'Rest! Rest!' she whispers. 'Everything is all right. I'm with you, my dearest; I'm not going anywhere. Rest, sleep . . .'

'Why are you in mourning, Anna?' I ask. 'Your old Papa isn't dead yet! He's not quite ashes and Charcot.'

Her faint smile strengthens a little. 'I never thought to hear your beloved voice again.' She searches my eyes anxiously, gnawing her lip. 'Are you in pain?'

I shake my head.

'Would you like Doctor Schur to –?'

'No. Just you.'

I add that I think the morphine has cleared my head a lot.

At this moment the door, which has been left ajar, is pushed open; Lün bounces in and flings herself joyfully at me, her tail wagging. I laugh, scuffing her behind the ears.

My smell must be less repellent, I suggest. Anna agrees, then blushes with embarrassment.

She starts to cry. 'You're better! You're going to live!'

'Don't let's exaggerate.'

I have to confess something, I whisper. I went to her desk, at 19 Berggasse, and took out her story to read. The one in which she and I were married.

She blushes furiously. 'Ah, my *wilde Phantasie*! Oh, Papa, how ashamed I feel!'

'No, no! It's I who feel ashamed. I read only two chapters, then shut it away. But it was indefensible of me . . . Well, let me confess the whole truth. I put it away after two chapters because I was too frightened of finding out how much you knew. About your mama and me that year.'

The blush on her pale face seems to deepen. 'I only knew you suddenly seemed very close. And then very angry and upset with each other. I heard sounds from your bedroom. That's all. I thought, perhaps, you were making love.'

'Yes, we were making love,' I confess. 'But that was the only time I was ever unfaithful to you, Anna. That year, I mean. A few months. And very irregularly. Well, the occasional session with your Aunt Minna, on holiday.'

Anna screws up her face. 'I guessed that; I knew it was nothing.' She makes a dismissive puff with her lips.

'You guessed a lot, I'd say. But not everything.'

'I remember, of course, that scene with – '

'– Herr Bauer. How could you forget that!'

'No, that was awful. Still, it's far in the past.' We have had visitors, she says, shaking off an unpleasant memory as a dog shakes off rain: Stefan Zweig and Wolfgang Pauli. They had looked down at me in what had seemed the final coma. 'Pauli', she says, 'told me something frightening. He'd spoken by telephone to Einstein. Einstein believes it may be possible to create an atomic bomb, with vast destructive power . . .'

'More destructive than Mrs Klein's breast-deprived babies?' I ask gaily.

'Much more! She wrote to my mother, actually, expressing her regrets. She has a nerve!'

'Ah, well . . . Forgive, forgive. No, don't forgive.'

'I won't. This emphasis on the mother's influence is absurd. They have little influence, except as objects of desire for male infants. You gave full weight to that; much more than anyone else. John Stuart Mill didn't even mention his mother in his autobiography; and when you think of *The Way of All Flesh* . . .'

'Mrs Klein wasn't even breast-fed!'

Anna looks down into her lap.

'We should have found a wet nurse for you, Anna. It was remiss of us.'

'It wasn't important. But I was saying what Einstein told Pauli. Einstein spoke to a banker who's spoken to President Roosevelt, and Roosevelt's set up a group to look into it. Because obviously, if the Nazis made such a bomb first . . . Pauli said you would be well out of this miserable world.'

And Salvador Dali had written. He remembered with great pleasure his visit to us last year. So *many* people had written. It kept her occupied in the evenings, answering them.

She had dreamt, last night, that an American called Fritz Kuhn had been interned for being viciously pro-Nazi and anti-semitic. The dream had depressed her and puzzled her. She woke up knowing she couldn't bring her dream to me.

She rests her head on my breast. I stroke her fine dark hair. The pressure of her against me constricting my breathing, I ask her to undo a button. Her fingers fumbling tenderly at my throat are my mother's.

'You have cause to hate me, my dear.'

'No cause! No cause!'

I can recall, very clearly, her lying on the couch; one arm over her face. A schoolgirlish red ribbon in her hair. The other arm attacking her stomach, as she relates her dreams of being beaten. Or of beating, fighting, with a male sword. A child is being beaten . . . There was much violence in my gentle Anna. Still she likes reading detective stories: the more lurid and corpse-strewn the better she is pleased.

She covered her violence with sentiment, writing 'nice' stories. Always in her stories she was a man.

Her blush when she first stammered out her compulsion to masturbate.

'I'm jealous that you are going to Sophie,' she murmurs. When I don't respond instantly she continues: 'It really hurt me when you wouldn't let me come home for her wedding.'

'I thought you needed to stay in Merano; you'd been overworking and were ill.'

'I know, but I should have come. And you even said, in that letter, I needn't write every day. You said it was so I shouldn't overtire myself, but I took it as you not being bothered.'

'That was silly, Anna.'

'Six months! It's a long time. Still,' she adds in a softer voice, 'you did weep when I came home after that pleasant visit to the Gestapo.'

'Yes, I wept.'

'You were so depressed after Sophie went away with Max. There was just me left. I couldn't have meant much to you for you to be so depressed. Your Sophie-Complex!' She sniggers maliciously.

'It wasn't only because of Sophie. Others had gone too, remember. Jung, Stekel.'

'Oh, of course, but it was mainly Sophie, admit it. I read your essay on the Three Caskets . . . "It is in vain that an old man yearns for the love of woman as he had it at first from his mother; the third of the Fates alone, the silent Goddess of Death, will take him into her arms." I was the third; I thought I meant only death to you.'

'And here you are . . . Anna-Cordelia . . .'

'And here I am.'

I strive to reassure her. 'I missed you dreadfully whenever you were away. Staying with Jones and his mistress, for instance, in England. When war broke out I was terrified you'd be interned.'

102

'Ah! Perhaps that's in my dream! Internment.'

Without the strength to lift my head from the cushion, I raise my hand in agreement. 'Actually, Anna, Loe Kann could be there. What was the name of that anti-semite? Kuhn? It's not so unlike.'

Jones's ex-mistress, married to the American Jones Two, declined to visit us after the war, saying if she did so she would have the feeling that my sons would have wanted to kill her husband. I tried to persuade her that, as Jews, we were stateless; but she wouldn't come. It hurt Anna. It hurt me. Loe's lovely, dreamy face and rare wit. I loathed attending her wedding in Budapest.

'By her refusal to come to see us,' I say, 'she was an anti-semitic Jewess.'

She pauses in her knitting, reflecting. I know she has a similar image of Loe's beauty. 'It may be.'

'You want to punish her.'

'I want to *beat* her!' She laughs.

'And I was worried that *Jones* would seduce you! I felt very angry and disturbed when you admitted your fantasies were full of Loe.'

'That was to punish you. I knew you loved her.'

Loe on my couch. Her eyes flashing up, back, at me; debating whether to leave Jones and marry Jones Two.

'I loved her because *you* loved her,' she adds. 'And I loved Lou Salomé because you loved her. I've always identified with you. That's why I could never – I mean, Jones was quite attractive, I was flattered, but you made it impossible. You made *any* man impossible.'

I groan.

'Not that many were interested; I was always so plain.'

'That's nonsense, Anna! Those dark, deep eyes are enchantment itself. And those full, sensual, yet intelligent and ironic, lips. You were lovelier than Sophie, in a way.'

She stops knitting again; her breast rises and falls. 'Thank you,' she whispers. 'I masturbated even more furiously after hearing those bedroom sounds. Hating you for them.'

'She was reaching the menopause, when women's libido makes a last surge. You will soon be reaching yours, darling. I'm concerned about it. To cease fertility, and never to have known what passion is – that's sad. Unless Dorothy and you have – '

We are silent for a while. Anna goes to fling a log on the fire. When she returns I say, 'Yes, I was worried for a few days that I might have made your mother pregnant. That would have been a disaster.'

'You didn't even want *me*. If there'd been decent contraception I wouldn't be here.'

'True, true . . . Yes, I was worried. I didn't realise I was worried till I forgot the word *aliquis* in a quotation.'

'Ah! I thought that just meant you'd fucked Aunt Minna!'

I smile, not at all shocked. 'Ah, you were always my *Schwarzer Teufel*, Anna!'

She giggles like an adolescent, her small pearly teeth flashing. She drifts into memories of childhood. Gathering mushrooms in the forest. How, when we approached a big one, I'd tiptoe and press a finger to my mouth, whispering, 'We must be quiet.' Then I'd drop my hat over the mushroom. That's got him!

'The quiet forest,' I murmur. 'You still have plentiful hair.'

A surprised but pleased glance at me, then down into her lap. 'So you were awake that night?'

'Of course. You are still attractive. There's really never been anyone else. Do you forgive me my brief infidelity?'

'Of course! Do *you* forgive that little adolescent fling with my tutor, Else? That's why you packed me off on holiday for six months, wasn't it?'

'Your passionate letter to her frightened us.'

'Oh, I always *wrote* passionately.'

I am tired. My eyes close.

'Sleep,' she whispers, kissing my brow. 'Sleep, dearest . . .'

17

The woman I married was of course not Anna but Martha Bernays, grand-daughter of a conservative Rabbi in Hamburg. Her father, Berman, moved to Vienna when she was eight. Herr Bernays was a swindler (jailed for fraud) and a respected bureaucrat. Upon his death, his tyrannical son Eli took over his bureaucratic post. Eli appointed my younger brother Alexander as his assistant. Our families thereby became acquainted.

Thus far in Martha's curriculum all the biographies will agree. However, the truth is otherwise. I discovered it only after my father's death in 1896. Out of the blue I received a poorly written letter in Yiddish from my old nurse, Monika Zajíc. She wrote to say she was sorry to hear of my father's death. She was delighted to learn that I had become a doctor, she had always known I was very clever. It pained her to tell me certain facts. My father had slept with her before and after my birth; at one time she had been expecting his child, but had miscarried while washing herself in the bath; I had come running on hearing her scream. That scandal had been responsible for my family getting rid of her.

My father (might he rest in peace) had continued to visit her from time to time, and she had again become pregnant. He had very kindly arranged for her to go into service with a very rich Viennese family, the Pappenheims, who allowed her to keep her baby girl. After a year or two Monika had fallen seriously ill and had to return to her family in Freiberg; but Frau Pappenheim, a kind woman, begged her to leave the baby, since Frau Pappenheim had lost two daughters in infancy and had grown fond of little Martha.

Many years later, so Monika discovered, her daughter (my half-sister) had been passed over to another family. And now she understood that her Martha had become my wife. It was a great shock to her, but of course she would tell no one. Now old and infirm, she hoped that in the circumstances I would see my way to helping her with some money. She wished us a long and happy life.

At first I did not believe her tale; indeed it seemed more far-fetched than that of Moses in the bulrushes; but under questioning my wife confirmed that she had been raised Martha Pappenheim, then passed on to the Bernays along with a substantial sum of money. I kept from Martha the identity of her mother – a woman who had been a second mother to me. As for my father, when he and my wife were together I was always struck by the resemblance. Though Martha had a rather long, camel-like face, and Jacob Freud the peasant squatness of Garibaldi, the family link could easily be discerned.

I have said that the Jews of Vienna were a clan. No family history could illustrate that more clearly.

I should tell you something about the Pappenheims, in whose wealthy, but orthodox and rather loveless home Martha passed the first ten years of her life. The father was a grain merchant, the mother came from the Goldschmidt family of Frankfurt, which included the poet Heine. The influence of the maternal family might account for Martha's poetic leanings.

Martha's adoptive sister in the Pappenheim family was named Bertha. The two girls did not get on, which was the cause of the former being 'disposed of' to close friends, the Bernays. Bertha Pappenheim, at twenty-one, developed a cough, then rapidly severe psychological disturbances. Her limbs contracted; her hair and ribbons became black snakes; she could speak only in English, etc. My colleague Josef Breuer tended her. Between them they created the 'talking cure'. Then 'Anna O.' thrashed about in a phantom pregnancy, saying she was bearing Breuer's child. Breuer rushed home terrified to his precious Mathilde, and they whirled off on a second honeymoon.

So Bertha was the mother of psychoanalysis, just as Anna, my daughter, was psychoanalysis herself, Anna-Lisa, conceived while I was undergoing my self-analysis. One could therefore say that Anna was Bertha's daughter rather than Martha's.

Wise Anna has never felt she was my wife's child.

Martha was the product of a passionate, ugly Moravian peasant (Monika), a poor wandering trader (Jacob Freud), a millionaire Jew family tainted by extreme hysteria (the Pappenheims), and Rabbis and jailbirds (in other words, for a Jewess, her background was fairly average. When our paths first crossed, I detected strength as well as sweetness. Almost immediately I sent her a red rose, and we clinched our fate with a handshake under the table, while she and her family celebrated the Sabbath. I loved her at first more than she loved me. I was extremely jealous of her suitors. She was also under the thumb of her 'brother' Eli, who had taken on the role of head of the family after the father's death. The mother was a possessive, spiteful woman – no love was lost between us.

My dearest wish was to remove Martha swiftly, but poverty stood in the way. We were apart for most of our lengthy engagement. I spent a period of time in Paris; and Eli, to forestall us, moved his family back to Hamburg. On one of my brief visits there, Martha burst into tears and confessed she and Eli were lovers. I believe she may then have told me she was adopted, but I was too distraught to pay attention.

A lurid, melodramatic scene from that visit: the three of us together; Martha with her dress pulled up to her waist, her drawers pulled aside, and Eli frantically unbuttoning himself. 'I'm sorry, Sigi,' he had the grace to mumble, 'but of course you know about us.'

With apparent calm, even indifference, but my hand trembling as it held a cigar, I watched them couple on the sofa. It was Martha's way of dealing with my insane jealousy. After he had withdrawn, he lay panting on her breast, between her thighs still. She stroked his hair, and said to him, 'This was the last. A farewell gift, so to speak . . . But I do love you. I love you very much.'

I was both distressed and excited by her daring remark.

Eventually he stumbled, drunk, to bed. She still lay with her legs wide, her eyes closed. 'Take me, Sigi,' she whispered. 'I want it again.'

Returning to Paris, to Charcot, to his writhing female patients under hypnosis in his theatrical displays, I think only of Martha, panting and dying under Eli's thrusts. She proved herself a true sister of Anna O. My jealousy eased; I well knew her saying it was the last time was a lie for my benefit; Eli and she had every opportunity for temptation, within the bosom of their family. Yet their incest made it somehow unthreatening. I knew he could not take her from me. In the eyes of society they were brother and sister; and in our way of life appearance was all.

Realising that, he married my eldest sister, Anna, and they emigrated to America. They joined the 'huddled masses, yearning to breathe free'.

When I eventually discovered the truth of Martha's parentage, I can't say it distressed me unduly. Most of the respectable Jewish couples I knew were in secret little less incestuous. I recall saying to Princess Marie Bonaparte, when she was contemplating sleeping, with her 24-year-old son: 'Sex is far too problematic to risk taking it outside the family.'

When I visited my half-brother Philipp and my (as it turns out) father Emanuel in Manchester, in 1879, they wanted to marry me off to my half-sister Pauline. The girl whose flowers I had plundered on the sloping green meadow.

I might well have consented to the marriage had I not had the experience of making love with a black prostitute, sheltering in a church porch from the pouring rain. She told me she had married a British soldier during the Zulu Wars. He had abandoned her. Sexually she was pure enchantment. In the space of twenty minutes I experienced the snows of

Kilimanjaro, the falls of Victoria, the Zambezi river, the sunless jungle of pythons and cobras. I learnt from her lips that woman is a dark continent.

18

Extracts from the private diary:

August 1914

Anxiety grips us, despite our assurance that Germany and Austria are fighting for the survival of European culture, and are bound to triumph. Martin is headed for the Russian front. He jests that at last he will be able to see Russia (it has been forbidden to Jews previously). Anxious too about Anna, in England with Jones. Will she be able to get back? . . .

Great rejoicing: Anna is home! Still, as far as I know, a virgin! . . .

September

(*Hamburg*) Wonderful to see our Sunday child again – Sophie looks blooming with health despite having given birth just ten days ago. Little Heinele is – well, a baby like other babies! Whole and healthy, that's the main thing. I see Hamburg for the first time as though it's not a foreign city, but one with us in a just endeavour against the barbarian East. If only England were not on the barbarians' side! I can't go all the way with the swoonings of Thomas Mann ('purification, liberation and enormous hope') nor Rilke's celebration of the 'great God of War'. Abraham, from Berlin, writes that France, England and

Belgium are finished, while the Russians have been totally defeated in East Prussia. Let's hope he's right; he's normally a cautious chap . . .

Ernst is called up. In the midst of our goodbyes, sad news arrives – poor old Emanuel is dead. He fell out of a train between Manchester and Stockport. Anna is full of passionate accounts of Jones's *mistress*. It appears that the attempt to cure my daughter by placing her with a notorious womaniser has not worked.

Write a letter of condolence (which may never reach them) to John, Pauline, and the others. Warn them they will feel as if they've moved up 'into the front line'. It seems inappropriate in view of the hostilities between our countries, and I start afresh. Yet it's only our childish relationship writ large – John's punches and hair-pulling in the dandelion grass; my gripping Pauline's arms so he could steal her flowers. The sixty-year-old woman will be crying now, but with less passion, though the loss is infinitely greater.

Dreadful depression. In my dreams keep falling out of trains. Martha is dead-alive; Minna not much better.

Did Anna's visit bring up painful early memories for the old man? As he sat in the train, with grim black factories drifting past, did he suddenly stop calculating how much the war would enrich his business? Did he instead start to think of Tysmenice and of Freiberg? Of Amalie? Of father? Of sexual abuse, suffered and/or inflicted? Was he filled, as I am now, with just this sense of evil and vanity? Did he then, with trembling fingers, remove his spectacles and put them in his case; did his frail legs carry him to the carriage door? Did he struggle to open it, then give himself to the darkness?

October

Ferenczi visits for some analysis. Dear, jolly fellow. While he is lying on the couch talking about a slight *folie* on his train journey, I mention poor Emanuel's death, on his way to his seaside holiday cottage. I say that one day some enemy may imagine I sent Anna off to England with a secret message and a sum of money for an assassin. This joke leads almost to a reversal of roles; Ferenczi gets me to confess I wish Emanuel had been my father, if only because he lived on and therefore gave me the possibility of murdering him. And, now, a powerful reason to do so, since he is, was, in the enemy camp. It is, of course, possible he was indeed my father; I tell Ferenczi that on my return to Freiberg at sixteen I consulted the town records and found my birth recorded as being in March rather than May – which would have meant a conception before marriage. What more likely than that Emanuel, panicking, persuaded his father to rectify the situation for him?

The good fellow is concerned for my psychic health. I tell him that the man who is not a little crazy at this time is truly mad . . .

Disturbing meeting, in the Prater, with Philipp Bauer, father of my 'Dora'. It's disturbing because I had believed him to be dead. We took a schnapps together; he's a charming rogue. Death can't be far off, however. Invited him to take supper with us. The encounter led to my remembering, in vivid detail, that astonishing year of 1900: my last congress with Fliess at Achensee, with its almost fatal climax; the first holiday with Minna, in undreamed of solitude, at Lake Garda. Also the suicide of my patient Margit Kremzer, after I had dismissed her with the correct diagnosis of paranoia. Then 'Dora' was brought to me; a disturbed girl who had threatened suicide. I undoubtedly believed her father Philipp too credulously at first, and was perhaps hostile to all would-be suicides on account of Frau Kremzer. (How many people have tried to murder me by committing suicide!) I disbelieved the girl's story that her father was sexually involved with a Frau Zellenka, and that she herself was disgusted by Herr Zellenka's pursuit of *her*. It seemed to me that if she yielded it would accord with her innermost desires; but she would have none of it . . .

112

Bauer comes to supper; confides to me, while Martha is out of the room, that his former mistress has spoken warmly to various acquaintances of our daughter Anna. He seems to be warning me gently. I tell him Anna is very sensible; he responds, 'That's what we thought about our Ida' ('Dora'); 'but that woman can have a disturbing influence on girls, as we discovered . . .'

A day of near madness. Am convinced the giant Aryan – can't bring myself to write his name – is projecting aggressive impulses from his Swiss redoubt. It wouldn't surprise me in the least if he had found a way to utilise the destructive energies let loose in Europe. I have more than once had to save my life by fainting in his presence – and then he was pretending to be my friend!

November

Dread that the war will go worse than expected. Humankind a folly. Anna disturbs me too by writing letters to Frau Zellenka, to whom a mutual acquaintance introduced her while staying in Semmering last year. Dangerous woman; not content with her affair with Philipp Bauer, introduced Ida, his daughter, to a knowledge beyond her tender years – and God knows what else, even sharing a bed with her. My attraction for her father, once a patient of mine too, has not died; he comes often to chat with Martha and me. His Ida, his 'Dora', is not happy in her marriage. The husband is an engineer and mediocre composer. Bauer has done his best to encourage him, even hiring orchestras to perform his works. Had to tell Bauer an unhappy marriage was to be expected, given his daughter's breaking-off from analysis prematurely . . .

My attraction for Bauer is taking the odd form, against my will, of telling him both Martha and I like him a lot. To Martha I say that Bauer obviously finds her attractive. My homely Martha is stunned – yet I can see flattered. This afternoon, when he called, I made an excuse to go out, leaving them together. Despite his syphilis, he still has a haggard charm.

He and his wife Käthe seem somewhat reconciled. Two years ago she was seriously ill with colonic cancer, so ill that her death was reported: a disturbing experience that her husband, too, suffered last year; the pre-war years, in retrospect, were unreal, phantasmal. Bauer's care of her made up to her, it appears, for the white vaginal discharge that has plagued both Käthe and Ida, and which they ascribed to his disease. He is terribly repentant about the sinister male dowry he brought to his marriage, like so many men before him . . .

Martha and I talked with Bauer. He and I have so much in common: Moravian/Bohemian background, the textile business (and another Philipp!), liberalism and culture. Am more convinced than ever I was right that his daughter suppressed incestuous wishes. He repents his infidelity of fifteen years ago; though it can hardly be called infidelity, given his impotence. He was blind in the one eye, then in the right – whereupon the other regained some of its sight. That history gives his fine eyes a mysterious, almost shamanistic, glow. I feel Martha is aware of it. I certainly am. He is the first male since Fliess who evokes my bisexuality . . .

February 1915

Martha, to my infinite surprise and even horror after so many years of abstinence, comes to my bed. A difficult, painful coitus. Psychologically painful. She feels to me both virginal and immensely old . . . Martha, all our married life, suddenly strikes me as a vast Arctic, featureless, cold . . .

Martha, love, joy, passion, beauty even . . .

I think she is feeling the blissful relief of infertility, her periods becoming irregular at long last. I had feared she would remain fertile to a Talmudic old age . . .

'Yes, I do find him attractive; I find him very attractive . . .' She says it as Anna enters the room, to Martha's embarrassment. I am amused at how well my little trick worked; yet it's no longer necessary, since Bauer holds little charm for me now. I am not discouraging Martha; if a little flattery from a friend encourages her to make the most of herself, and feel a menopausal surge of libido (as, my God, is happening), I am grateful to him . . .

Anxiety over rising costs, falling fees. Martha continues to take every opportunity to 'bump into' Bauer. It's extraordinary and rather delightful to see this ethically pure woman a prey to such fires. I am in favour of an infinitely free sexual life, though I have myself not followed my own precept . . .

Martha in bed with a very bad cold all day, but rises in the early evening, elegantly dressed. Am flattered that she has done this for me. Says, after dinner, she is just going out for some fresh air, and vanishes. An hour later she's still not back. Minna tells me not to worry; but the weather is bitterly cold, the ground covered in snow. I march out. After tramping the streets for an hour, I catch sight of two figures in a small park, lit by the light of a gas lamp. My heart misses a beat. It is they. They are close, walking side by side, making a zigzag motion, up and down over the snow. I see he has a dog with him, the dog is pulling him in contrary directions. But in fact it's not Bauer's Alsatian dog but passion, desire, that causes them to walk agitatedly up and down. They are planning an assignation, or they are agonising together over whether to begin an affair. I feel I have wandered on to an operatic stage, with the *Liebestod* playing. I beat a hasty retreat. My heart pounds. When I let myself into the house I walk straight upstairs to our room. Martha arrives twenty minutes later, radiant, her coat streaked with the watery snow. Says she bumped into Bauer, walking his dog . . .

When Bauer is leaving, after a long afternoon conversation, she says tenderly, 'I'll see you again soon, I hope.' *I'll* see you! It seems he is no longer our friend, but hers . . .

Cannot listen to my patients. See only him and her in the park that night. They seemed so right together, so bridal, like my mother and Philipp (Philipp!) strolling together in Freiberg; I feel reduced to the size of a two-year-old child, helpless, longing for its mama . . .

Feel stifled, strangled, by the overwhelming hysteria of this city, this Empire. It's not new, but with war it seems to have risen to an unbearable crisis. Mostly women, of course: full of tics and writhings and compulsions of one sort or another. Why? Why? They are well off (in the affluent class), taken care of, and spared the stress of professional work. Why can't they bring up their children and enjoy their tranquil existences? It's driving me mad. I want nothing to do with them. Would prefer to be a pathologist . . .

Eros has nothing to do with beauty or even youth. I want to *become* my darling Marti; to take up residence in her. I want to feel the blood falling from her – her period very late this time, and its arrival brought relief. She asks if I mind her sleeping in the other room again, just till the flow stops. I regret it but of course say it's all right to do so . . .

Evening with Bauer and Frau Bauer at the theatre. Supper at the Ronicher. Käthe subdued, mouselike; does she not notice her husband and Martha flirting, gazing at one another? I disgrace myself by showing boredom (actually raging jealousy). Martha screams at me when we have left them for my rudeness. I say the play brought up a memory of my father seducing my sister Anna. Nonsense of course; but it calms Martha . . .

Tell Martha I've had a dream in which I saw Philipp, looking the image of my father, and I shot him with a rifle. She looks scared . . .

Martha angry. Her period long over, but she remains apart from me at night. I feel childlike, lost, deserted. Beg her to invite Philipp so we can discuss my dream of my father, and the seduction of my sister. He may be able to help, since he has thought deeply of Herr Zellenka's attempt to seduce Ida; realises she was probably telling the truth. That in fact he and Frau Zellenka may unconsciously have condoned it to leave them free to meet. Bauer comes; I tell my story; move quickly on to sexual fantasy. Bauer is embarrassed, says he has no fantasies, his sexual life dead. Extremely drunk, rising to my feet, I lean towards him and shout, 'I know one fantasy you have, Bauer! You want to sleep with Martha!' I hear him say, 'I don't, I don't!' I pitch into unconsciousness. The next I know, Martha is shaking me, trying to pull me up from the floor. Somehow she gets me to bed.

19

It is necessary to interweave my spasmodic diary of that period with my more uncertain memory . . .

By the next morning I had forgotten my provoking challenge to Bauer. Martha tartly reminded me. I groaned an apology. 'Well, he said no, he didn't want me,' she said; 'and he was very drunk, which is supposed to be when you tell the truth; so I would say you were wrong, wouldn't you?'

I made no response; instead, asking her if he had stayed long after I'd passed out.

Only a few minutes, she replied. She had been upset, and apologised to Bauer because it had looked as if I was offering her to him. She felt very angry. I said again I was sorry.

She is very withdrawn. We have probably lost Bauer's friendship, she believes; she would be surprised if he will visit us again very readily. To have come at *my* request, to help me with a psychological problem, and then to be insulted! Obviously it had been my intention to do that.

She sleeps in her old room.

Her distant anger makes me feel all the more like a lost child. I follow in her footsteps, adding to her annoyance with me. I can't think of anything but her: literally. It is infinitely worse than when I first fell in love with her, in our youth. My eyes cling to her, with an obsessive desire which she will not satisfy; and with fear, not understanding what has happened. I know it is a kind of breakdown, and I cancel all my professional engagements. My patients have gone temporarily to others. I had started work on an essay, 'Mourning and Melancholia', but can't proceed with it.

Martha was right, Bauer doesn't visit.

I consulted Lou. She was, as ever, deeply sympathetic and comforting. 'It's torture, Frau Lou,' I said; 'yet I would not have missed this experience. It's not just libido; I have learnt how to love, for the first time. She is lit by a kind of aura.'

'She does look younger and more vital,' Frau Lou agrees.

'I always said the criterion for health was an ability to love and an ability to work. I've discovered the first, but at the expense of the second!'

'It will come back.'

'I hope so. But it's wonderful, to discover I can love.'

She smiled a little sadly. There was perhaps a touch of jealousy. 'I also feel she is much more narcissistic.' She heaved a sigh. 'And your capacity for love all came from a fuck! How wonderful!' She spread her arms wide, then made them come together above her lap. 'With us women, it all starts everywhere and ends here. With you men, it starts here, and ends everywhere.' Her arms spread wide again.

Martha was irritated by my constant attention, and expressed her irritation by using a coarse word, for the use of which she had once sternly scolded little Martin. She encouraged me to leave her for a week or so; to go off somewhere with Minna. Minna and I travelled to Gastein. Amidst the splendour of the snowcapped mountains, Minna tried to console me physically, but I found myself as impotent as Philipp Bauer. She tried to be understanding but I sensed her disappointment. I could think and speak of nothing but Martha, Martha, Martha.

When we returned to Vienna, there was a kind of radiance about Martha, and she greeted me with affection. That night I was in my study when she came in armed with a bottle of champagne and two glasses. 'I thought we should celebrate your homecoming,' she said, kissing me on the cheek, stroking my arm.

Yes (in answer to my inevitable and anxious question) she had seen Philipp. They had sorted everything out. There would be no more problem. She had a slight confession to make to me. After I had accused him of wanting to sleep with her, Philipp had not left almost instantly as she had said. She was crying, and the arrogant fellow had assumed it was because he'd told me he didn't want to. 'But I do, I do!' he had burst out. Only he couldn't. Not merely his impotence, but honour. His friendship with us both; his duty towards a wife barely recovered from cancer.

'He did kiss me,' she said. 'I was waiting for the right time to tell you.'

Her words frightened and excited me.

'It was unexpectedly good. Well, it's the first time anyone's kissed me since before our marriage. But we sorted it out when we met this week. We agreed the kissing had been very pleasant; we might possibly wish to go to bed together if you and Käthe, and Anna and Ida and so on didn't exist; but they do. So everything must be in the open. We can flirt, perhaps, but no more.'

As I was absorbing this, she said shyly: 'I've been writing; one or two poems. I'd like you to read them. They're in our bedroom.'

I stumbled after her up the stairs. Minna and Anna had gone to bed and their lights were out. As she took a few pages from a drawer and handed them tentatively to me she said, 'They're the first I've written since I was a small child at the Pappenheims. People encouraged me to write then because of Heine being in their family. These are hardly Heine. They're not much good.'

I read them, and they were love poems. Obviously to Philipp. She started to undress. I read them trying to stop my fingers from trembling, my eyes from veering towards her. In one poem, using the metaphor of Dido Queen of Carthage, she wrote that all her life she had been searching for love, for a love beyond mere fantasy. Yet now her hero, Aeneas, was sailing out of harbour, pleading duty. Did *her* feelings not count?

'They're good,' I said shakily.

She screwed up her mouth, not believing me.

120

'You are still searching for love?' I questioned in a hurt voice.

'Oh, you know how artists exaggerate. *I'm* not; no of course not.'

She came into my arms and we loved. In her pleasure she parted her lips, exposing her teeth in a way that looked at the same time predatory and passively abandoned. We loved until the dawn was breaking. I rubbed champagne into her vulva and drank. I had the feeling of leaving my own body and psyche and entering hers. No Marti any more, no Sigi. And I started to float outside of the two of us. I thought of Lou's expressive gesture with her arms.

Resting quietly side by side, hands clasped, we talked. *She* talked mostly. She'd wanted passion. In the early days of our marriage she had been too shy; then the children had come. She'd been a pretty good *hausfrau*.

'But then last June, Sigi, Minna confessed something that made me terribly dissatisfied. It was on her birthday; she was entering her fiftieth year and feeling downcast. She showed me some of the letters Fliess wrote to her. She wanted to show me, poor dear Minna, that she *had* known passion and devotion. And to remind herself, I expect. I know you knew about it – I don't blame you for keeping her confidence; it was up to her whether she told me or not.

'I was amazed Fliess could feel all that; he always struck me as rather stiff. Bless you, your letters were sweet but you never wrote like that.'

'You'd have sent me packing if I had!'

She laughed. 'You're right! – though I think you'll agree you weren't the most passionate of men, dearest! Anyway, I decided I wanted some of that passion. Not the disgusting things, but the passion, the desire! I got some new clothes, new cosmetics; you didn't notice. Philipp started giving me the odd glance, which boosted my morale. Well, the rest you know . . .'

After climbing out of bed to use the chamberpot she returned to the subject of Fliess's passion for Minna. She didn't wish me to think his grossness hadn't revolted her;

121

indeed she couldn't imagine how Minna could have responded to it. She was grateful for my gentlemanly delicacy; *I* would never, thank God, have asked to be sent menstrual napkins and so on. All the same, that urge to plunge into a woman's most intimate life had stirred something in her, an ache, a craving.

She turned towards me, touching my spent penis, stroking it; and kissed me. I hardened again and entered her. Her eyes were closed, dreamy, and I had little doubt she was imagining I was Philipp; but it did not matter.

The next day, a Sunday, we went together to my mother's. Mama was in her usual dictatorial mood, making life hell for my poor, nice, hard-done-by sister Dolfi. But Martha was at her most charming to them both. When we left, around four, I suggested it was too early to go back. We took a carriage and drove into the country. At a tavern we gazed at each other with open lust. It was disgraceful and astonishing, an old couple like us. When we left, she grabbed my arm and pulled me into a doorway and kissed. We walked on with our arms around each other like young lovers; indeed, as we had never dared to do in our youth. We were laughing and giggling; I kept grabbing at her dress trying to pull it up, and she made only half-hearted attempts to stop me.

'Lust! Pure lust!' Marti cried.

The Bauers, she informed me, were at Grundlsee, staying at a luxurious hotel with their daughter and son-in-law. A 'treat' for the young man, who had been called up into the Army. They were due back tomorrow. Philipp had hired a hall and orchestra to perform some of his music, as a farewell gift. We were invited.

I am not fond of any music after Mozart, but I felt I should go for Martha's sake, and to make amends to Philipp for my boorish behaviour. The Bauers, with their daughter Ida, greeted us warmly; my 'Dora', despite her rude exit, has never shown me anything but friendliness. We were introduced to the nervous husband and wished him well for both the concert and his patriotic service. Martha and Philipp contrived to sit beside each other with complete naturalness. The music was appalling, as expected; I shut off from it, conscious only of the touch of Martha's arm, and the touch of Philipp's on hers, the other side.

We walked the short distance to the Bauers' elegant home, set in expansive grounds off Heisenburgstrasse. I enjoyed what an English poetess has called 'silence, more musical than any song'. Martha's hand in mine. Over supper, she and Philipp again contrived to sit beside each other with perfect naturalness. He ignored his wife, or spoke to her curtly. As a result she withdrew into herself. It did not surprise me when she announced she had so much enjoyed her holiday she was going off again somewhere, with her sister. Bauer said to her irately, 'You can go where you please.'

One could understand his surly attitude; Frau Bauer punished her family with over-cleanliness; Ida told me, during her brief analysis, that her mother locked the living rooms at night, so as to keep them tidy. Who would not be pleased rather than sorry to wave goodbye to such a woman?

I felt a caress at my knee, and was thrilled; but putting my hand down to cup Martha's I found it instead being licked by the Bauers' Alsatian.

The conversation, to avoid the topic of war for the sake of Ida's husband, revolved around trivia. Notably bridge. Philipp had been teaching Ida, who was proving an expert at it. Martha said she would like to learn (a complete surprise to me); she said to Ida, 'Would you teach me?' I thought I saw a glance pass between father and daughter. Ida said she would love to, but she was going to Semmering with some friends, she and her little boy – it would cheer him up after saying goodbye to his father.

20

April 1915

News of huge Allied attack on our forces at Ypres. We seem
to be holding them, but casualties (reading between the lines)
heavy on both sides. Cannot, however, give much thought to
anything but the situation with Martha. Philipp, she informed
me, has offered to teach her bridge. She suddenly announced
she was going to his house. Why couldn't he come here? I
asked. Why should he? she attacked: it was he who was doing
her a favour. Her argument was a blind, and she knew I knew
it. Who else would be there? – The servants would be there:
why should I worry? Wondered how on earth he could teach
her bridge with only two people present at the table. Using
two dummy hands, she said. Grabbed her coat and stormed
out . . .

Martha: 'We played bridge, that's all. What do you expect
me to be doing with an impotent man?'

I: 'There are other things. He could suck you.'

Martha: 'I don't know what satisfaction that would give
him.' . . .

Martha has been at Bauer's all afternoon. I spend it pacing
up and down, tormented. Käthe Bauer is still away. I decide to
beard them in their den; set off, on a crisp spring afternoon – but
wintry thoughts in my head. As I turn the corner of their drive,
I see them vaguely framed in a window, their heads close. Bauer
catches sight of me, waves. I wave back; feel foolish. A servant
shows me in. Bauer greets me affably; Martha less so. I plead
boredom; since I am not working, can't work, I felt like a little

company. Bauer says, indicating the scattered cards: 'Do you want to learn bridge, Professor?' I decline. Martha assumes a brittle animation, hiding anger . . .

Spend a whole evening with Martha discussing her relationship with Bauer, sometimes querulously, sometimes amicably. Martha: 'What matters most is the friendship. Surely it should be possible, if there is sexual attraction, to burn through it somehow?' . . . 'I'd be quite happy if we could meet somewhere outside, once every month or so; but he's too frightened. *You* have your private friendships with women. With Frau Salomé, for instance; with Frau Eckstein. I don't question you; why shouldn't I be allowed the same?' . . . I: 'Is my anxiety irrational?' Martha, after long thought: 'Not irrational; I understand how you feel. But it's far in excess of the facts.' After another minute's thought: 'If I ever felt that *you* were a little bit involved with someone else, I would hope I'd trust you to work it out. I'd trust you that you would be faithful. Or, if you weren't faithful, that it would be short-lived. Of, if it were not short-lived, that it wouldn't be the end of the world.' She talks now with the chillingly rational tones of a psychoanalyst; of me . . .

Tonight she gives me a warm kiss good night before going to her room. It is some promise. I have told her I've fallen in love with her afresh. She says she is pleased, but does not return the compliment. 'I've been concerned with the problem of sex in a long marriage,' she says. 'And what's wrong with using an attraction for someone else to stimulate some excitement? Fliess presumably used Minna to ginger up his marriage sexually, and gave her a lot of pleasure and fulfilment too. Is there any great harm in it?' I: 'But *I* find you enough.' She: 'You don't; you have used Philipp.' It's true I have occasionally spoken of her and Philipp, the possibility of their having a (limited) liaison, during sexual intercourse . . .

I search for her poems while she is out learning bridge. Can't find them: she has taken them with her – to show *him*! I do find the start of a letter: 'It doesn't seem just an hour ago that I sat talking with you. Why won't you introduce feelings? Who gives a damn about bridge? I gave myself a migraine wanting to talk to you about feelings and sentiments, and not suppress everything . . .' A chill torpor descends on me; I'm no more alive than my statuettes. When she returns, looking calm, I confront her with it. She's taken aback; is silent, searching for some excuse, the bitch – she's very good at rational explanations these days. I shouldn't have been rummaging, she says. I agree. I'm like a child. I agree. She says, 'It's a theme for a poem. If you'd let me finish it before reading it, you'd have realised that. I might well have shown it to you.' . . .

I hide in the Bauer shrubbery, staring through binoculars (Russian Army, sent home by Martin) at the window where they are imaged. It's a strange feeling seeing them so close, their lips moving, smiling, without any sound. Without depth too, or perspective; so that their bodies and faces, one behind the other, seem fused together. Nausea stirs in me. I want him to reach out and touch her hand, yet dread it . . .

21

Martha was a totally changed woman. Since Minna had taken herself off, unable to stand the atmosphere and, probably, her jealous feelings, the house was in disarray. Our normally reliable and hard-working maids found themselves left to their own devices and took advantage of it. At times, relatively pleasant to me, Martha would be reassuring: it was no more than a flirtation; I had nothing to fear from her and Philipp (though spoken in such a way as to isolate them from me, as though they were a 'couple'); she had only developed the migraine that day because he wouldn't allow her to break off from the cards to discuss matters sensibly. She feared only that *he* was concealing more dangerous feelings.

'But he's extremely honourable,' she said; 'since the kiss, he's not put a foot out of place; and *you* encouraged him to kiss me.'

At other times, when angry with me, she made remarks which sounded coldly considered, almost biblically awesome, and which reduced me once more to that small infant in Freiberg: such as 'If you continue to be suspicious, that which you presumably most fear is likely to take place.'

One day when strolling in the garden I asked her if she was in love with him. After a pause for reflection she shook her head and said, 'I've thought about that, of course; because it does feel a little like being in love in an adolescent way. But I decided I'm not. I am very, very fond of him; he's my closest friend; he's important to me and I am, I think, to him; and I find him very, very sexually attractive.'

I said rather drily, 'That sounds awfully close to being in love, Marti.'

'Yes, but it's not. I could say I love him – I have loving feelings towards him. In any case, since when have you been interested in love, Sigi?'

It was a good question. I have always felt that love is an unknown, as mysterious as gravity.

She looked radiant, triumphant, her crimson lips open to draw in the dewy early-morning air. She had begun to paint her lips at the start of her relationship with him. I thought at the time it was to make herself more attractive to me – in that brief period of sexual frenzy. Now she regularly spent two hours on dressing herself up and painting her face, before her bridge lessons. She preened herself before the mirror, torn between vanity and dissatisfaction. If I was two years old, Martha seemed sixteen – younger than Anna. Anna, increasingly cut off from us, regarded her mother with stupefied contempt and bewilderment.

Anna was highly serious; could not flirt, did not want to. She announced that, having seen my colleague Helene Deutsch in her white coat in hospital, she would like to become a doctor. Perhaps an analyst too. Gazing at us as if to say, I can practise on you two.

I too wondered, with anguish, what strange illness was affecting Martha. How I regretted my condescending remarks to Sophie's bridegroom Max: 'I have really got on very well with my wife. I am thankful to her above all for her many noble qualities, for the children who have turned out so well, and for the fact that she has neither been very abnormal nor very often ill.' Two years later she was both very abnormal and very ill: but an illness which made her glow with sexual vitality, a sparkle in her eyes and the bloom of a rosy peach in her complexion. I had fallen hopelessly in love with my wife, just at the time when she was falling in love with another man. I felt the humiliation deeply. At the same time I was racked with sexual desire.

Her excuse for not sharing my bed was that I was with her too much by day. All that clouded her happiness was that her sons were away (and in danger) and I was present. I felt that, had her sons been at home and I on the Russian front, her happiness would have been complete. She could not wait for the afternoons to come when it was time to go to Philipp's. Her bridge, she told me, was improving by leaps and bounds; the dummy partners very rarely won. She spoke that goadingly, with a mildly sadistic gleam in her eye and a grin on her painted lips. Then condescendingly brushed those lips against my cheek – and I was grateful for it!

One comfort was that Käthe Bauer was due home shortly after her holiday.

Even when she was not with Bauer, but engaged quite innocently somewhere out of the house, I mourned her absence. I lived through mourning and melancholia, feeling my life suspended while she was gone. Myself a corpse until she returned (with that look of slight irritation that I had done nothing, was still here to bother her).

Attempting to pull myself together, I accepted an invitation from an artistic society to address them on the subject of Leonardo. Philipp passed on a request, through Martha, that he would like to attend. I had to agree to it. I wanted to agree with it, since his presence would make her blossom into a gardenia.

'I have to warn you,' she said. 'It will look as if Philipp and I are together, since you will be in the front or surrounded by your admirers. I don't want you taking this amiss.'

'I won't.'

It had been quite obvious throughout the evening that they had gloried in the appearance of their being together. I had kept my eyes on them as I stumblingly explored the image of the vulture in Leonardo's painting; they leaned apart, ostentatiously. After-wards Bauer drove us back in his new Mercedes-Benz motor car. He at first declined Martha's invitation to come in for a nightcap, saying that his wife was due to arrive home from her holiday. However, a disappointed *moue* from Martha made him change his mind.

She has never looked more elegant and desirable. I could see they were restraining themselves with difficulty, wanted to leap on each other like goats. I too wanted to leap on her.

The conversation was halting: the rising price of paintings and antiques. No one was interested. So I deliberately moved it towards Eros. The female nude. I brought out art books for Bauer to look at. Michelangelo, I said, turning the pages for him, had no conception of how to sculpt or paint a breast. The gigantic female figures in the Medici Chapel in Florence had breasts that looked as if they were stuck on as an afterthought; and in fact he had used male models.

Martha kneeled up, resting her arm on his knee, to see. 'Is that how they are?' she mused, touching her own bosom, glancing down, inspecting. 'Are mine like that?'

'You can hardly tell with your clothes on,' I said, dry-mouthed. 'But no, they're not.'

'Yes, I suppose you can't tell with clothes,' she reflected. 'I don't *think* they're like that. But perhaps they *should* be. Michelangelo should have known. Perhaps I'm a freak. Do you think?' She smiled at me.

'Well, let's see.'

She undid a button of her bodice; hesitated; removed her hand. Bauer, hunched towards her, legs apart, his ape-like arms hanging down between them, said quietly, 'Yes, let's see.' More buttons were undone; and in the dim lamplight a white breast appeared. A nipple, engorged, hurriedly covered. She stroked her breast, examined it like an art expert.

Bauer's hand holding his cigar shook.

Covering up her breast, she rose to her feet. 'Coffee, I think,' she said. She left the room. Bauer hunched forward, staring into his glass, his eyes red and manic. His silence, his apartness, his secretive lust, unhinged me. I said with apparent casualness, 'So how do you feel about Martha, Philipp?'

I half-expected him to say, crudely, 'I'd give half my fortune to be able to fuck her!' Instead, he burst out, 'It's hard, it's hard! Especially when she does something like that! But I wouldn't! I couldn't betray you. Nor Käthe, for that matter. Oh, we're fairly cool with each other, but I don't know that I'd want to hurt her again.' He had slid close to me, laid his hand on my knee. 'If it were some wench in a tavern, I wouldn't think twice. It's hard, though; damn hard!'

Convinced by his words that only his strength stood in the way of an affair, that Martha had made it clear she was willing, I lost any pretence at dignity. With moist eyes I begged him not to take her from me; told him I loved her so much, needed her so much. 'I know, I know!' he said compassionately; 'I wouldn't do it! You must believe me, Freud!'

I glimpsed Martha's skirt, and raised my eyes. She held a tray of crockery. 'What are your feelings towards Philipp?' I demanded.

'I'm very attracted to him,' she said evenly. 'You know that. It's no secret from you. And he's attracted to me. You've been talking about me; what have you been saying?'

So it was out! No more concealment, no more camouflage when the three of us were together. And the words said to me, You're in the way; we tolerate your presence only because we have to. As parents tolerate a troublesome child's presence. I felt ready to burst into tears. In the silence that followed Martha's statement – or rather understatement – I saw Eros hold them in a theatrical glow, an absolute enchantment.

'I must go,' Bauer mumbled, and got unsteadily to his feet. Martha saw him out and, when she returned, raged at me for my interference, my distrust, my childishness. Sitting down, she buried her head in her hands and sobbed. 'That's the end of us!' she snarled. 'I'll leave you.' I rushed down the stairs and out of the house. The motor car was still there; Bauer was sitting behind the wheel, his head slumped. I pulled the door open: 'Please, come back and talk to her: she's distraught!'

He grumbled, but finally came. Martha was slumped in an armchair. She glanced up with surprise. 'Talk to him, Martha,' I said. 'I'm sorry; please sort this thing out between you.'

'Then go to bed,' she said coldly. 'Leave us in peace to talk.'

'I will.'

I undressed, put on my nightshirt, and got into bed. I heard Anna's door open, and her footsteps. I tossed and turned for a while. Anger flooded through me. They had reduced me to an infantile state: an unwanted infant. I sprang out of bed and rushed from the bedroom. Anna stood guard, in her dressing-gown, plain sleep-dazed Anna, over the closed living-room door. 'Let me through, Anna,' I shouted. 'Let me get in: I left my book in there. I want to read.'

She looked scared. 'I'll get it for you, Papa; Mama told me they're not to be disturbed.'

It enraged me even more. 'He's stolen my wife,' I shouted, 'now does he want to steal my living room too? Let me past, there's a good girl!'

'No.' She licked her pale lips, stood squarely before the door.

'Damn you, Anna!'

One of our maids appeared, nightcapped, frightened. 'Go back to bed!' I snarled at her. She scampered off. I pushed Anna roughly out of the way and opened the door. Martha and Philipp were on the sofa, their heads almost together. Martha shouted to me to leave them alone to talk. I shouted back, 'You bitch! You whore!' Philipp sprang to his feet, his arms spread in a quietening gesture.

He laid a hand on my arm. 'Please,' he insisted, 'you're hurting the people who love you.' I shrugged him off and gave a tug at his neat greying beard.

'He's having a nervous breakdown, and he's blaming every-one else,' Martha said coldly.

'I wonder how Käthe will like being told she and I are the dummy hands,' I snarled. 'You syphilitic swine!'

Anna, stealing up behind, seized me by the arm saying, 'Come along, Papa, come to bed! Leave them in peace, please!'

I don't remember collapsing into bed.

22

I am lost on a mountain, a blizzard howling; can't see more than a few feet in any direction, yet I have to blunder on. Any moment I could plunge off the mountainside or into a chasm. It's like that storm Anna and I blundered into once, in the Dolomites, only much, much worse, and I am alone. I call out to Anna. A simple cry for help becomes a romantic plea for her love . . .

My eyes open. They see first the statuettes and the 'Gradiva', then focus on Anna. She is sitting on the floor in front of my desk, her grey skirt spread out around her. Surrounding her is a mass of papers. She is picking them up, sorting them through, sliding them into folders. At times she pauses to read something: not briskly, in her businesslike way, but slowly, thoughtfully; then gazes out of the window.

'Anna,' I whisper.

Her vague face, misty eyed, turns in my direction. 'Papa. Dear Papa!'

'You're sorting my papers through.'

'Yes. It has to be done.'

'Of course. I have a dream I want to tell you.'

I describe my wandering around the mountainside. She murmurs, 'I hate to think of you lost and bewildered, dearest.'

My dry mouth cracks into a faint smile. 'You remember what I told you about that.'

'Yes.'

'Anna.'

'Yes?'

'Promise me you'll destroy those private papers from the war. My diary, notes, and so on. Or at least have them embargoed until even our grandchildren are dead.'

She has started to read them, I know.

'Of course I'll do that. Rest again, my dear; close your eyes. I'm here. I'm not going to leave you.'

After the post-Leonardo scene, I endured several nights of savage assault from Martha. I say deliberately 'nights', because by day there was a cold silence mostly. Such assaults were not new, they had occurred at intervals for several months. Martha had fallen into the pattern of waking early, around five; whether or not she was sharing my bed (and by now she wasn't) she would wake me up too and 'resume' a conversation we might have started at midnight – as though she had thought of nothing else during her brief sleep.

At first there would be an ominous reasonableness in her tone, almost like the first faint gunfire, at the front, which might have been distant thunder. But soon the full range of the batteries would be unleashed with devastating ferocity on me. I was a vile man, I was manipulative, I wouldn't let her have a life of her own, and so on. I would try to stay reasonable, keeping my head down in the trench so to speak, but occasionally I would be goaded into launching a much weaker battery on her.

Martha had never shown such a ferocity and power of obscene invective ever before. I wondered if it was an inheritance from Monika; or whether the Judith who smote Sisera sleeping had been an ancestress. When I thought I could stand no more, and would go mad if the guns kept it up, there would be a lull. She might concede a point, calm down. As soon as I began to breathe more easily, an even more ferocious assault would be launched. This pattern could last for two or three hours. Strangely, at the savage height of the bombardment, I would enter a surreal realm where I felt a masochistic pleasure almost; a kind of weak, female orgasm would ripple through me. And when the bombardment fell silent at last, I felt a wondrous relief.

134

I think she did too; a few times she moved almost straight from her rage to desire, opening her legs and pulling me into her. But not post-Leonardo, in the spring of 1915: now she merely stood up from the bed and went to her room to dress.

Now, in this period of nightly assault, the day was glimmering outside the window as she came in and started. They were 'dawn attacks', like those our sons were enduring in the East.

23

May 1915

Terrible atmosphere. Martha barely speaking to me by day, after nightly 'dawn assaults'. Anna reserved with me, while refusing to utter a word to her mother. Wrote to Minna begging her to return to try to restore some harmony. Martha refuses to see Bauer, but in a way that punishes me. It's only until I've started to learn how to be an adult, she says. Then she has every intention of being friendly with him again; intimate friends. Says I've grotesquely misrepresented, and tried to destroy, a relationship that involved one kiss, given and taken in a tense situation induced by me. In contrast, I've spent most of our married life locked away in a room where young women lie on a couch and pour out their secrets and their desires to me. I brag, she says, of breaking down their resistance; I call the treatment a cure through love; I acknowledge shamelessly that they are likely to fall in love with me and I with them. This is a travesty of the truth, but difficult to counter given her present irrationality . . .

I stare for hours at the savage, still face of Seth. As he tore Osiris into pieces I would love to dismember Bauer. Later, a chilly conversation with Martha:

Martha: 'I had so many resentments you should have seen Philipp as a necessary evil. Because he was too honourable to have tried anything. Even if we had slept together, a few fucks would have been trivial compared with your massive intimacies with Salomé, Deutsch, and so on, not to mention all your patients. Including Philipp's daughter! You were obviously obsessed with your "Dora" . . .'

She returns to the same subject over and over, with a 'compulsion to repeat': 'Then there was Fliess. It wouldn't surprise me if you'd had an affair with him; you were all over him, it was quite revolting, you thought the sun shone out of his arse . . .' But these coarse assaults are welcome, like a water hole in a desert, as a break from her contemptuous silences. It feels not good but ominous that her night attacks seem to be petering out. I wake at dawn and long to have her enter, if only to attack me . . .

At breaking point. Every moment I feel psychologically like poor old Emanuel as the door he was leaning against burst open and he was torn into chaos. Death would be welcome, were it not for Anna – who is a shade kinder to me. She's still writing passionately to Frau Zellenka. All from a chance meeting at Semmering. Am a prey to vicious thoughts: such as telling Frau Zellenka she can have Anna if she will contrive a meeting with Martha and tell her some home truths about Bauer. There's nothing like a former mistress for spreading dirt about her ex-lover. Such fantasies are a sign of my moral degeneration, and death would be preferable. I'm no better than Lot, offering the angels his daughters . . .

I fall back on the Egyptians for comfort. At mealtimes, in the deathly silence, I stroke Horus, Seth or Isis. They connect me to the childhood world of caresses and touches. Sometimes I feel, when in my study, all my divinities will lift me into the air and carry me away. I want it to happen . . .

It's a relief I can grieve over the hundreds of women and children drowned after the sinking of the *Lusitania*. I'm not totally corrupt, though sometimes I feel that a devil, a *dybbuk*, has occupied my corpse. Or perhaps has occupied Martha . . . The *Lusitania* is a terrible tragedy, and one that will probably cost us dear in the long run . . .

Helene Deutsch calls, to discuss with me Anna's hopes of taking up medicine. She grieves to find me in such a plight, and has no sympathy for Martha's discontent with her domestic and maternal role. At the same time, though rather plain, Deutsch has a strongly erotic nature, and betrays poor Felix often. With both sexes. Nature blessed her with the anomaly of giving her both male and female genitals at birth. She has shown me them. A real anatomical marvel! They allowed her to be both her father's nice little girl and clever boy. Not quite clever enough, of course; but her present sympathy is most welcome . . .

A letter from Bauer, in response to one of mine asking me if he will meet me to discuss the absurd situation. He expresses anger over my attack on him; but admits he was somewhat to blame in finding Martha so attractive in that she found *him* attractive. 'If she had been the wife of a friend I less respected and admired I would not have hesitated. As it is, I assure you I would never have attempted a seduction. I must assure you, though, Martha gave me no indication she would have said yes. I agree this is quite absurd, and I will suggest to Käthe that we invite you both for a meal sometime. I hope you have had good news, or at least not bad news, of your sons. I rather think Ida hopes her husband will not return . . .'

Rather strange evening with the Bauers. I am sure Käthe knows something is up. She wore a drab dress, her hair was unkempt, and she made almost no attempt to join in the conversation. Her technique, whenever there is a threat to her marriage, is to withdraw. One saw this when Philipp was having his affair with Frau Zellenka; Käthe became all but disembodied, it would appear. Yet she gives no obvious sign of suspicion. At great cost to my peace of mind I drew her away at one point on to their veranda, so that the enamoured couple could talk privately. Afterwards Marti smiled at me for the first time in weeks, and informed me that Philipp will resume his visits to us . . .

June

Martha pleased that I am more accepting, and can discuss her friendship more rationally (a weird reversal of the truth!). It must be perfectly possible for three people, in our situation, to get on, she suggests with a cold, bright smile. 'I regard my relationship with Philipp as quite separate from my relationship with you.' In other words, we are equals; except that *he* will be the one who excites her sexually! . . .

Good news from the East: the Austrian Army has regained Lemberg. We wonder if Martin was involved in the intense fighting and, if so, if he has survived. Have good reason to believe Martha says prayers and lights candles for our boys. If it helps her, so be it . . .

Entering Anna's room, in her absence, to see if she had typed a piece I had written, I inadvertently read part of a letter to Frau Zellenka. It upset me. Not only is she clearly enamoured of the woman still, she referred to her mother's amorousness. She calls Herr Bauer 'the Cough-Man', *der Husten-Mann*, since when he is here taking tea with Martha, and Anna approaches, they seem so raptly *tête-à-tête* she has to warn them of her presence with a cough. 'Your old flame' is another term she uses; 'My mother is making a fool of herself with your old flame, and my father does nothing about it. I am terribly unhappy, and long to be able to talk to you.' This can't go on . . .

Have no intention of being the dummy hand, however Käthe feels. I telephoned Ida, whom I knew through Martha to be back in Vienna after her stay in Semmering. She was somewhat surprised, but responded quite warmly. She is not without vanity at being the subject of a famous case study – a revised edition of which was my excuse for telephoning. I softened her by taking a highly sympathetic approach. I suggested that possibly her father had misused her much earlier in life also: in childhood. She failed to rise to that challenge. I then hinted strongly that he had taken his philandering nature elsewhere. She said she'd guessed as much. I said it might be fairer to her mother if she were warned of the danger. It would not be appropriate for me to do so. 'I shall be visiting Mama this afternoon,' Ida said, 'while Papa is consulting a urinary specialist. I'll point out to her that bridge can be a dangerous game to teach someone fairly late in life, and perhaps she should put her own cards on the table . . .'

Philipp writes to Martha; he is *forbidden* to see her, though I am welcome to call on them! Martha weeps and rages, and I comfort her . . .

Minna returns. She is sunburnt and well. Has evidently missed me greatly. Is glad to find a calmer house. Had begun to feel, as had Anna and I, that our house was collapsing around us, like Europe's. Anna quotes to me her favourite Rilke poem beginning: 'Who has no house now, long will so remain . . .'

Attend the B'nai B'rith, quite as in old times. They are good, kind men, however archaic in their beliefs . . .

Letter from Ernst. Thank God, he is safe so far. Martha goes out for a walk in the glorious day, returns looking a little sad. 'I was thinking,' she says, 'in the past I'd have told our good news to Philipp, and he'd have been pleased for us. But now . . .' I know, I said; I feel that too . . . And it's true; life seems awfully quiet . . .

He did kiss her a second time, she admits. It was the night when I started abusing them. After I'd been bundled off to bed, she had told him he probably wouldn't want to see her again; heading for the door, he had turned and stumbled towards her saying, 'Just one kiss!' Martha repeated to me 'one kiss', with scornful emphasis. This time, she said, the kiss was rough and crude, not at all as pleasant as the first time . . .

Marti very depressed. She denies it's because of Bauer; points out unnecessarily, though with some sarcasm, that we have sons who might be killed at any moment. Also points out (I had not, to my shame, thought of it in connection with her) it's much easier and more comfortable to be obsessed over a lover than over sons in danger. She is more concerned about Ernst, just *because* he has always been the luckiest, always found the best mushrooms, etc. She's convinced his luck will run out. My fears focus on Martin. As the eldest, he has much Oedipal aggression; if I service intellectually six or seven women on my sofa, he will service at least a dozen carnally; if I slay a hundred philistines with an essay, he will do his best to slay a thousand with his rifle and bayonet, heedless of danger to himself. It was indeed more comfortable to worry myself sick over Martha and Bauer . . .

She who has never shown the slightest interest in my work, who regards it as pornography, has been reading 'Dora'. 'What a wretched man!' she says. 'He was as good as saying to Herr Zellenka, with a wink and a nod, OK, you can do what you like with Dora – Ida – so long as you let me fuck your wife! . . . Or suck her at least, if he was incapable of anything more . . . My God! I wouldn't give him the time of day. He can rot in Hell! . . .' Her bitter, unpainted mouth withdrawn into her fat jowls, which I adore. Thus grief over his disappearance, and anger over his timidity, strive together and suppress the underlying fear. I too, oddly, am angered by his desertion . . .

July

(*At Altaussee*) Letter from Martha with the news that Martin was wounded on the very day (8 July) on which I dreamt he had been killed. Fortunately he was only slightly wounded in the arm. Huge relief . . .

August

Have stayed mercifully clear of the diary this holiday, apart from the entry about Martin. I say mercifully, because even to keep one is a neurotic symptom. Anna and Martha have returned to Vienna (Martha only stayed for ten days), and now Minna and I are here on our own for the final week. Martha was extremely cool and lethargic; with the result that I have weakened in face of Minna's evident need. Lying with her, I could almost imagine it was a stouter Martha; they are so remarkably alike in feature, though not in spirit. The coitus was unsatisfactory from my point of view; Martha, in her brief season of plenty, has spoiled me for her sister, or indeed anyone. Minna has helped me a good deal with 'The Unconscious' and 'Repression'; she believes Martha has behaved very badly and wishes I had married her instead. 'Two men have given meaning and a stoical happiness to my life: Fliess and you,' she said. Fliess gave her an experience of passion, and it hardly mattered that it was unconsummated; I, of high intellect. 'That isn't to say', she added hastily, 'that Wilhelm did not have a fine mind, nor that I don't enjoy sex with you.'

September

Minna's porcine face gazing at me unblinking across the hotel dining table: 'I feel so guilty, because if I hadn't, in a moment of weakness, showed her those letters, you would have gone on in your comfortable pattern of life. They gave her a glimpse of something beyond mundane existence. Only my sister, much as I love her, is incapable of rising to it. It's not too late for you to leave her, my dear. You and I could have twenty years of happiness. I'll share your work and your bed. Who cares what anyone else says or thinks? You're used to the anger of the mob. Be braver than Wilhelm was . . .'

Vienna, full of war-wounded, feels like a prison house. A note from Ida Bauer asks me to call on her. I had almost forgotten the Bauers . . .

24

These diary entries I am quoting may not be word for word; I have no means of checking them; but they are fairly reliable, since I forget very little of what I have written, however long in the past.

Recalling those particular entries, I realise I gave a very inadequate account of Helene Deutsch's visit. I was both too unkind to her and too kind. Of course I am speaking now from the vantage point of the Jungfrau peak of one's dying breaths. (Ah, how Jung creeps in! I parted from him in 1911, about the same time as Helene Rosenbach painfully gave up a decade-long relationship, beginning in adolescence, with a married man, the Polish socialist Lieberman. So, when she turned almost simultaneously to psychoanalysis and to a new, marriageable man, Felix Deutsch, she and I had certain shared emotions.)

I was unkind in that she wasn't really plain. Plenty of men thought her truly beautiful, with 'luminous' eyes, glowing complexion, and so on. But for me she looked rather too bovine. Ah well, there's no accounting for taste. She was just thirty at the onset of the war, in the mature flush of womanhood, and I am quite sure she thought I was in love with her. It must have been painful for her, that visit, finding how intensely, if temporarily, I craved my wife.

I don't know what made me say she had female lovers. No, no, I don't think so. Nor did she have the organs of both sexes, though she dreamed that she had. What lies we tell in our diaries!

I was unkind also in saying she betrayed Felix often. Physically I don't think that was the case, then or later. A few light affairs. But in her *imagination* she betrayed him constantly. That was what I had in mind. I doubt if she ever slept with Felix without imagining she was with Lieberman. Felix wasn't passionate; he suffered from premature ejaculation – no doubt because he'd have preferred (to be crude) to have it up the arse himself. Well, one can't have everything in a relationship. He worshipped her and, later, Martin their son. He looked after Martin much better than she. All Sunday he would devote to taking care of him. A motherly man.

Which of course was extremely helpful to Helene, enabling her to pursue her career; and she was highly ambitious. Yet she complained constantly that he wasn't a real man! What do women want?

They had a remarkably free marriage. Helene, on the occasion of that particular visit to me, was making one of her rare appearances in Vienna. She was working and studying with my old boss Kraepelin in Munich, and would remain there for most of the war, while Felix stayed in Vienna. Hardly an entrapping marriage!

She had had her first miscarriage, I recall; and, mixed up with practical advice for Anna and sympathy for me, she complained at length about the plight of women, torn between work and motherhood; or, in her case then, the urge to become a mother.

And laments, in a German still execrably corrupted with Polish, over Lieberman still!

'Can my marriage work, Professor?'

'You must make it work! It's good for you; it gives you freedom to be yourself, to develop your talent.'

'Yes, but . . . It's not the same; there's no passion.'

'Passion doesn't pay the rent.'

'Yes, but you're finding now how important it is . . .'

It was always 'Yes, but . . .' with Helene. She could never be satisfied. Hell would be an eternity in her company, listening to her laments, her confusions, her self-analysis and analysis of those close to her. Whenever she says or writes, in presenting a case, 'A female patient of mine . . .' you can bet your bottom dollar (as she learnt to say in America) she's referring to herself. Terrible narcissist.

I've always admired poor Felix for tolerating her absences and her ambition. Martin is not so tolerant; he absolutely hates his mother.

What I did not express in the diary sufficiently was the ambivalence of her sympathy. She was exploding with anger inside, at my daring to declare that I thought Martha beautiful and desirable. You could tell she was thinking, She's old, she's rather ugly, she's dull! Has the professor lost his marbles?

Nothing of that came across as she hunched her rather plump body forward in the chair, her thighs under a too-tight frock slightly parted, reassuring, comforting, in that soft Polish-German voice.

Also she was jealous of Anna, while pretending to like her. She made an interesting comparison that day, I recall. 'She's a bright girl,' she observed. 'I see a lot of myself in her at eighteen. We have a lot in common, Professor; we are both third daughters of loving and brilliant fathers. Our older sisters have used up the incest threat, now we can use our masculine identification to forge ahead and make something of ourselves. Don't you agree?'

I neither agreed nor disagreed; my mind was on Martha. I could feel her thoughts churning about Philipp.

'But Anna has a good mother too. I had to marry Felix to find a good mother. If only he was also good in bed! It's fine him milking the goat and warming a drink for me when I'm tired, but I want a good strong penis too! I was so looking forward to coming home and being with him, but . . . it makes it even harder.'

She stretched languidly, and her dress tightened. She always wore very tight-fitting dresses. Later, when she started sailing off to America and became rich, she wore the finest silk; and whenever she sat down you could see the outline of her corset. I think she meant it to look seductive. The Americans, of course, now that she's chosen to live there, will be lapping her up!

All the same, I like her.

As she rose to leave, and I held out my hand as usual, she took it between both of hers and pressed it to her ample, stiffly stayed bosom. 'Don't, don't let Anna find a Lieberman!' she said.

'I'll try to discourage her.'

'I was her age when I fell into bed with him. I'd loved him much earlier. I've wasted the best years of my life. Although . . .' her body shivered . . . 'he gave me such joy, such joy.' Her gloved hand briefly touched my cheek as I moved back. 'I wish I were staying in Vienna so you could call upon me.'

The temerity of it!

'That's kind of you, but your patients need you.'

'Yes. And your pain will pass. And when this insane war is over, my dearest wish is that you might conduct my training analysis.'

'It will be an honour, Frau Deutsch.'

She brought my hand, which she had continued to hold, to her lips. She has great warmth of heart.

I think later she came to disbelieve 'the Bauer affair'. In her paper 'On the Pathological Lie' there are possible hidden references to it. I did not much mind, since it was an exceedingly interesting paper. It argued that fantastic lies, or tall stories, could bring creative release, and were a kind of poetry.

The Achaeans set sail because of tall stories about how beautiful Helen was.

Fear on behalf of my warrior sons, muted somewhat previously by erotic anguish, became stronger and at times overpowering. I would 'see' Ernst or Martin fighting bayonet to bayonet with an enemy, and 'feel' the cold steel penetrate my heart. I was convinced, and still am, that I was in telepathic contact with my sons at that time. During a walk in the Prater I saw doubles of them both on the same afternoon. I wrote as a consequence of these experiences an essay on 'The Uncanny'.

Minna was again helpful. The whole experience with Fliess had been uncanny for her. She recovered quickly from my tactful rejection of her proposal. It was just as well, she said; she was really wedded to Fliess. Lovable though I was, she could not happily settle for anything less than that passion. I said, 'Yes, if you'd ever actually met and made love, you'd have both turned into the Shekhinah!'

'Oh, it would have been *incredible*! You please me enormously, but we don't *explode*, as he and I would have done.'

'I'm too rational and cautious for that, Minna.'

'Well, we are as we are.'

Martha and I made love again. She was rather passive, still under Bauer's spell; but it felt good.

'Käthe is the power in that house,' she murmured, her hand clasping mine in bed after our lovemaking; my thoughts were a long way from the Bauers. 'She waits like a spider, ready to pounce on him. *Forbidding* him! You and I never forbade each other to do anything.' She's forgetting the Sabbath candles, but no matter, she's right in general. 'He's so fucking timid! He kept saying he wanted me, how he wanted me, but he didn't dare.'

'It would have been dangerous for you,' I murmured.

'Oh, of course, but my life has never been dangerous. It appealed to me. And an impotent man would have been quite a challenge!'

'But you said you never contemplated sleeping with him.'

'I didn't. I knew he wouldn't.'

Her face a faint glimmer on the dark continent of womanhood, her lips parted in a smile. 'I did stroke his genitals that night when you threw your hysterical fit, Sigi!'

'You *what*?'

A chuckle. 'After he'd kissed me. I grabbed him down there and fondled him. I thought, what the hell, it's probably all over. He said, "Why are you doing this to me, Martha?" And I said, "Because I feel like it!"'

147

I chuckled. 'That's wonderful!'

'Actually, I thought I felt a slight erection.'

'Impossible!'

'A stirring, at least.' A sigh. 'Life is so fragile.' She turned away from me. 'Good night, Sigi.'

The next night she would not come to our room. I made her edgy, she said, by making it so obvious I wanted her. Men were so obsessed. 'You have sons who may be dying of wounds and you want sex, sex, sex!'

Instead of coming to bed she would go out into the garden. I would steal out behind her; she would be sitting, gazing thoughtfully up at the stars. It frightened me. Martha has never gazed up at the stars. She seemed suddenly in her own world, indifferent to me. 'I am me!' she snarled once. 'When I felt erotic again, you thought it was for you! It wasn't! It was for me!'

She confessed to having kissed him on a third occasion. I must have stolen away from their grounds, with my binoculars, before it occurred.

'If only he had agreed to meet me outside – say in some country tavern – that would have satisfied me.'

'Just to talk?'

'Well, perhaps a kiss or two afterwards in his precious motor car.'

'That would have left him terribly frustrated,' I pointed out. 'But you could have – relieved him. – If, as you say, he's capable of an erection.'

'With a handkerchief. It sounds very sordid, doesn't it?' She screwed up her mouth.

'No, I don't see that it's sordid. It would have been even restrained. The sexual life should be infinitely free. I wouldn't have objected.'

But even after this exercise of fantasy, Martha had a headache.

Occasionally she did visit me. Our lovemaking had none of the passion of those brief pre-Philippian nights.

We were the Masurian Marshes after the tumultuous battle.

And – just as our brave Austrian armies were fighting on the ground of our superstitious sidelocked Shylocked ancestors in Galicia – so Martha and I had been fighting a war whose origins lay deep in the past: our own. It was the war of the nursery. Whether or not you believe what I have told you about her background – and you must remember, should documents be produced to 'disprove' my revision, the Bernays family were well versed in forgery – Bauer and I were for Martha *dramatis personae* representing past conflicts and seductions. He and I too had our private theatres. My drunken challenge to him – 'You want to sleep with Martha' – had been merely the Sarajevo incident, the *incidental* spark.

I was starting to think the fearful artillery bombardments had been worth enduring for the sake of the occasional blissful interlude. We both became obsessed with revisiting the battlefield.

'Did you ever talk to him of love, Marti?'

'Only on that night when Anna dragged you off us. I said it felt a little like being in love, in an adolescent way. He misunderstood, and said, I don't love you. I said, I didn't say I loved you. – But then we heard Anna approaching the door again, coughing rather obviously, so that was that.'

If I came in on her dressing for dinner, I imagined how it might have been, watching her dress to go out with Philipp. 'Will he like this?' she would say, stroking her underclothes. I would respond, 'I'm quite sure he will.' I became Martha, in fact, kissing me on the cheek good night, before leaving the house to climb into the Mercedes-Benz. He waved cheerily to me; he knew I knew what they were going to do.

Over a Saturday night game of taroc one of the players mentioned Bauer, without malicious intent, I think: something to do with a charitable fund he'd set up for the families of war casualties. I slid to the floor in a faint. This caused great concern, and was seen as my response to the mention of war dead. It was the sixth or seventh time in my life I have fainted, the earlier occasions being with Fliess and Jung.

The English broke through our lines at Flanders. The leaves began to turn brown, like the leaves in Rilke, for those still without a house, those who restlessly wandered.

25

I am well enough to be be pushed by Anna around the garden for a few minutes. The ground is still crisp with frost; it is so good to see the trees begin to bud. Of course it is only remission. I meditate on the dream I have had: It is a newspaper headline, saying the new *Queen Elizabeth* has made a secret crossing to safety. Anna is in a way my Virgin Queen, and I am grateful for her deliverance.

Yet I have a sense of the crossing being a physically greater one, such as an Atlantic crossing. The renaissance English queen was renowned for her fire as well as her ice; there may be a glancing reference to our maid, Martha, who at the onset of the war and her menopause veered unpredictably between passionate warmth and cold fury. One might say she was storm-tossed like a ship on the Atlantic, yet came through finally to safety.

When she thinks I am asleep, Anna sits in my hieratic, rather Egyptian chair and reads my neurotic war diaries. She is clearly fascinated and horrified by what she learns of her parents' relationship at that time. Her reading makes me uncomfortable, and that's why I seem stuck in that minor (not to say embarrassing) episode of my life, when there are so many much more important events I should be narrating. For example, the amazing mediumistic *séance* that Jung, Ferenczi and I took part in during our voyage across the Atlantic: *we* took our 'virgin queen', analysis, across, that's true; it's probably in the dream, now I think of it. There will be time; I will get to it.

But I must keep on to the end of this, since it's at the heart of our science. I wanted at the same time to abolish Bauer – murder him, if necessary – and have Martha confess to me, with tears in her eyes, 'I'm sorry, but I love him deeply and passionately; as I have never loved you.' And give me 'the ocular proof' of it. And this ambivalence is in my diaries and Anna is reading them. She is still kindness personified, but treats me with just a touch more reserve.

Such ambivalence is why prosperous nations destroy themselves with wars; and it's why I responded as I did to Otto Bauer, Ida's brother – you'll read it in a page or two, if Seth doesn't intervene.

Anna wants me to have an analysis. Apparently a very remarkable analyst called Doctor Tod has moved to England. She is willing to take me, but lives in Dover, which is too far for me to travel.

26

'I'm so grateful to you for calling, Professor,' Ida greeted me in her home near the Rasumovsky Palace. She looked gaunt and hollow-eyed, as when her father brought her to see me, fifteen years earlier.

'Not at all; it's on my way to my weekly dissipation – a game of taroc.'

'I would have called on you, only I didn't think the Frau Professor would welcome one of our family.'

'She's still angry with your father,' I said; 'but you would not have been made to feel unwelcome.'

She blinked several times, and it seemed to me she had probably been crying a lot of late. 'Perhaps that was my excuse,' she said; 'perhaps *I* would have felt uncomfortable visiting your family.'

'Tell me what's wrong, Ida. Your son is well, I hope?'

'He's very well. Came second in his school exams.'

'Then what's wrong? You've been crying.'

She took a handkerchief from her cuff to dab under her eyes. 'We've had bad news from the War Ministry.'

'Your husband?'

'That would not have been such bad news, I fear,' she said with a wry smile. It was her brother, Otto; he had been reported missing in action; it was thought he'd been taken prisoner by the Russians.

'I'm so sorry, Ida,' I said. 'But I'm sure he will return unscathed to take up the causes he believes in so idealistically.' Otto Bauer had consulted me briefly; he was a passionate socialist. I had warned him not to try to make people happy; they didn't want happiness.

'I hope so.' She ran a hand absently over her straight black hair, pushing a strand behind her ear. 'But I didn't ask you to come to commiserate with me on that. I don't know how to cover up what I wanted to ask of you, so I'll plunge straight in.'

'You always did.'

She looked pleased, amid her sadness. 'Well, I tried to be honest. Though I found my honesty was leading you to extraordinary conclusions. I never loved Hans Zellenka, you know; but as for Frau Zellenka, yes, you were right about her.' She was silent, gazing at me with a wistful expression before saying: 'I have a – a romantic problem, connected with Frau Zellenka. I am still attached to her.' Her cheeks reddened. 'And she *was* attached to me. However, all her thoughts for the past few months have been on someone else. Your daughter.'

I sighed. 'So that's why you were reluctant to visit us; you didn't want the risk of meeting Anna.'

'Yes. Our holiday in Semmering was a complete disaster; Frau Zellenka simply wasn't with me; she just lived for letters from Anna. Ever since they met, she hasn't been able to think of anyone or anything else. I would like you, I beg you, to put a stop to it.'

I spread my arms helplessly. Anna was strong-willed; in any case I did not believe I had the right to forbid her a friendship.

That was weak of me, Ida snapped. The girl didn't know her own mind. Anna would do anything to please me, if she felt I really cared about something strongly. I should surely be steering her towards some steady young suitor. Was there no one interested?

'There's a young fellow called Lampl,' I conceded. 'He seems decent enough; not too bright, but decent. She quite likes him, I think.'

'Well, then!' She tugged a bell-rope. When the maid appeared Ida asked me would I like coffee, and I said yes, thank you.

'Please, dear Professor,' she pleaded, stretching to touch my hand.

'Let me think about it.'

She seemed content with that. She begged me to forgive her rudeness in not asking after *my* health and well-being. Both were fair, I replied abstractedly, my mind working. I was really quite unhappy, with Martha in a dreary, lacklustre mood. Sexual intercourse was infrequent and spiritless on her part. I knew she grieved over the lost lover and even more the lost friend. It had been a savage blow to her narcissistic pride that Bauer had dismissed their friendship as of no account.

The maid brought the coffee. Ida poured.

'Thank you. I will do my best with Anna,' I said slowly, 'if you will help my wife.'

'How can I do that?'

'This quarrel between her and your father is stupid. Their friendship was important to her. I have written to him twice, urging him to pay us a friendly visit, but have had not even an acknowledgement. You could use your good offices with your parents; perhaps invite us and them to a simple luncheon here, or something. Your father wouldn't deny you – he feels too much guilt for having used you as barter.'

She held her cup in mid-air, gazing vaguely past me. 'I don't think it would be wise. Frankly, I think the Frau Professor stirred his sexual feelings to their depths; but he has too much honour -- now, at last – to have done anything about them. He felt it best never to see her again. For Mama's sake.'

'So, is he happy, with his honour intact?' I asked ironically.

'No!'

'Well, there you are! We make so much fuss and nonsense about sex. My wife is on the verge of menopause; she has been as fluttery as a girl in her menarche. Your father wanted her; she wanted him. Supposing they'd had each other, once or twice? Would the heavens cave in?'

She veiled her gaze, and touched a black, white-crossed prayer book that lay beside her on the sofa. Ida had converted soon after her marriage: from one absurdity to another, even more absurd! With a refinement of rebellion, she had chosen the minority Lutheran brand.

'It could actually have helped your father, healed him,' I said. Her eyes widened in astonishment as I explained.

'I'm sure my mother wouldn't come,' she murmured. 'She was dreadfully hurt, just when she'd begun to trust him.'

'You must persuade her we should face our demons; and assure her we are really just a boring old bourgeois couple. Her greatest risk is an hour's moderate boredom!'

'I will try.'

27

Leaning over Anna's shoulder I see she is writing to her friend Dorothy in New York. 'I beg you not to risk the voyage,' she writes, 'though I long to see you. I can't help remembering what happened to the *Lusitania* in the Great War. In any case, you will find me a disappointment. Life, I feel, is like a farm that I'm just visiting on holiday. I used to think I was like a wandering Indian monk, belonging to another world than this. Now I *know* it, my dear. My place is with him . . .'

I am touched by Anna's devotion, but also troubled.

As fate would have it, after my visit to Frau Ida I was visited by a Martha who had much of the vivacity of several months before. She no longer gave a thought to Bauer, she declared; riding me, her sagging breasts jigging, she panted that she quite liked being the man for a change!

I rejoiced.

When I opened Ida's letter, inviting us to luncheon with her and her parents, I had a mind to toss it in the waste-basket. I no longer needed Bauer. But then his powerful image rose before me, and I decided I had quite missed him. I took the invitation to Martha. She affected casualness, but could not mask a flush of pleasure. 'Ah, he misses us! He's got his daughter to invite us. Well, do we go? Or teach him a lesson by refusing?'

'One feels like teaching him a lesson.'

'I agree. On the other hand, you've something of a reputation for falling out with your male friends and colleagues.'

I shrugged. 'Yes, I think we might as well go to Frau Ida's. It's all deep in the past.'

'I suppose we might as well.'

She suddenly beamed radiantly. 'I'm so relieved I regained my zest, Sigi, before this arrived! Otherwise you might have thought . . .'

'Yes, I might have,' I said drily.

'One should feel sorry for him,' she said. 'Our flirtation was probably his last – ' she spread her arms, leaving her sentence unfinished.

'Yes. Perhaps you should give him one of the drawings I made of you.'

She coloured. 'I did.'

'You *did*?'

'I thought you wouldn't miss just one. You have *me* now: surely you don't begrudge him a picture?'

'No. Poor wretch. You know he's masturbating with it, Marti?'

'So what?' She shrugged.

'Yes: so what!'

Oh, and he'd seen her piss, she said. Well, not actually seen: it was the night they'd met in the park, by chance, when he was walking his dog. It was cold, and she'd simply had to go. They'd laughed about it; he'd pretended to turn away, but didn't; however, the darkness meant he could have seen nothing, or very little. She'd thought to herself, Fliess would have liked to have watched Minna do this . . .

I telephoned Frau Ida with our acceptance. 'If the weather holds,' she said, 'we'll have a picnic lunch in the garden.'

'That will be very nice.'

'I hope there won't be a strained atmosphere. I'm still dubious: Father was in two minds and I had to bully him. Even though he does miss you – both. But there's still the problem of – you know.'

'I know – the attraction,' I said.

'And Mama can be so withdrawn.'

'It won't be easy for us either, Ida. But I'll bring you

something that should help.'

Martha became cool and detached again in the fortnight leading up to the lunch party. It was nothing personal, she said; just a touch of nerves.

28

I can predict only too easily the reaction of Freudians to this book. While grateful for the revelations about Emanuel and about Martha's parentage, as shedding light on my romantic views of industrial England and the discovery of the Oedipus Complex, they will refuse to believe I could behave as childishly, as over-emotionally, as inconsistently, as the Freud I have depicted in the Bauer episode. If I was not raving from morphine, I was trying to portray certain of my mental characteristics, notably masochism, by inventing a symbolic action.

They will point out I confessed my *Leonardo* was a kind of novel; that's why, when I found out 'vulture' was a mistranslation for 'kite', I didn't bother to correct my text, didn't give a damn. Likewise I wanted to call my last work, *Moses and Monotheism*, a historical novel. Moses an Egyptian! Sacrificed by his followers! Jesus Christ! . . .

(Speaking of that book, I really got a great kick out of writing something so offensive to most Jews; imagining their faces when they read it, I would almost forget my pain.)

So – the case will be made – in my 'memoir' I'm informing the reader, fictionally, theatrically, that my inner life with Martha wasn't entirely smooth, and I wasn't fooled either by her overwhelming conventionality – as though she, uniquely, was not a prey to universal ambivalence.

Others may go for what seems to be Helene Deutsch's explanation in her 'On the Pathological Lie' of 1921: or rather, in the uncensored version, presented to a private audience the following year. She writes there, you will recall, that 'an eminently truthful physician' created an unreal 'triangular' erotic situation which he himself half-believed; he was 'temporarily unhinged' by fears for his son, or to be precise 'fears that his unconscious destructive wishes towards him might be all too terribly realised. He knew he would not be able to support his guilt as well as grief, should it happen, and so fled into the lie.'

Purists will reject the notion that I could have had some kind of nervous breakdown; they will argue that Frau Deutsch, as so often, was writing about herself. No one, they will point out, was more constantly involved in triangles – her father and her lover Lieberman; Lieberman and his unfortunate wife; Lieberman and Felix; Felix and his bisexual friend Paul, whom she also slept with. No one had more ambivalent feelings towards children: the abortion of her child by Lieberman; the mysterious death of Lieberman's baby son, conceived when Helene's lover was claiming a sexless marriage, and possibly killed by the vengeful mother; Helene's son, Martin, adored but neglected. And she was forever telling her friends about non-existent affairs.

All of which is undeniably true. Helene could still burst into tears, twenty years later, about the death of Lieberman's baby boy: loathed at first, as cementing his bad marriage; then loved as their own fantasy child, with hopes that the ailing Frau Lieberman might die; then bitterly mourned yet also resented, since Lieberman had to comfort his wife.

Enough of Frau Deutsch. With her stiffly corseted, silk-dressed figure and melting eyes. Enough of her – or the suspicion will arise that I've disguised an involvement with her and Felix. They'll know Helene paused outside our house one day and said to herself, 'What *will* the poor Frau Professor do!' Could Freud have been her established lover, and then she made him jealous by finding poor Felix attractive for once? I have to admit, Helene has crept mysteriously into this narrative.

The multitudes of my enemies, of course, will find no

difficulty whatever in believing the Bauer affair, and will refuse to find anything that might extenuate my bad behaviour – whether that Martha was acting in a provocative manner or that I genuinely wished for her happiness.

To get back to the question of truth and lies in this memoir: I'll be honest – I *have* sometimes fictionalised. Martha never slept with Eli, for example. I was representing my jealousy, and they *were* attracted to each other. I've lied symbolically, as a defence, for dramatic effect, from embarrassment at my quiet, uneventful life, and from a puckish, teasing sense of humour.

Also because memoirists lie while pretending to be honest. I prefer to give scholars, those fleas on the head of a giant, every chance to check dates etc. and say, with blazing spectacles, It couldn't have happened!

But this, the business with Dora's father – well, all I can say is, Eros is a powerful god. '*Some guy!*' as my delectable 'Kat' said on one occasion; and Psyche was '*some gal!*'

She, a poet and a woman, was my *alter ego*; I shared everything with her, including *l'affaire Bauer*. She seemed to understand. She thought the Frau Professor misunderstood me because, like most people, she was a day person; whereas I, like Kat's father, an astronomer, did my best work at night.

The day of the reunion with Philipp Bauer proved blissfully warm and cloudless, and Frau Ida's walled garden was a sun-trap. Bauer's greeting of us was a little over-hearty; looking remarkably fit and content, he was wearing a white suit and straw hat. Käthe, much more reserved in her greeting, had on a pale lilac dress that chimed in with her unassertive personality. Ida – I almost said Dora – was in gay pink, a colour that suited her youthful vitality; yet in my eyes – not to mention Bauer's – there was only one desirable woman present, despite her years: my Martha, who had spent all morning making herself beautiful while lamenting her lack of beauty.

And it's true, as I've said before, she wasn't beautiful; she became, you could say, almost ugly. 'Old and ugly', as was said about her mother, Monika. Yet probably Monika too could have looked attractive if she hadn't been run off her feet all day, and too poor to buy glamorous clothes and cosmetics.

Wait – I am getting tired of this *jeu d'esprit* about Martha's birth. I have to confess my new genealogy for her was a pure fiction. That chapter was a pack of lies: except that her father was indeed jailed for fraud. I'm starting to understand how my analysands could get trapped in a 'creative' lie; and how one can adapt to it quite gaily, since it opens up a certain freedom. Crime can spring from the same impulse: Herr Bernays' fiddling of his accounts, for instance. He, the son of the Rabbi of Hamburg! Anyway, I recant – Martha wasn't Monika's daughter by old Jacob Fraud, and never lived with the Pappenheims. Her background is utterly normal; that's to say, she would like to have born a child to her father, and felt intense jealousy of her small-minded, whining, domineering mother.

Perhaps, if I reflect on this particular lie, I wanted to fuck my old nurse and impregnate her. But I really believe it's more to do with a frustrated imagination. I should have been Rabelais or Cervantes.

Where was I? The picnic . . . Mature stone walls, a blaze of autumn shrubs, an ornate pond, a fig tree, wrought-iron picnic table and chairs; two highly mature 'blooms' with parasols, one maturing bloom serving cold drinks from a tray; grey-bearded, dark-suited Freud and white-suited, raffish Bauer. Ida and I strolled to admire the yellow star-shapes of a superb *Rudbeckia fulgida* (there is one also, less resplendent, in our Hampstead garden); and, as we bent over together to smell, she slipped a small packet into her handbag.

Maids came, bringing a lavish cold buffet, curtseyed to Frau Ida, and left.

Sitting round the table, we drank a toast in lemonade to our absent sons. Their son had been confirmed as a prisoner of war, so at least would be safe, one could assume. Anxiety, however, gave Käthe Bauer an excuse for silence. She poked uninterestedly at a salmon salad. Her liveliest contribution for half an hour was an irritated wave at a wasp investigating her lemonade.

I was watching Martha. She was talking to Philipp and Ida with equal pleasantness, showing no sign of the tumults of the past.

There was a friendly disagreement about the death penalty that had been enacted upon a British nurse, Miss Cavell, in Belgium. Bauer argued that she merited it for her behaviour in helping enemy soldiers escape; Martha, Ida and I believed the punishment had been cruel. 'What do you think, Käthe?' Martha asked, trying to involve her.

'It's war, isn't it?' she snapped. She dabbed her tight thin lips with a napkin, and gazed away into space.

There was stillness except for a scraping of knives and forks. Ida picked up a second jug of lemonade and filled five clean glasses. 'You must try this,' she said; 'it's a recipe one of my church friends gave me. I think it's rather pleasant.'

I sipped, and tasted for the first time in many years that slightly bitter tang, changing quickly to a delightful coolness. Bauer licked his lips. 'It's good,' he said, 'but a bit odd; my lips and tongue feel sort of tingly – what's in it, Ida?'

'Ah, that's a secret!'

'It's good though.'

'Yes, it is,' Martha agreed. 'But I know what you mean. My tongue's gone a bit numb.'

'It's sort of warm in the mouth then cool in the throat,' said Käthe, like a flower suddenly opening. 'But I like it. You must give me the recipe, dear.'

'I will, Mama.'

A few minutes later I felt sweep through me that light, exhilarated, powerful feeling as if anything is possible to you. I could see the others were feeling the same; the tension eased. Philipp told a joke, and chuckles danced around the table. His lips gaping at his own joke, one saw all too clearly the sparkling white teeth, and the bright-eyed vivacity, which had charmed Martha.

'I've been meaning to say to you, Käthe, I do like your dress,' I murmured across the table.

Her eyes lit up. 'Do you, Professor? Oh, it wasn't expensive.' She glanced down at herself admiringly.

'I do, very much. The colour suits you. It's a dress meant to be worn by such an attractive woman – I hope you don't mind my complimenting your wife, Philipp?'

He flushed, uneasy. 'Not at all.'

Käthe's blush was rather becoming. She really *wasn't* a bad-looking woman, I decided. 'Philipp doesn't think I'm attractive,' she said.

'Oh, come now! I'm sure he does.'

Ida broke in tactfully: 'Shall we make ourselves more comfortable?'

We moved to swinging seats near the pond. 'Come and sit by me, Käthe,' I suggested; 'that's if you don't mind cigar smoke.'

'I love it. It's very sensual.'

'I didn't think you enjoyed sensual pleasures,' I said. 'Do you mind? I've wanted to do this for a long time – while we were dummy hands, so to speak.' I stroked her neck. 'Your skin is so wonderfully soft.'

'I don't mind.' Her eyes were shut, her head tilted back. Ida, sitting on the grass by the pond, called to me. 'Come and see my fish.'

'Excuse me,' I said to Käthe; 'I'll be back.' She nodded, her eyes still closed, tilted back, drinking in the last of the sun, of the year, of her life. I knelt by Ida, gazing down at the twisting carp.

'What are you doing?' she hiss-whispered.

'Cheering everyone up. Does your mother look unhappy?'

'No. But you're practically inviting *them* to . . .' I followed her glance across to Martha and her father, sitting in apparently normal conversation. I said that, with the coca as with hypnosis, no one did anything he did not actually want to do. That might well be, Ida countered; but she felt like a conspirator.

'And have you forgotten your father conspired against

you, Ida? Bartered you for your friend Frau Zellenka? And your mother simply withdrew into her chores, leaving you in the lurch.'

'That's true.' She frowned; then her lips struggled to suppress a smile. 'What does it matter anyway? Life should be fun! I feel extraordinarily light-hearted! I think I shall leave you to it, and go and telephone Frau Zellenka.'

'Why don't you? But before you go, I have a question I must ask you.' I wished to take advantage of her exalted state of emotion. 'Do you now admit, Frau Ida, that you were in love with Herr Zellenka when he embraced you and made a proposal? And that your disgust at his pressing against you concealed feelings of desire?'

She reflected, eyes closed, face tilted towards the sun. Then she said, 'I would hardly have accepted flowers from him every day for a year if I had not loved him; nor been so interested in his children. And as for concealed desire – well, I have never felt disgust in my husband's embrace. And you know how much I desire *him*!'

Smiling gaily, she kissed me on the cheek, then stood up. She went to her other guests, pleading a slight headache. She left us, closing the heavy door after her.

I returned to Käthe. She had closed her eyes again after the brief word with her daughter, and lay back on a pile of cushions. Stubbing out my cigar with my foot, I began to pay court to her seriously: stroking an arm, then her thigh; leaning close and kissing her neck. I started to unbutton her dress. She made a half-hearted attempt to appeal to her husband, crying that the professor was being very amorous – a touch of sun. Philipp, smoking, merely stared, as did Martha. They might have been watching the mating ritual of butterflies.

This, I reminded myself, was the loathsome father who had probably (though Ida refused to confirm it) brought on her childish bedwetting by abusing her. This was the miserable, impotent adulterer who had polluted the woman who was now toying with both Anna and Ida.

Martha and I were in the spell of our family romances. She

was triumphing over her imbecilic mother, in the person of Frau Bauer, by having her husband caught in her web. And I . . . I pulled Frau Bauer to the ground; she made little protest. A breast was cupped between my hands; I bent to suck at the nipple. She gave a moan, and her hand went to my beard, gripping it, drawing me in tighter to her soft breast.

As I raised her dress she struggled a little; though wordlessly. I soon realised she was embarrassed by a colostomy bag and, when I whispered that it was of no concern to me, she yielded totally. I took my time at each stage of seduction. Kneeling before her spread thighs, I enjoyed drinking her juices without any particular need to go further. My only regret was that I had positioned us carelessly; in order to watch Martha and Philipp I had to glance back over my shoulder. They were still clothed but in an embrace. He was gently stroking her back, and her head lay on his shoulder. I envied them the appearance of established intimacy, of a peace long desired. They seemed to have melted naturally into each other, like Rodin's *The Kiss*.

I took my mouth away, moved myself up, and entered Käthe. I felt myself to be spry and agile, twenty years younger. She moaned that it was wonderful; but for me it was merely pleasant – the wonder was to look over my shoulder and see Martha lying on the grass, her dress up to her waist, her legs spread to engulf Philipp's head. My breath quickened; Käthe took it as a sign of rising excitement at our union. She moaned louder. Her eyes were open, gazing into mine; I could not without insulting her gaze at the other couple. At last I buried my head in her loosened hair, in a way that allowed me to glance aside. To my immeasurable joy and pain I saw Philipp thrusting in and out of Martha.

'Don't stop!' Käthe cried; however, I withdrew from her. I sat back down on the grass, facing Martha and Philipp. Käthe too sat up, pulled her dress over her knees, embraced her legs with her arms and observed. Her expression was blank. I saw Martha's lips move in a whisper. She was telling him how wonderful this was, at last! From her passive, dreamy face, and from his obsessional thrusting, I could tell that it was wonderful. I was receiving him, moving to his unfamiliar rhythm, feeling the sweetness of being filled by him, of sharing his unbearable excitement, his desire to spurt his seed into me, yet to prolong the desire – for in love we desire desire. My contracting vagina willed him to rain the cool seed on the neck of my womb.

29

This is an ecstasy such as, Eros apart, only a religious visionary can experience, or a child. It combines joy and terror. As I watch Martha and Philipp, and feel their blissful fulfilment, I move with light's speed back to the sloping green meadow, and to the forest. I get shakily to my feet and am impelled across the grass, paddling like a two or three year old, to where my Mama and Philipp are lying entwined. I kneel down beside them; stroke her thigh, as if to say, I'm frightened, don't leave me!

'Piss off, Sigi,' Martha hisses. Her mouth is buried in his beard.

Philipp, without pausing in his stroke, turns his head to exclaim angrily, 'Yes, beat it, Sigi!'

(Another reason for introducing lies – of which this is not an example – into this book: it's true to life, to history. History is full of delusions, fads and shibboleths, that soon are scattered and tossed, like restlessly wandering autumn leaves in an avenue. Take Communism – someone once told me it would mean terrible hardship in Russia for fifty years, followed by perpetual happiness; I said I half-believed it. Nor is psychoanalysis exempt from the follies of one's epoch, though I believe its core will survive.)

I rise to my feet and walk away from the intent couple to the farthest side of the walled garden. I confront a grinning stone gargoyle, poking his tongue at me. My blood boils in my veins. I'm aware what a ludicrous spectacle I am, an infant of almost sixty, wearing just a shirt in a garden in October. I stride back towards the couple. Käthe is still staring at them blank-faced.

Leaning over the lovers I snarl: 'No one's going to say beat it to me while he's fucking my wife!' I seize him by the shoulder, and pull. He tries to shrug me off, but I seize him with both arms and pull him out of Martha. There, in a brief glimpse, is the fully erect, strong member, glistening with Martha. In his surprise he staggers, falls back on the swing-seat. Then he leaps to his feet and moves towards me, muscular, bull-chested as Charcot was, his hands up for a fight. Käthe and Martha seize hold of him, and with surprising strength for two woman cling on to him. 'Let me get at him!' he shouts. 'I'll kill him! You're a selfish bastard, Freud! You fucked my wife, you've had your fun!' His face is bloated and flushed, his eyes demented. 'Let me go! I'll kill him!' He strains forwards, the women grunt and sway in the struggle.

I feel curiously calm and strong. Walking up to him, just out of reach of his flailing arms, I say, 'What is your problem, Bauer?'

He snarls with pure rage. I hear the garden door open and a rush of footsteps. Ida appears, accompanied by two maids. They come to a halt, horror-struck. As for me, I'm filled with loathing for this syphilitic, womanising monster. Do Martin and Ernst feel like this when locked in bayonet-to-bayonet combat with a Russian? No, nothing personal; just fear and the survival instinct. I step up and clip Bauer on the chin. It is the first time in my life I have ever struck someone. We Jews don't like physical violence. He staggers back, howls, and bursts from the arms of the two women. He is upon me, hammering my ribs. I feel no pain; am amused by such a turn of events. Bauer is seized by Ida, a maid and Martha, and pulled away. He is forced to the ground, where he lies flailing like a beetle. Ida pulls his shirt down over his genitals.

Martha is screaming abuse at me. I loathe her too. When she slaps my face I slap back, much harder. She flinches. Her lover struggles to rise, screeching invective at me for my cowardice in striking a woman, the woman he loves. Ida and the maid sit on him.

I back towards the wall as Martha stalks me, her eyes mad

with anger, all the muscles of her face twitching. 'You bastard!' she cries. 'You bastard!' She punches me in the chest, around my heart, punches like a piston, regularly. I make no attempt to stop her. Her eyes are inches from mine; they tell me she would like to murder me. Staring into her crazed eyes and taking her punches, I feel vaguely like laughing.

30

A low fire flickers in the grate. The bushes outside are hung with a thin coating of snow. Winter has set in early. Anna has confessed to reading those diaries and I've said, Of course, I knew. Now her knitting needles click furiously, telling me she's feeling badly hurt. Anna's whole psyche goes into her knitting.

'It wasn't true,' I say weakly.

'Nonsense!'

'Yes, there was a situation involving Philipp Bauer, as you well know from that evening when you had to intervene; but nothing like so dramatic. I was exploring fiction.'

It is a lie, of course. Any sensitive reader will have had no doubt the love scene between Martha and Eli was imaginary, the one between her and Philipp real. But it seems kind to offer Anna an escape, if she wishes to take it.

'But obviously you did feel passionate about Mama.'

'Only for that brief time, dearest.'

Actually there was an intensification – painful, with my bruised ribs – after her adulterous *coitus interruptus*; she was excited; felt a certain respect for me; I tried to persuade the Bauers to repeat the 'four-handed' experience, to a therapeutic and peaceful completion; Käthe was keen but Philipp had had enough. Martha became angry again. But eventually we rubbed along well enough once more; whereas Bauer never recovered from his humiliating experience. He suffered from severe depression, according to Deutsch, who treated him. A year or so later general paralysis of the insane came on.

It is not a condition I would wish on my worst enemy; but I can't say I wasted too much grief on him. I had tried to help him, by virtually offering him *carte blanche* with Martha for an afternoon or two. But he pretended jealousy over his wife, and craved now a private affair with Martha – actually wrote to her suggesting it, pleading *love*. Martha honourably refused. Still we urged on him the fairer and more reasonable alternative, as did Käthe, but he sulked like Patroclus in his tent. Some fellows it is impossible to help.

'War has a strange effect, Anna. Yes, the libido surged for a while. But it flattened out. And after that, once more, it was only you.'

Her face softens, just a shade; her fingers at the needles relax.

'And in the last twenty years', I add, 'I've slept with no one.'

I've chosen the number carefully; in 1919 I made love (yes, I confess it) with Helene Deutsch, on one isolated and crazy occasion, on my couch. It was the day after Tausk's murderous suicide, for which we both felt slightly responsible, and we were in a state of shock. His body swung from the curtain cord and his head spurted blood. Her silk-stockinged legs wrapped around me tightly, we wanted to say, 'Fuck you, Victor!' She murmured wildly in Polish – I guessed about Lieberman's baby son, killed either by meningitis or infanticide. She wanted to hold me in, but I broke away as my seed spurted. A stocking had loosened during our struggle; sitting up, poised in the act of fastening a suspender to the stocking, she hissed in German, 'I'm so glad he's dead!' and jerked the silk into its stranglehold. She ruffled her dress down, reclined, and we continued with the analysis.

'In any case, my dear, it was mostly aggression. Against Bauer. He'd lied to me when I was treating Ida, denying any sexual entanglement with Frau Zellenka. At first I believed *him*, unfortunately, rather than Ida; consequently I was rather harsh with her. In other words, he was willing to sacrifice her *again*. I don't forgive such a monster. So I *unleashed* your mama on him!

To finish him off!' I give her a questioning smile. 'Wouldn't you say that was it?'

Anna shrugs, lifting her brows, not displeased by the idea. I think she has the image of Frau Zellenka in her mind, and remembers how jealous she once was of all her lovers. Anna stares into space and her fingers move quite languidly. Gradually a Leonardo smile tilts her lips. I ask her what is amusing. 'I was thinking of that *fictional* scene. You pulling him out of Mama.'

Dora's garden shimmers before me.

'They must have been surprised.'

'Yes.'

Her smile broadens; I smile faintly too.

'A kind of reverse rape,' she murmurs. Her eyes and her fingers dance wickedly. She chortles; and I too chuckle weakly.

'Herr Kofman!' I croak gleefully; then, breaking into English: 'The Cough-Man!'

'Ah, yes!' And she goes on rippling with laughter.

'I do recall', she says when we have calmed down, 'your ribs were all strapped up and you could barely move around. You said you'd had a fall.'

'That's right; I had.'

'And Mama fussed around you.'

'No more than usual.' '*You were a* mensch, *Sigi, I'll give you that . . .*'

Her fingers speed up as she concentrates on the pink sweater she's knitting for Dorothy. Frown marks appear between her eyes. 'I was never seriously interested in Frau Zellenka; you needn't have worried.' Then, scornfully: 'Lampl! You'd have had me married off to Lampl!'

'Not really.'

'He did propose to me. On our doorstep. And tried to kiss me. I turned my head away.'

Blinking rapidly, she turns her head away. She becomes meditative, statuesque; I recall a photograph of her, just post-war: seated at my desk, gazing at a vase of sunflowers, her porcelain skin accentuating her short dark hair and intense dark eyes, the mouth trembling between intellect and sensuality.

'I've ruined your life, Anna.'

'No. Only my sexual life. And that wasn't really your fault. I became you; and you had chosen to live without love and sex – at least it seemed to me – so I felt obliged to follow suit. And yet – Lampl and the others seemed so sexless compared with the overpowering scent of sperm and vaginal juices exuded by your patients. Or by your gods and goddesses; I don't know which. From your consulting room, anyway. Nothing was going on, yet it simply reeked. We all smelt it. When you walked through at the stroke of one, the smell overwhelmed that of the onion soup. I knew I could never live up to it, nor any possible husband.'

I bury my face in my hands. 'Too late! Too late!'

'It's not too late.' Dropping her knitting she falls on to her knees and takes my hands between hers. 'Make up a *wilde Phantasie*! Release me! Fulfil me! Fill me full!' Her eyes are burning like Rebecca's. I see the sternly kind teacher of children that she once was. 'My God! I've done everything for you! I give and give and give! Do this one thing for me. Make up a truthful fiction; never mind facts!'

Ah, to be liberated from facts!

'Simeon ben Yohai', she says in a pedagogic tone, 'believed that a good man, at the hour of his death, could if he wished live another life through his youngest daughter. If she gave him a daughter in her turn, the process could go on endlessly. By this he explained the farsighted wisdom of the prophets: they had already lived many lives.'

'I haven't read Simeon ben Yohai. I wasn't aware you were so learned in the kabbalistic authors.'

'I've glanced through Grandfather's library. It astonishes me; how did we get from a Galician *shtetl* to Hampstead? From superstition to psychoanalysis? However, that's not important now. We are starting out in life, you and I, together . . .'

It's not at all a plot I would have chosen. I would have chosen to be the brother-in-law of Ilona Weiss, 'Elisabeth von R.'. When she heard her sister was dying, she came post-haste by train, distraught at knowing her sister's death would leave her free to marry the handsome widower. My 'Elisabeth' would have burst in, her fur coat and hat draped in snow, and flung herself into my arms, consoling me.

I would have taken Sabina Spielrein from that dreadful lying womaniser Jung. What did she see in him?

I would have been one of Lou's lovers – Rilke, preferably, or Victor Tausk; in which case I'm damned sure I wouldn't have committed suicide, only because Freud had declined to analyse him and had instructed Helene Deutsch to terminate his training analysis. I'd have shown more manliness. These women analysts, Lou and Sabina and the Princess, Anna and Deutsch and even the choleric Klein, have the balls.

I would have been Schliemann, uncovering Troy. Moses, receiving the Shekhinah. That Russian poet who imagined himself sleepless beside the Mediterranean, watching the Achaean ships sailing off towards Troy . . . 'The sea, and Homer – everything's moved by love . . .' I can hear Lou's voice reciting it. I have a thousand plots ready; and I am truly tired of this life; truly tired. 'I have counted all the catalogue of ships . . .' Yes, I would like to be a poet, a knitter of dreams . . .

But I have to become Anna's lover. The incest taboo is strong; it will be difficult. Yet I must try to please her. She's right: she has given me so much.

'Give me a fairy tale, Papa!' she cries. 'In which we sit and read and write long letters . . .'

I begin: 'I recall, as if it were today, our arrival in Rome. I was ill; cancer had just been discovered in me. Death seemed as close as my shadow, and was only kept away by my beloved's beauty and fresh youthfulness. One evening, when blood suddenly gushed from my mouth, spattering a tablecloth and her white dress, I knew, even though she was my daughter, I . . .'

I pause. This isn't truthful, this isn't honest, it doesn't suit me. What I really remember are the hikes in the mountains with her. A sudden blaze of gentians. A cloud's shadow

176

stealing across a green valley. The joyous sense of freedom; Anna laughing like the winged Victory, her hair tossed, her apron-skirt blown back, pressed against her thighs; one's leg muscles aching, the air like pure oxygen. If I must start the fairy tale anywhere, it's there.

A plane drones overhead. We hear the sudden wave-like wailing of a banshee. Even though Anna's voice reassures me that she will not leave me, my eyes close, I drift off.

31

I am finding it is harder to die than I had anticipated. I am reminded of that evening with Lou when she described how the cloaca and the vagina were very close, like death and life: a statement that Princess Marie echoed strangely when she told me about her operations to have her clitoris brought closer to her vagina. For her, she said, the former represented life and the latter death, and they were too far apart in certain, mostly tall, women, with the result that the vagina remained frigid, however passionately the clitoris wished it to grow warm and alive. (Of course her operations had no effect on her frigidity.)

Still, in the case of life and death, I am finding that the clitoris, so to speak, continues to be agitated. Asleep, or more probably in a coma, I continue to have vivid dreams. It seems to me it may be a universal experience. In my fortieth year I plunged into self-analysis, deeply exploring my dreams, in order to try to make sense of my life. Perhaps before the trauma of death we need again to explore dreams – in order to make sense of our non-existence.

I am in a city of canals. I think I recognise Amsterdam. All around me are ruined buildings, people with pale, shocked faces silently watching columns of tanks pass by. Storm-troopers and motor-cyclists, all in black uniforms with the symbol of the swastika, surround one tank in which rides a proud general whose name is Guderian. He is the author of this triumphant advance.

When I consider this dream, I am puzzled first of all

by the name of the victorious general. It sounds vaguely Armenian, and so suggests Mount Ararat and Noah. There is something cataclysmic in the dream's atmosphere. I am further reminded of the Gadarene swine, into whom Jesus cast devils, precipitating them over a cliff to their destruction. It is a legend which characterised the primitiveness of Christianity for me. I think it may have been my old nurse Monika who told me the story; I suppressed my sense of injustice on behalf of the poor pigs.

Dora's conversion to Christianity relieved me, in a sense. I could see that her rebellion against me was not an isolated event, but part of a pattern of rebellion against her own kind. Like her mother, she had been greatly affected by the father's syphilis; felt herself tainted by it, since she produced a white vaginal discharge (as did her mother). The Low Countries on which this successful attack took place suggests we are in the realm of sexuality.

The swastika, an almost universal symbol among the most ancient peoples, represents, according to Schneider, the succession of the generations. Alternatively it may symbolise the fertilising sun, or the action of the Origin upon the universe.

The city of canals, Amsterdam, has no personal association for me. Two other such cities, however, have had some bearing on my life: Petersburg, indirectly, as the birthplace of Lou Salomé; Venice, from a delightful holiday I spent there with my brother Alexander. This was around the time of my self-analysis, in the final years of the nineteenth century.

Who can fail to be stirred by that unreal, illusory city, in which stones seem to be founded in water? It occurred to me, while we strolled on the Rialto, that all culture is fragile, since it is born out of perilous repression of instincts. The 'cloud-capped towers' of civilisation could melt as easily as these great domed buildings could collapse into the lagoon. I recall saying to Alexander, 'It would not take Noah's flood to overwhelm all this. It's a precarious balance of opposites.'

I recall also a certain contempt for the mass of sightseers, many of them no doubt on the 'grand tour', pouring aimlessly over the bridge. I would not have minded if they had been swept away by a freak wave. It would not have been surprising if, in that place of many churches, I thought of them as the Gadarene swine.

My brother was named after a great general. Canals are water, the primeval life force, under discipline. Any city built on water has had to be compelled into existence. If humanity is to survive, we must show respect for the primitive instincts that constantly threaten us, but not be overwhelmed by them. In Venice, the city of glorious flamboyant prostitutes, I had to be aware of strict balance. I have had the reckless imagination of a conquistador or pimp, and the caution of a bourgeois Amsterdam diamond merchant or canal engineer.

But a canal engineer cannot construct good canals unless he knows the chaotic forces at work in the Mindanao Deep. In Venice I read Vergil instead of hunting after whores. I decided on my epigraph for my book of dreams: *Flectere si nequeo superos, Acheronta movebo* . . . If I cannot bend the higher powers, I will move the infernal regions.

'Guderian', in my dream, sees himself as a necessary sweeper away of corruption, and in a sense he is; yet he has a bewildered, self-ignorant air, since he has never looked into his own infernal regions. He looks for culprits to drive over the cliff, but he finds only innocents to destroy. The devils remain where they were. People are still infected.

One can really only hope for a single righteous man.

– Yet these gloomy thoughts seem a long way from today, sitting with my brother in a canalside café, the sunlight sparkling on the water; San Marco proud overhead, as the fleecy high clouds scud by, scarcely interrupting the blue. We shall live for ever. I light a cigar, sit back at ease.

'So how are Martha and the children, Sigi?' he asks.

'Fine. Little Anna is still taking the bottle well.'

'That's good. No more children!'

I reply by breathing out smoke and raising my eyes to the heavens.

My brother goes off to look at some jewellery, and I

open and re-read a letter from Minna. She has had another marvellous but disturbing letter from Wilhelm. She is writing this while sitting with Anna in the garden. What a lovely baby, no trouble at all!

I feel a stab of guilt that I'm not interested in little Anna. I resent this stretching out of one's responsibilities. If I die at fifty-two, as is quite likely according to Fliess's calculations, she'll be scarcely menstruating; if I reach sixty-two, by miracle, she may still be unmarried. Josefine is a good nurse, and Minna will be a help. But one is drained of energy and resources.

Must go to Murano to buy Martha some fine glass. What is the purpose of it all? 'We see through a glass darkly.' The blinding flash of inspiration – or delusion. I look for it. It won't come. It's maddeningly close.

32

A most unpleasant dream. I am standing on a railway station platform, somewhere in a rural area. Stations always agitate me, but this one is rather cheerful and comforting, full of welcoming baskets of flowers. I glance up at a round clock, fearing I'm late; the hands reassure me. I hear the slow chug of a train in the distance. A man in a white jacket and cap, holding an Alsatian on a leash, smiles at me and says, 'I shouldn't bother to consult that – it's stopped.'

A goods train pulls in and stops. A mass of people, all of them Jews, tumbles out. Many are just bloated corpses. I see my sisters, Dolfi and Pauline, and am very pleased to meet them again, even though they are in a miserable state. I embrace them. We are being invited to walk along an avenue. Someone says to them, 'You are going to have a shower and get cleaned up.' Everything is pleasant, yet over all hangs a horrid smell of putrefying flesh. My sisters are worried, but I try to cheer them up. Dolfi says, 'Thank God Mama did not live to see this.' I reflect that it would have been unlikely, since she would have been well over the century.

I am with them in a large, densely packed bath-house. My sisters have had their hair removed, and are as embarrassed by their naked heads as by their naked bodies. I haven't seen them naked since Mama bathed them as little girls. They wait for the warm water to drench them, but instead they are gasping for breath, clawing at their throats. There is a smell of gas. Everyone in the room is dying, turning blue.

– The dream obviously expresses my guilt at having had to

leave my sisters behind in Vienna. I left them 'naked', however much I convince myself I took care of them financially and could not imagine four old ladies could come to any harm.

The flowers on the station platform, in the midst of countryside, take me back to Freiberg, the green meadow dotted with yellow flowers. The stopped clock needs no interpretation; the beginning and the end of life are clearly enunciated.

The cheerful man with the Alsatian puzzled me at first. I managed to dredge up his name eventually: 'Stangl'. The name, and the white coat of a doctor or laboratory worker, conjured up Anna's only serious suitor, a young man called Hans Lampl. He was in his youth a schoolfriend of my son Martin; he became a serologist and a bacteriologist, before becoming interested in analysis – and Anna. He proposed to her, but Anna and I decided he was not suitable.

There is another association with him, through the Alsatian. When Lampl announced his engagement to a Dutch woman, Jeanne de Groot, in 1925, Anna felt very relieved. We were amused by a newspaper's banal comment that 'Lampl got his Jeanne and Anna got her Wolf'. In that year I gave her an Alsatian whom she called Wolf.

The 'Stangl' who replaces him in the dream looks happy enough. He may feel that, when rejected by Anna, time did not stop for him but it did for her; that at almost thirty she was declaring herself a dried–up spinster – like Pauline and Dolfi, Rosa and Mitzi, her aunts. That's unfair on Mitzi, who is a widow, but she has that spinsterly look since Moritz's death. Henceforth, in terms of woman's biological destiny, Anna may feel there is for her only her aunts' one–way route to death.

There may be incestuous impulses, long forgotten, in the bath scene. Martha and I used to fear that our sons would be rendered blind and helpless through gas attacks in the war; yet I cannot accuse myself of having worried more over my sons' fate than my daughters'.

In connection with the horror of the 'shower' becoming 'gas', and the screaming, contorting bodies, I can only think of certain infernal scenes represented by German painters.

I fear I may have consigned Anna to a sterile life, relatively cheerful and busy on the surface (like a rural station), yet an internal hell of unfulfilment. Her hairless baby skull was born out of my head, as Athene from Zeus.

And of course 'Pauline' is the cousin–niece whom I deflowered in the meadow.

'Stangl' – I catch a memory. *Stange*, a stick. (He carries a stick in the dream.) Lampl saying to me, crestfallen after another rejection, 'I intend to stick to the point, persevere, Professor Freud.' (*Bei der Stange bleiben.*)

I offer him a cigar, and say, as I light it for him: 'Well, Anna is very determined. There comes a point where it's better to move on, Hans.' I take out my watch, glance at it, wind it up.

Mama – 'more than a hundred': relief when she died at last, aged ninety-five. My growing horror at her immense age and continued hold over me. She turned, long before the end, into a Gorgon. I could not bear to think that she still possessed, in shrivelled form, vagina and womb. In her dying moments, gas escaping from her cloaca. An embarrassment with my sisters present. The same happened to me yesterday with Anna, a fart I could not prevent. Anna's face didn't change, yet I sensed the same instinctive embarrassment at the reminder that fathers have the same vulgar bodily parts as other, lesser mortals.

A goods train. Why on earth should my sisters arrive in a goods train? – Because, I think, I was trying to evade guilt. My thoughts were, I left them with plenty of money; it's their own meanness, so typically Jewish, that has prevented them from travelling in a decent train. They travel like pigs. And the bloated corpses that tumble out with them?

No, it does not come.

Perhaps I'm thinking of the bloated corpses from the Seine, whose brains Charcot asked me to explore. But it doesn't make sense in relation to the other elements.

Only that I think of one such young woman, a prostitute and a suicide, as I stand later amidst the wondrous stained glass of the Sainte Chapelle; thinking of so much beauty, so much splendour; and so much pain and misery.

There seems almost no end to the connotations of this unpleasant dream.

33

A third dream: an old man, possibly Japanese, sits on some steps in the sun. There is a very bright light, and he becomes just a shadow on the stone step. All round is a city flattened to the ground. Into the sky rises a cloud, which forms a mushroom shape . . .

I was probably thinking of the Buddha, sitting cross-legged on my desk. The Orient, and particularly Japan, defies incorporation into Western values. I have simply no idea if the Oedipal Complex of a Western family could survive translation to the land of samurai and geishas. Therefore the dream reminds me of the limitations of my science and my thinking. I am no more than the snail crawling up Mount Fujiyama. No more than a shadow cast on a stone.

The figure sitting on the step is not merely a man, but Man. In the light of infinity he is nothing, and his proud cities are swept away.

The mushroom recalls Anna's memory of mushroom picking with me. My shushing the children to be quiet as I tiptoe towards the giant mushroom in the forest, to drop my hat over it. Anna is laughing delightedly. Perhaps nothing in my life has been worth more than that occasional gift for making Anna laugh in delight.

It can be said of me that I loved children.

34

On the other hand, there are so many hatreds. The question of
an analysis still hangs in the air. Anna doesn't think it's right for
a daughter to analyse her father. Jones, the little Welshman, is
much too dull. Tod is a possibility, but I don't know her.

I have been moved to the top of the house, to Anna's
work-room. She is talking to a boy of about ten. At last he
gets up from his seat and she accompanies him to the door.
She touches his shoulder affectionately as he leaves the room.

Now, her face losing its brightness, becoming sorrowful,
she returns to her desk, picks up a letter and scans it. A tear
glistens in her eye.

'Anna.'

She comes to me, holding the letter. 'We've had dreadful
news,' she murmurs. 'You'll grieve as you did for Sophie and
Heini. Eva has died in Nice.'

'Eva! Eva Rosenfeld?'

How I hoped it was she: Anna's close friend and nearest
rival to Dorothy.

No – our Eva.'

Silent tears gathered. Our golden grandchild. I moaned
That she should die before me, who have had my time.

'How old was she, Anna?'

'She was twenty. She would be twenty-four now. The news
has only just reached us. It was influenza.'

'Ah! Like dear Sophie! And even younger . . . How sad.'

Overwork and suffering have etched Anna's face and thinned
it. 'You must take care of yourself, my dear,' I whisper.

'I'm all right, I'm all right. But the best have gone from our lives. And there's still no news of my aunts; we're trying to find out.'

We old ones, I say, are ready to move on. It's when the young die – Sophie, Heinele, now Eva – that it leaves an unhealable wound. My eyes close again; I want to sleep, to blot it out. That wailing in the apartment when the word came from Hamburg. Sophie, our Sunday-child . . . I feel the profound difference between a daughter gone, at times almost forgotten in the activity of living and working – and that daughter dead.

'Is the letter from Oliver?' I ask.

She nods; the tears trickle down.

'How dreadful for him and – I've forgotten her name.'

'Henny. Yes.'

I could have spared Oliver – our youngest son, our handsome 'Italian' child, our obsessional neurotic, Martha's favourite – rather than our sweet Eva. But far, far better than either would have been Eva Rosenfeld. Given the choice, to save Eva, I would gladly pick up a gun and shoot Eva Rosenfeld – that nice woman who endured many tragedies, deaths of children, and went on to help the children of others. True, there is some hostility, since she once, when entrusted with our dog, the first Lün, lost control of her at a railway station and the poor creature was run over. It was a pure accident; and I like Eva. But still I would shoot her, saying, I'm sorry, Frau Rosenfeld. There is guilt at almost every moment of a life; in the end it reaches unbearable proportions and we have no choice but to die, to escape.

35

Schur professes himself well pleased with my progress; though of course we both know I am merely in remission. He does not dissent when I say to him and Anna that I have a desire to see my parents once more before I die.

I have been warned on the way that the Galician forests are dangerous, with many brigand bands lurking. It has seemed sensible therefore to wear a wolf's skin and an eagle mask. Human bones along the lightless track indicate that the warnings were well founded. Snow falls, but the wolf-skin keeps me warm. I am inevitably reminded of my patient the Wolf Man. I can remember clearly the moment when the aristocratic Russian turned the tables on me in my consulting room: leaping from the couch, spreadeagling me over my chair, hoisting up my skirts, and thrusting painfully in.

The experience of anal intercourse was intriguing. Though I was conscious of something missing in my vagina I also felt a decided pleasure in the violation; there was a sense of a second defloration in mid-life.

The journey through the forest was long and dark. Only a sliver of moon glimmered between the tops of the pines. I followed a rough path, moving by hope rather than judgement. I was beginning to think myself lost when I saw three or four figures heading towards me along the path. The leading figure turned out to be my mother. She was masked by a bird's beak; the two or three misty figures behind her were antlered. I was reminded of a dream I had at eight or nine about my mother. The only difference was that in that dream she had been carried on a bier, and was calmly sleeping. In the present actuality, by what power I know not – but possibly hypnosis – it was I who found myself falling to the ground, dazed.

My mother said, 'Since you are a great healer, Sigmund, and a maker of dreams, we are going to turn you into a shaman. But first I must know: do you now believe in the Spirit?'

She used the word psyche, I said yes. 'Good,' she said. 'First, in order to re-create you and heal you, we shall have to kill you.'

My eyes closed, I felt my limbs being taken from me and my entrails being removed. I heard my mother say they were putting stones inside me. A drum was being beaten. My eyes opened and I was whole. 'Now you can fly like a bat,' my mother said. Flapping my wings, I flew into the tops of the trees. When I returned to earth my mother said they must take their leave; my stay in this world was not over. In time I would be given a spirit wife, or wives if I preferred. They would assist me in my healing.

'This is a promise of what is to come,' she says, and her bird-beak bends to my penis. I feel her soft lips within the beak close over me, her tongue warm against the tender glans; in a moment I am erect. I think of Isis, fellating Osiris to bring him back to life. My mother and the two or three figures accompanying her bid me farewell.

Travelling on, I found the ground becoming increasingly swampy, and could walk only with difficulty. The swamp became a mud-coloured, murky stream, as wide as a street. Fortunately someone had left a rusty old boat tied up with rotting rope to a trunk; as I stepped into the boat it almost overturned and took in water; however, with the aid of a pole I was able to make my way across. Moving on again, I saw a figure in a long ragged robe, barefoot, crouching under a tree. His hair and beard were long and wild. With a surge of emotion I recognised him; he was known to me intimately, yet his name, for the second time in my life, escaped me. I stumbled towards him; seeing me, he gave a wan smile, rising to his feet.

His name was – Botticelli? Boltraffio? Palinurus?

'Sigmund!' he exclaimed, holding out his arms.

Three times I tried to embrace him, and three times my arms passed through him unresistingly.

'Signorelli!' I cried: recalling the likeness in our names.

We sat down and chatted. I thanked him for having painted those representations of my theories in Orvieto Cathedral: those frescoes of naked men and women, many undergoing sadistic torture; that wild-haired woman with the orgasmic expression as she rode a leering devil through the sky. Signorelli, my helmsman.

I told him I had seen my bird-beaked mother. 'A *dybbuk*,' he commented; 'someone who's stolen her body. I hope you weren't taken in?'

'Of course not.'

'This is a terrible place,' he said. 'Where have you come from?'

I hesitate, the name escaping me. 'Vienna,' I respond inaccurately.

He winces. 'Not the best, either. Well, good luck.'

Soon, after I leave him, the swampy forest dries out, and turns eventually into a parched land of white skulls. I stumble across the barren soil for many hours. I see two figures approach from the horizon's heat haze. As they near me I recognise, to my astonishment, Martha and Minna. Martha is carrying baby Anna. The two sisters look exhausted.

Why are they here? Why didn't they tell me they were coming?

From their excitement and gestures of relief they appear to have found a waterhole. I try to run to them; but am rooted to the spot – my feet having become soldered, so to speak, to the earth. Along with helplessness comes fear: I know what lies at the bottom of this waterhole; the python Yulunga.

I have been here before, as the saying goes.

The women have made a fire and gathered vegetables to put in a cooking pot. Unfortunately all the vegetables leap out of the pot and scurry away into the sand. The women look disconsolate.

Martha nurses Anna (something she never did in reality). Minna squats over the waterhole. Blood pours from her cunt, to use a word that Fliess taught her to use. I am relieved she is menstruating.

The sky grows dark; rain pelts down and lightning flickers. The sisters dance and sing around the fire to try to keep warm. In their ecstasy they cannot see the great python Yulunga coiling out of the waterhole. *I* see him, and am too terrified to scream out a warning.

They have taken shelter in a hut, with the baby. I can do nothing as Yulunga opens his jaws and engulfs the hut. I watch hut, sisters, child, visibly snag their way down the snake's throat. And a snake is nothing *but* throat.

I must have fainted, as twice I fainted under Jung's aggression. But Yulunga is yet more sinister than Jung.

I wake to a clear sky. With grief mixes the thought that the Dreaming is authentic – as Schliemann found Troy authentic. It happened, it happens.

And now relief floods through me. As creatures of the Dreaming, they do not die. And I recall that Yulunga vomited them up. Or at least the children. That is what matters: the child.

The rest of my journey proves uneventful. Towards nightfall I enter the city of Lvov (Lemberg), and find an inn.

I interrupt the banal narrative to record a dream. In it I am wandering around the city seeking fellow Jews from whom I can solicit information about my parents, Jacob and Amalie Freud. There ought to be innumerable Jews, but in fact I find none for a long time. Even the ghetto is deserted. At last, in a hovel, I stumble across three Hassidic Jews, two men and a woman. They tell me all the Jews of the city except themselves and a handful of others have been destroyed. The survivors escaped the common fate by hiding in sewers. All endured unimaginable suffering, they say, over several years: the elder of the two men, his grey beard almost to his waist, relates how his three brothers were put in a barrel of water one evening, in the midst of winter, and he himself had to cut out from a block of ice their corpses the next morning, using a pick-axe. But even more terrible, they tell me, was that the Jewish council itself was made responsible for selecting the victims of deportations.

The faces of my three hosts were shocked, zombie-like; they scarcely seemed living creatures. European Jewry, they said, was extinguished.

This is undoubtedly a wish-fulfilment: the wish that one could extinguish all one's Jewishness. The guilt arising from that 'wicked' thought is partly assuaged by my being told the Jews were part-authors of their own sorrows (our own council making the selection of victims). But, of course, to cut away all Jewishness from the three male members of my family – my father, my brother, and me – would be like trying to cut flesh out of solid ice.

I reach my parents' home town, Tysmenice. Yet what is a home town? They came from the Baltic; before that, from the Rhineland, centuries ago; before that, Israel; before that, Egypt; before that . . . Well, Eden: the primary Oedipal family of God, Lilith (or the Shekhinah) and their son Adam. Here in Tysmenice's narrow rutted streets I see Jews at last; I smell the Jewishness. It is the festival of Pentecost; girls are parading in their best gowns; the men, returning from the baths. I stop one man in his satin gaberdine, fur-trimmed velvet hat and white stockings, to ask if he knows Jacob Freud. He nods, pointing down the track, muttering curt instructions in Yiddish. I thank him.

I am outside the small ramshackle house. I peer in. The window is decorated with cut-outs of flowers, doves; silver and gold twigs bear small birds with dough heads. At the corners are reeds, symbolising the gift of the Torah on the Mount. There is a delicious smell of chicory and pastry coming from inside. In the dim interior I catch the fleeting form of a woman. She notices the shadow at the window; frowns. My heart suddenly sinks. I realise I have made a stupid mistake. This is not my mother; my father did not, presumably, meet my mother till he arrived in Moravia. This is Sally, or it may be

Rebecca – though I think I would have recognised Rebecca. My half-brothers are probably around somewhere: I hear boyish voices in play, faintly. My father was always too indulgent.

I move away from the window just as the woman, wiping her hands on her apron, moves towards the door. I am quite a way down the street before the door opens and the swarthy, buxom young woman appears. She calls after me, in a melodious voice: 'Were you looking for someone?'

I shout, 'No! Thank you.' And hurry away.

I have no wish to meet my father without my mother being present.

Lying tonight on the uncomfortable straw bed at the inn, I contemplate why I made the elementary mistake of seeking my father and mother here. Of course Amalie came from Galicia too, but I've no idea which town. It is one of those inexplicable errors I tried to study in my *Psychopathology of Everyday Life*. A superstitious person might take from it that even the Angel of Death is prone to odd ellipses and stumbles; that he is not at all certain of himself, but carries the psychic wound of early trauma, such as perhaps the shocking sight of his parents engaged in copulation; an act which, through clumsy contraception, gave rise to an undesired universe: to Anna, as it were.

36

On the homeward journey – but where is home? – through the forest, I find succour from danger in a wolf pack. They seem unperturbed by my eagle's mask; take me as one of them. They are gentle creatures, padding through the snow. I share their reindeer meat, sitting in a circle under the tall bleak pines, the snow falling in thick flakes. They are much preferable to the mass of humanity.

I sense, however, a sadness among them. I discover the reason: their homeland is diminishing, the forest growing smaller. It will not be long before they too require psychoanalysis. I could happily end my days in trying to help them come to terms with reality.

I leave the pack and trudge on. Approaching the broad stream again, I see a barefoot woman in a long red skirt drifting aimlessly among the trees. Drawing close, I recognise the smouldering eyes of Rebecca, my father's second wife. Gladness at seeing me changes swiftly to sorrow. 'I'm not allowed to talk to you,' she says, speaking in an educated Galician Yiddish. 'Why do you bury all knowledge of me, Sigmund? You could so easily have been my son.'

She starts to turn away with a hopeless expression but I say, 'Wait! Don't go yet! What *happened*?'

'Don't you know?'

'I've heard tales, but I've no idea if they're true.'

'Then I can't enlighten you. Families are a mystery. Everyone is a mystery. Did you ever truly get to understand anyone?'

I shake my head.

'Those famous patients in your elegant tales – Dora, the Rat Man, the Wolf Man, Little Hans – they are *dybbuks*: wonderful likenesses but not the people themselves. Isn't that true?'

I nod, and my back bows, as under a burden.

'Did you ever truly understand *yourself*? You were jealous, weren't you, when Minna wrote to Fliess to say how close she felt to him? Even though you knew it was a chimera. Your jealousy baffled you. You see, I've followed your life very closely. And Martha – you still hide away from how much she means to you, how much you love her: don't you? You could only write it to Minna, as from someone else; you felt Martha wouldn't understand, wouldn't respond.'

A choking feeling enters my throat.

'In your engagement, in Paris – my God! – you wanted to breathe with her, eat with her, bleed with her, shit with her . . . But the genteel world said otherwise. I know how you felt – I felt it for your father. But alas . . . And you had a second chance, late in life, but . . . again the world intervened. That's to say, *you* intervened.'

Sobs start to rack me: as when Anna came back from the Gestapo, or as when Mama smacked me.

'Even Anna doesn't understand you, and never will.' More softly and gently she adds: 'But you tried. My God, how you tried to understand the soul! Nobody more so.'

She hurries away with downcast head, disappearing into the conifers. Exhausted, I sink down and rest my back against a tree trunk. I sleep; I dream. We dream because we need to escape. In my dream I am in a tea shop. It has a very solid English look, nothing at all like the cafés of Vienna. I am sitting at a small table with Anna and Kat. Kat was my name for her, though others knew her as H.D. She looks more gaunt, more hollow-cheeked than I know her. A third person joins us, apologising for being late. She is dressed in a severe mannish suit, her hair is cropped and sleeked back; I recognise Kat's lesbian friend, Bryher; though, like the other two, she looks older than she is in reality. Tall Kat, especially as she is wearing a high broadbrimmed hat, dwarfs Anna and Bryher.

I am the dumb, unnoticed onlooker. Anna's friend, Dorothy Burlingham, comes in – probably returning from the ladies' – and takes my chair.

The two lesbian friends (though Kat is bisexual) are praising me glowingly, making Anna look both proud and uncomfortable. They say I was so wonderfully kind, like an old-fashioned doctor who would come out in the middle of the night and in all weathers. But then, I was also a god-man, like so many of my mythological figurines. Kat, with a chuckle, says I hated being a mother to her in our analysis.

'But your father was so wonderful, Anna! I was crazy about him. We talked in *vers libre!*'

A shadow crossing her face, she says she's been unwell, has spent time in a Swiss clinic, because someone called Dowding, a retired Marshal of the Air Force, let her down badly. They had become close friends after she'd heard him lecture on his conversations with dead airmen. But when she'd contacted airmen too, and received warnings of nuclear horror, he'd broken off their friendship. That had brought on another breakdown; she'd wished I had been around to help her.

Anna simply nods, her head bent over her plate, her finger dabbing at crumbs. A man reads a newspaper at a near-by table. I see the front-page headline: SUEZ CRISIS ROCKS EDEN. Anna says she is frightened about the world; she has had a New Year card and note from Helene Deutsch's son Martin, who had been involved in the Manhattan Project. He is now guilt-ridden about it.

'How we need your father; yet it's extraordinary, how he lives on in you,' Kat says: drinking in Anna's face as avidly as a schoolcapped boy was drawing in a milkshake through a straw.

'He is in me,' Anna agrees, returning the gaze.

What strikes me about the dream is that I am being discussed very much in the past tense. It reminds me of my *non vixit* dream in the dream book. I am obviously dead in my dream yet still there. As I wrote in *Totem and Taboo*, 'It is impossible to imagine our own death; and whenever we try to do so we can perceive that we are still present as spectators. No one believes in his own death; in the unconscious every one of us is convinced of his own immortality.'

I interpret the praise of me as an expression of my wish to be spoken well of even in my absence, my death. Kat's praise is particularly welcome. For my shy, delightful American patient I felt tremors of absurd desire. The last, the sunset desire.

The death of loved ones strikes us down savagely. So primitive man created the idea of spirits. Kat suffered many deaths around the time of the war: a stillborn son, caused she believed by the shock of the *Lusitania*'s loss; a brother in the trenches; her father as a result of *that* shock. It wasn't surprising that she hallucinated, and came to believe in spirit survival.

I tried gently to steer her away from those fantasies; and our conflict is recorded in the dream. 'Dowding' is an anagram of wind-god; insubstantial Aeolus. It also suggests 'dowsing', a dubious 'supernatural' technique for finding water. The dead airmen are clearly angels. I wished for her to be disabused in a way that would leave her morale, her essential faith in life, intact. It was clear from her occasional smiles and laughs at the tea table that this has happened.

Doubtless her stay in a Swiss clinic has a glancing reference to the mystical Jung.

Anna dabbing at crumbs – I fear this is how she may regard life, when I am gone. This part of the dream depresses me. Dorothy will be some comfort; but as a 'nuclear' family, once Martha and Minna are no more, the two women may feel a certain horror of sterility.

– And I recall a forgotten fragment of the dream. Anna and I are in a taxi, presumably driving away from the tea meeting. I say to her that she and Kat betrayed a mutual attraction; both are with long-term partners, which inevitably leads to a slight sense of boredom. I would not blame her if she and the American poetess started a relationship.

Suddenly Anna has turned to face me, enraged. With tight

knuckles she starts to hit me repeatedly in my left eye, hissing, 'You bastard! You bastard! A child is being beaten! A child is being beaten! . . .'

Well, it is inevitable that underneath all the tenderness and love she hates me with a terrible hate.

But eating one's food down to the last crumb also brings back the dreadful hunger towards the end of the war. None of us has forgotten how we huddled in our greatcoats and mufflers at the table, and scraped our soup bowls clean. I tried to eat less than my due, since I was convinced that February of 1918 would see my death: it marked sixty-two years since my conception, and so according to Fliess's calculations it was the time for me to die. However, Martha's hawk eye saw to it I ate my full share of what little there was – and deprived herself. I spent the last day of February in a blank, phantasmal state, wondering at what moment the heart attack or stroke would arrive.

Yet I felt also a serenity, a resignation. Expectation of my death was like a glorious morning at Gastein compared with the reality of death when it did strike, two years later, and twice within a week. First my dear young friend and colleague von Freund ended his long agonised battle with cancer; then – the news of Sophie.

There are no words for that. If only, to use Kat's pun, my 'goods' were indeed 'gods', and I could believe.

And not long after Sophie – her son, our little Heinele. For a long time after I could take no joy in my other grandchildren. In fact I simply wished to die too. Life really is pretty unbearable. You love someone much more than you love yourself – then they are gone. For ever. I felt this when I said goodbye to – I think it's Oliver's daughter, Eva, a few weeks or months ago. She was being taken to France. I knew I'd never see her again. It was far worse than that dream in which I was forced to take out my guts, to analyse them on a laboratory slab.

Wounds. War wounds. One's body and psyche a mass of them, and still bleeding.

I step into our garden at 19 Berggasse, and come to a halt, seeing Martha, sitting, gazing up at the stars. She is wondering, in awe. Wondering what lies at the mysterious heart of it all; why we suffer so much. Dreaming of other lives that might have been possible; in which, God knows, she *might* have loved someone else more passionately.

Where is the root of it? If there are no gods, only goods, what was the original primal scene? And why?

Those questions are surely in the one unanalysed portion of this dream, the newspaper headline, SUEZ CRISIS ROCKS EDEN. There's Monika's Red Sea, faintly. But far more centrally it contains Zeus and Isis, the king and queen, though in different pantheons. At the very end, then, the miraculous conception of the firstborn son.

The bedroom in Freiberg is dark. Jacob (if it is he) shudders and is still; rolls off Amalie, panting. Her arm cradling his neck, she stares up at the ceiling. In the next room, the other side of the house's divide, Frau Zajíc is lightly snoring; her husband, who has listened to the faint sounds, sighs, makes the sign of the cross, and turns over to go to sleep. These damned Jews, he thinks, they're always at it. And this Jacob more than any. First that nice Rebecca – and then suddenly Amalie, half his age. It's not fair. Always fucking, fucking, fucking . . . While the dead woman's spirit wanders, sobbing, tearing her hair. Zajíc wouldn't be surprised to find it had been murder.

37

The musty, down-at-heel railway carriage is hot and airless. I have always hated airless railway carriages. I recall a journey in my youth when I opened a window and my travelling companions turned on me, saying Gentiles had consideration for other people, not like us filthy Jews. I stood up to their anti-semitic taunts, unlike my father. I wrote and told Martha all about it.

This time my fellow travellers, quiet, poorly dressed, do not demur as I open the window. I have to close it again as the filthy smoke from factories billows in, covering us with sooty flakes. We arrive at Leipzig. The hairs on my nape rise as I remember the gas lamps: these are the very same, I think. We stopped here during our year of wandering after leaving Freiberg. I thought the burning lamps were Hell. I must have been recalling some dire warning by Monika.

The train moves on slowly. In the heat and airlessness I doze off. The subsequent dream is mixed up with sudden, brief awakenings as my head lolls to one side, until I'm on the point of overbalancing. I'm trying to reach Hamburg. I would like to visit Sophie's grave. The journey should be straightforward, but at one nondescript station there is an interminable wait as military police roam the corridors checking people's papers. When they come to me, they go into a suspicious huddle. I am forced to leave the train and continue the interrogation in a hut. Eventually they decide I'm Austrian and let me back on the train.

The carriage is now empty, all of my former companions

having got off. A whistle blows and the train moves off again. At the next station a plump businessman gets on. I ask him what the problem was at the last station, explaining how I was closely interrogated. He regards me with an amused, amazed look. 'It was the border,' he says. 'You mean you didn't know Germany is divided?' He waves a plump ringed hand back the way I have come. 'Over there', he says, 'darkness; here – light!' He grins, his splendid white teeth flashing.

I can see in the last statement a memory of an atmospheric painting by Chagall, called *Between Darkness and Light*. It was in a book given to me by Salvador Dali, who visited us recently. As far as I can recall, Chagall's painting showed the faces of two lovers, pressed close together, inseparable. I have an impression of snow, eeriness, desolation.

This dream is so obviously death-haunted as to be almost banal. I became aware in early childhood that train journeys brought death and life close together. My mother's nakedness; the burning gas lamps of Hell. Yet in the dream, as in Chagall's picture, it was quite difficult to tell which was darkness and which light.

Yet even at this late stage I am still clinging to my identity. Austrian! And they let me back into the light – to be joined by a rather complacent fat German businessman. Both sides of the border seem equally stuffy and airless.

Of course it's I who am divided. A German, a Jew. Which is the darkness and which the light?

A man, a woman. A scientist, an artist. A puritan, a Casanova. An atheist, a believer – for who would try so fiercely to murder his Father without in some sense believing in Him, fearing Him?

Bear in mind these stress fractures, this duality of Berlin and Vienna, Aryan and Jew, nose and vagina, asceticism and passion, scalpel and quill, mind and soul, when Fliess's controversial love letters to Minna are published. If I hadn't written letters to myself at that time I'd have gone mad, strangled an infant in its cradle or thrown myself out of a speeding train.

*　　*　　*

I am joined, in my walk through the seemingly endless swampy woods, by a familiar figure, small, plump, spectacles flashing in the sun – my old enemy Adler. My initial repulsion is disarmed by realisation that Adler is dead, and that this must be a *dybbuk*. He confirms it, cheerfully enough, and proves an entertaining and pleasant companion for an hour or two. A distinct improvement on the original!

A chance remark of his brings back a forgotten fragment of the dream. I was in Israel, a land governed by Jews, but in the present day. It's a prison cell. I mean, the setting of the dream-fragment is a prison cell, not the state of Israel. (Though, unlike Martin and Ernst, I have always had doubts about a Zionist state, unless it were set up in a remote and uninhabited region of the earth.) A swarthy, muscular guard, in shorts and a short-sleeved shirt, a holster at his belt, enters the cell which is occupied by a pale, nondescript man. He sits at a table. He looks mild, yet somehow I know he has been accused of killing millions of Jews. His name is Eckermann or Eichmann.

There is a book on the table. I see its title, *Lolita*. The prisoner hands the book to the guard, saying, '*Das ist aber ein sehr unerfreuliches Buch.*' ('That is quite an offensive book.')

This fragment too seems to be about one's identity. As the prisoner, as a German, I the Ich-Mann have produced offensive books. 'Lolita' sounds like a frivolous extension of 'Dora' and 'Gradiva'. With *Moses and Monotheism* I have been accused of spiritually killing millions of my race. But the Jew here, the guard, seems unperturbed. Perhaps his tolerance proceeds from his very unJewish appearance. He is remote from the pallid, blinking, thick-spectacled 'ideal' of Jewish manhood, stooped over crumbling books in the prayer-house, as inimical to sunlight as a bat. Here the supposedly athletic Aryan is stooped and short-sighted, the Jew has reverted to the manly ideal of a David.

After Adler's *dybbuk* has left me I trudge on, lost in thought, lost in that shadowland where memories and fantasies blur. *Lolita* has the same pattern of vowels as my nursemaid and sexual teacher, Monika. I, the Ich-Mann, was the most sensitive and even feminine of us children, and therefore drew her to try to save my soul. She dandled me on her lap in church and, as the priest intoned the Latin phrases, quietened my restlessness by secretly stroking my little penis. She baptised me in her blood, and made me kiss, very crudely and clumsily, the most holy of places. It is thanks to her that I hovered for years just outside Rome, prevented from entering, prevented from shedding my obsession to enter.

With my nephew and playmate John she was rougher, more sexually voracious, which aroused my envy. Even at three, John was the manly Jew; it was he who did the lion's share that day we molested Pauline. I would love to know what happened to him when, at sixty-four, a prosperous businessman, he gave me the quiet satisfaction of disappearing from his Manchester home.

Monika, so caring for me, so certain I would achieve great things, may have persuaded my father not to subject me to his custom of getting his infants – Alexander and four of my sisters – to fellate him, thus causing their adult hysteria. (And with poor little Julius, much worse, causing him to choke to death.) Or perhaps my father could see for himself that I was more sensitive, and decided to spare me.

The 'offensive book' . . . The Philippson Bible . . . The Day of Judgement. Burning, burning, burning. The lights of the Leipzig station. Leipzig was where Uncle Abae lived. Of his four children only one was not insane. My parents talking about them in low, distressed tones as the train waited; father dabbing his eyes. Uncle Joseph in prison for counterfeiting: and would Emanuel and Philipp escape to England safely? Criminals and lunatics . . . and a psychoanalyst! The little Ich-Mann crying because beloved Monika was gone for ever, and so were Emanuel and Philipp, my fathers. The 'bird-beaked woman', my mother, lying in post-coital ecstasy with two, and possibly three, men.

All this in the stuffy, choking carriage, the flickering lights and darkness, my head compressed like a newborn babe's.

38

My return journey continues to be relatively uneventful. As so often, it is sleep that brings the most intense experiences. My dreams now are vivid and crowded, as though over me were that 'shadowy giant elm' in Vergil, where dreams 'beneath each leaf / Cling and are numberless.'

For instance: a group of young soldiers are sprawling by the side of a village track, smoking cigarettes or eating chocolate. It appears to be somewhere in the east: there are bamboo trees and paddy fields. Not far away from the peaceful soldiers are dismembered bodies of natives, some still twitching. A few of the young soldiers, hardly more than boys, get to their feet, stub out their cigarettes, and move to a little girl wearing a black pyjama jacket, with nothing on below the waist. She is being guarded by a soldier with a rifle; she shakes with fear. The men order her to lie down, spread her legs. One of the men begins intercourse with her, while a second puts his penis in her mouth. As they finish and button their trousers, others take their place. When all have finished, someone says, What do we do with her? Another says, Blow her away. But instead, a gun is placed against her ear and her head explodes into fragments.

They speak in English. I think their accents are American.

The atmosphere of this dream is puzzling. I remain convinced these soldiers are 'nice boys'; that what they are doing is a deserved (and rather unimportant) reward for a hard morning's soldiering. One of them is riding on the back of a water buffalo, quietly stabbing it with a bayonet.

I am accustomed by now to violent dreams. One should not expect tranquil visions at the end of one's life.

I discern a reference to repressed violent feelings against my sister Anna when I was studying for my examinations. She used to protest that too much fuss was made of me, that I was given preferential treatment in the family. Allowed to eat on my own while studying, and so on.

Without the thin veneer of culture and civilization we are all capable of raping and fellating and murdering without much thought. The exotic oriental setting is a defence: an attempt to distance it. But it is an impossibility. The horror of the scene with the young girl is vastly increased by one's awareness that it provides a perverse pleasure. I do not believe that even the most morally pure are exempt. The kindest, most generous woman I know, a French princess, has spent her life in fantasy about sexual murders; her imagination a torture chamber beyond anything in Poe, whom she reads constantly.

Just the same, I am as much the girl being ravished and killed as I am the soldiers enacting the barbarity. The unconscious is bisexual, and not limited in time or space. Mine certainly spills over into Anna's; when she nears the end of her life, she will grieve, I think, more for the final cessation of my life than of hers.

We are like two climbers roped together, like those English climbers who vanished, a year or two ago, while heading for the peak of Everest. She is dimly present even in this dream. The victim's black pyjama jacket reminds me of Anna's black silk blouse that she sometimes wears when representing me at Congresses. The fearful eyes remind me of Anna's when Martin, home on leave, showed her his bayonet. Martin too was a nice boy who inevitably became a killer. Only, with this girl, fear becomes shock then the glaze of death.

39

In another, there is no violence, but what appears to be an idyllic scene of untrammelled sexual delight. Perhaps because I have been thinking about my sisters in the bath-house, another bath-house provides the new setting. A bath-house, however, with no sinister overtones, but rather considerable comfort and luxury. Slim and muscular men rub oils into each others' flesh. Attendants flit round with warm towels. The single preoccupation of everyone here (and there must be hundreds) is sexual pleasure, expressed in homosexual acts. Everyone has everyone else, via fellatio and buggery. I see entire arms vanish into rectums.

I undress and join in. There is no individuality; faces are anonymous, often completely unseen. Erect organs are poked through holes in thin walls, to be immediately fastened on, so to speak, by mouths or anuses. Moans of pleasure echo through the marble halls.

In some ways this dream disturbs me more than the others. Here is a paradise without a serpent. It seems to be a comment on my belief that the sexual life should be infinitely free. Fittingly, given their democratic spirit, the setting is American. Through a window I can glimpse a bridge spanning the sea; it glitters and sparkles in a golden haze. I think of the 'Golden Gate', the popular term for the San Francisco bridge. It is a city I have never visited, nor wished to visit.

While I cannot deny the pleasure of this dream, which granted me a young man's arousal and potency, it left me, on my waking, with a mournful heart (as well as an erect penis):

as if I had exposed my most licentious fantasies in a newspaper interview. If sex cannot be in great part secret, hidden, furtive, it is devalued. Were I to have kissed my patients openly – or more – as Ferenczi made a practice of, I should have lost the great happiness of seeing muffs, fur hats and satin gloves turn into vulvas before my gaze.

The 'golden gate' to fulfilment is an illusion. The illusoriness and falsity are clearly indicated by the unusual sharpness, clarity, realism of the dream, in which – apart from the arms disappearing into rectums – nothing was actually impossible.

All the same, I have to confess with some shame, I masturbate. The object of my fantasy during this act shall remain private. Not everything needs to be spelt out in a memoir.

40

The train has just passed Zurich. There, a smartly dressed professional woman of middle years entered my compartment and immediately opened a briefcase to take out some papers and begin to work. But now, setting it aside, she addresses me: 'Excuse me: aren't you Anna Freud?'

Smiling, I shake my head. 'Her father.'

'How stupid of me! Of course! I'm so sorry.'

'It's all right. As one ages – there's less difference.'

She nods, gravely. 'You treated my mother – Fanny Moser. "Emmy von N."'

'Ah, you must be – her elder daughter? Also Fanny?'

'Yes. *Doctor* Fanny Moser.' I understood her stress on the title. Her mother, an admirable though severely hysterical woman, had not wanted her daughter to enter a stressful male occupation. 'You were very unfair on us girls,' she continues evenly. 'Mother hated me in particular, as you know: my father died just four days after I was born, and she always thought I was to blame. She tried to keep us in that stifling luxury my father bequeathed to us; and also resented that looking after us meant she couldn't have as many affairs as she wanted. She was *insatiable*, I hope you realise that now.'

I find myself flushing. 'I would have reacted differently now, Doctor Moser, that's true. I was very young when she came to me – my first patient, in fact. I could not believe sex played such an important part in life. In your mother's anyway – she was so moral, such a good, benevolent woman.'

'Christ!' blasphemes the doctor. 'At seventy she was still desperate for men!'

'I *may* have taken her side too much against you and your sister. How is your sister? What's happened to her?'

'Mentona's very well. She became a Communist and opened a home for abandoned children in Moscow. At present she's working in East Berlin.'

'And you?'

She gives an ironic smile. 'I followed you, in a curious way. I became a research zoologist; but increasingly the mind drew me. I had some amazing occult experiences, and so now I'm studying ghosts.'

'Ah! If I had my life over again I'd have devoted it to the paranormal.'

She nods, staring at me, through me. She has very bright blue eyes, unblinking.

I drowse; I dream. This might be called 'The Dream of the Gigantic Delicatessen'. Here is a store, stretching away almost endlessly, in which the shoppers are not served but help themselves to the goods. They mill up and down the long 'alleys' of merchandise, pushing huge wire trolleys which they are busy filling, tossing the goods in with careless abandon. There are many couples and single men among the normal women shoppers.

An impression of relentless, meaningless animal frenzy; a concentration on the displayed trivia which Goethe might have expended in writing *Faust*.

I catch sight of Anna, looking frayed, stooped; she carries only a wire basket. She chooses carefully, and there are few items in her basket.

As in the previous dream, though less overtly, mankind is sating its libido without reference to morals or other inhibitions (the absence of shop assistants). These people gorge their appetites indiscriminately. The confusion is increased by the casual attire of both males and females, who seem to blur into each other.

Anna alone deprives herself of that dubious plenty. Her self-discipline and her asceticism make her appear a sad and lonely figure.

Here is exhibited my wish that she should never join the herd. But at what cost to her?

There is another discomfort for me, which for a long time escapes my understanding. Then I realise I am looking at an exaggerated representation of all that I have consumed in my life; yet I have never once had to bother with how it reached the table. The men who are (absurdly) shopping with their wives, tossing washing-powders and fancy cakes into the bottomless trolleys, symbolise an uneasy conscience. Yet would I have discovered the secret of dreams and the unconscious, and earned the money to feed and keep my extended family, if Martha – instead of putting the toothpaste on my brush each morning – insisted I went out and bought my own paste?

But this in any case is not a major component of the dream. Would they like me not to have written so much but have helped Martha and the servants with the laundry? Could we tolerate losing *The Magic Flute*, consoled by the knowledge that Mozart peeled vegetables for Constance? Not that I am comparing myself to Mozart; I struck it lucky once in my life, and built on that with hard work.

Just the same, I have to confess these are excuses. It was much more enjoyable writing *Gradiva* and *Beyond the Pleasure Principle* than helping with the laundry. Martha had a better time instructing the maids than the maids in scrubbing and polishing. Life is unfair; but a common justice awaits us.

Interestingly, Anna's only 'extravagant' purchase, among bread, cheese, and the like is – *stwawbewies*.

A fragment just dredged up: near the strawberries is a meringue dessert which bears the name Pavlova.

I recollect Jones telling me of a ruined country-hotel liaison as a result of his eating Pavlova containing rancid cream.

A dream has a fantastic economy, hitting several targets with the one arrow. I am not fond of ballet, but my sister Mitzi did persuade me to take her to see Pavlova when the great ballerina visited Vienna. She danced with such marvellous naturalness that I recall admiration mixed with a touch of envy. I wondered if I could bring that same naturalness to my writings, and feared I could not.

There is also Pavlov here. According to an American professor who visited me a few years ago, Pavlov told him in Leningrad he owed most of his success in researching conditioned reflexes to my discoveries. I observed tartly to the American that Pavlov might have made this known several decades ago – for example, when he was awarded the Nobel Prize. Easy enough to win the Nobel if you're prepared to torture dogs.

In connection with both Russians then, I exhibited an unworthy vanity and envy.

It leads me to understand that I am jealous of so much spontaneous greed in action. I would like to have grabbed life as determinedly as these shoppers were doing. To hell with culture and civilisation! – Let's take all the delights on offer. Let's take Pavlova (I wished to, when I saw her dance). Let's take Lou Salomé, also from Petersburg. Let's take Yvette Guilbert, the delicious *chanteuse* I adored, starting from my Paris years. Let's take Anna, Sophie, Mathilde (I observed to Fliess, of my daughters, 'I have them all!'). Let's take everyone and everything. I should have been more like my easy-going, self-indulgent father. I burnt the midnight oil, studying, to become a worthy son for my mother. Like every Jewish mother she lived through her smart, educated son. She was the oppressive shadow throughout my life, coming to resemble more and more a teak-hard, sharp-nosed, Sicilian matriarch and *mafiosa*.

This dream is the very incarnation of the dreaming process. In our conscious life we have to ask for everything via the shop manager or assistant. How embarrassing it was to ask for condoms! Whereas in the unconscious we 'just throw everything into the vast trolley of the libido. The store offers delicacies from all over the world: from Italy, France, Russia, India, China, Japan . . . I wanted it all.

As if to stress that universal plenty, another fragment swims up. The woman ahead of Anna in a queue (one of several) to pay for the goods has a magazine on top of her mountainous trolley. It is called *Cosmopolitan*, with a bright cover of a beautiful girl. I read next to her smiling lips *Are you as happy as you should be?*, *How good is he at O-level?*, *Brighter Periods*, and *Everyone for Singles?*

Instead of this dream's cornucopia, I had my game of taroc at Leopold's on Saturday nights! Apart from that, everything was duty. Up at seven; patients from eight to one; dinner on the stroke of the hour; a constitutional to buy cigars; more patients from three until nine; supper, followed by a stroll with one of the family, or a short card game to entertain Minna; then reading, writing, editing, until one. A two-hour lecture at the University every Saturday; the visit to Mama every Sunday morning, followed by correspondence.

And at night – dreamwork!

No time for Venusberg.

But at least the genteel bookshops, antique shops and bakeries of Vienna had a delicious smell – which is noticeably absent from the superabundant delicatessen.

What I noticed too was – the 'shoppers' should have looked happy but their faces were sour. It's because, as I told Otto Bauer, people don't want happiness. Otto didn't listen to me; released by the Russians, he worked with that scum Adler's brother-in-law, my school-friend, becoming a leading socialist politician but ultimately a failure; endured a complex double life rather like that earlier socialist, Helene's Lieberman, and died a broken man last year after the *Anschluss*. While his sister, my 'Dora', survives, sipping champagne and playing bridge!

How some of us scurry around trying to make people happy!

Anna, content with bread, milk, cheese and *stwawbewies*, is a chip off the old block. She can write my memoir. She knows what's in my mind. The child is mother to the man.

Later the same night I am with Anna in an art gallery. We are looking at an oil painting of a nude young woman, her legs wide apart. 'This is one of Lucian's,' she says to me. 'It's his daughter. He paints all his daughters like this, his diverse and scattered daughters; as well as wives, girlfriends, transvestites, drag artists. I can't approve. It's as if he's trying childishly to overturn all your moral restraint.'

Lucian is Ernst's son. He's only seventeen, and a bit wild. I know he has artistic talent, like his father. I persuaded Ernst that art was too uncertain as a profession. Perhaps I feel guilty about that, and imagine his son as compensating. As for the subject matter, the sexual plenitude . . .

41

How strange it is that America is a recurrent theme in these death-dreams. In the next one (dreamt at an inn by the Rhine) I was back in Hampstead. Anna – an old and white-haired, frail Anna – was engaged in emotional conversation with a brash American professor. The professor, who was editing my correspondence with Fliess (an absurdity, since Marie Bonaparte, who purchased the letters from a dealer, would never let them out of her hands), was telling Anna in very forceful tones that the whole basis of psychoanalysis was faulty, and that I had been a betrayer of the truth. Anna was arguing and weeping.

My betrayal, according to the good professor, lay in my *pretending* to believe that my patients' accounts of childhood seduction were merely a screen for their own early fantasies. I was covering up, he said, the extent of family incest in Vienna – or indeed anywhere. I had distorted the truth, he asserted to Anna, fundamentally out of fear of causing offence. (As if the bourgeois Viennese, or people generally, were happier knowing they had wished to sleep with their mothers or fathers!)

The meeting ended stormily, with the professor being dismissed by Anna and threatening legal action.

I tried to comfort Anna, but she was inconsolable. He was destroying the Oedipus Complex, she said: destroying *me*. She could foresee a witch-hunt of fathers, with children being torn from their homes and subjected to painful intimate examination. 'Look how you used to dandle us girls on your lap, even when we were quite grown up; and we loved it. But of course', she added, drying her eyes, 'there are so few real families any more. So many broken homes, so many unmarried mothers . . .'

I wake in the dawn's murk and light a stumpy candle. I suppose it is not so surprising that one of my death-dreams should cast doubt on the whole fabric of my science. I can't hope everyone will be as generous as H.D. and Bryher. It will undoubtedly happen that people will want to sacrifice the patriarch. I must warn Anna to be ready for it. The attack, as in the dream, will probably come first from the American continent.

Anna feels betrayed by the American professor, whom she has trusted; and I am betrayed by my friend the princess. My life has been full of betrayals; in the end we can trust no one but the family.

Her final sad remark (a considerable exaggeration of what is undoubtedly a weakening of the family in these post-war decades) must simply reflect the break up of our own family, scattered and diminishing. Perhaps also a sensing that at times Anna herself might have wished, not for the trammels of marriage, but for the normal fulfilment of motherhood, even were it the result of a brief, meaningless liaison.

Or, cunningly, she may wish to persuade me to provide her with a living and breathing legacy.

42

Again America! This time it is on American soil. We're in a house – a whole gaggle of analysts. Everyone in dark suits or frocks. A funeral gathering. I become aware it is the funeral of my faithful disciple Helene Deutsch. Someone reads out very solemnly a telegram from my Anna, who starts by saying she would have been here but for the stroke that has made journeys impossible. There is a murmur of sympathy.

Someone refers to a 'great age': presumably referring to the dead woman. The figure of ninety-eight is mentioned.

There are hostile shouts from outside and we crowd to the windows. We observe people outside, women mostly, demonstrating. The placard I catch sight of bears the seemingly nonsensical words: LET'S HAVE SOME HERSTORY FOR A CHANGE.

Apart from my affectionate and respectful feelings for Frau Deutsch, I feel it is I who am just-dead in this dream. I who am being mourned, I who am being reviled. It is not so surprising, this identification with her. Her husband carried out the very first operation on my cancer. Helene came originally from Galicia, like my parents and half-brothers. One of her brothers seduced her in childhood: helping to set up masochistic fantasies. She dreamt that she had the organs of both sexes. (This is perhaps hinted at in the androgynous appearance of the demonstrators.) None of this is particularly alien to me. My background too is like a myth, which I have explored fictionally in my imagination – but the truth, as Rebecca intimated, is forever hidden.

The Deutsches anticipated our exile from Vienna by emigrating to Boston in 1936. Helene is in her fifties; the figure of 98 has a symbolic meaning: they add up to 17, which can be spelled out as the Hebrew word for good. As a boy I chose the number 17 in a lottery that was supposed to reveal my character; it concluded (on no evidence) that I possessed *Beständigkeit*: constancy, persistence, steadfastness, faithfulness. I made sure Martha and I got engaged on the 17th, and have always celebrated that date. I have had a fortunate life – as, in the main, has Helene Deutsch. That's not to say there wasn't a good deal of suffering. Her marriage was fairly sexless, her son didn't get on with her, she had miscarriages and love affairs. But she survived, soldiered on, was steadfast and true to herself.

Her first and only child bears my first son's name, Martin. I did not see her Martin in the dream – the only Martin there was a stooped, grey-haired man, speaking almost pure American, who was a nuclear physicist. But how Oedipal to have such an explosive son! Martin may not have been Felix Deutsch's offspring. Helene and Felix were mixed up in a triangle with an actor.

And if some wish to imagine I was indeed hiding her and Felix in my account of a wartime triangle, that she was the hidden, tormenting love of my life and I grieve still over her departure – so be it; dream away.

It's all there in her given name, Helene. '*The sea, and Helen – everything's moved by love . . .*' Ours is a cure through love. Health is the ability to work and to love.

So HER STORY, Helen's story, is HIS STORY.

Wait! I do recall a recent dream in which my Anna and Frau Deutsch were together. I had it in Paris, when excitement at revisiting old haunts quite drove it from my mind. I recall a farm, isolated amid full-leaved summery profusion. If I were not growing used to seeing familiar figures looking decrepit, and were not aware it's an effect of my own condition, I would have been shocked at both Anna and Helene. I recall just scraps of conversation . . . Helene: 'You must excuse me for not getting up from my chair . . .' Anna: 'I had no idea New England was so beautiful . . .' Helene: 'I've had good reports of your Harvard lecture; I hear it went down wonderfully well . . .' Helene again: 'No, I'm not sorry to be out of it; it's so pseudo-scientific now; not as in your father's day. It's all analysis and no psyche . . .'

Still-glinting, still-cunning eyes, peering out of a crone's wispy-haired face. She looked older than my mother at her death. I should have gone to Mama's funeral, it's inexcusable. Even Helen of Troy came to this. They wouldn't have sailed if she'd been old, and Troy would have become just an ordinary city, not set in imperishable lines. *Were it not for Helen, what would Troy be to you, O Achaeans? ...'*

43

In Paris, on this last journey, I was alone and lonely – just as I was over fifty years ago. How different from last year's arrival at the Gare de l'Est, when I was staggered to see crowds of well-wishers, journalists and photographers. A shy, attractive girl stepped forward on the platform, curtseyed, and presented me with a bouquet. If only she had stepped forward to greet the young, black-bearded, spring-footed Freud in 1885! Such miracles don't happen: that's the iron law.

I felt bewildered and unworthy at the reception. Life is farcical.

Then I tottered forward into the embrace of Ernst and the princess. We relaxed for a few hours on her sunny terrace, and she gave me Athene.

But now, my steps echo on the pavements of Paris. No one gives me a passing glance. This is better, more fitting. I find myself, to my surprise, in Pigalle.

Victor Tausk is my unexpected and unwelcome companion during the Channel crossing. I saw him hunched over a table, looking decidedly ill – the sea is rough today, and travellers keep to their seats or grip hold of rails as they attempt to walk. I thought I couldn't be mistaken about that moustached, rather handsomely arrogant face: looking no older, despite his nausea, than at his death in 1919, twenty years ago. His mouth opened in a gape of astonishment as he saw me heading towards him. He had heard I had moved to England, so was coming to try to find me.

I groaned inwardly. That insatiable craving he had for me to love him! But I let him pump my hand.

'How are you, Professor?' he asked.

'Dying; otherwise, fine.'

I looked for signs that this was another *dybbuk*. But no, Tausk died too long ago; it must be he.

I can't remember if I've mentioned Tausk. Brilliant fellow, up to a point. Threw up a legal career in Slovakia to come to Vienna and join my crew. And quickly made an important contribution; only I became irritated at the way he would seize hold of one of my ideas, sometimes even before I had quite got hold of it myself, and take it over. He was unstable, divorced, an absent father. A lover of Frau Lou: mainly to try to invade me through her.

I kept him off. He made another attempt just after the war. Said he wanted a training analysis and obviously expected me to take him. Instead I suggested Frau Deutsch, whose analysis I myself was conducting. Well, it didn't work out; she talked of nothing but Tausk when with me. I had to tell her either to stop coming or to give up Tausk. She gave up Tausk.

Wishing to kill me, he committed suicide, twice over. He still bears the small bullet hole in his temple, and the marks of the curtain cord round his neck.

I try to be pleasant to him on this short sea crossing; but one can't be pleasant with some fellows. He very soon picks a quarrel . . . 'Why did you instruct Frau Deutsch to give me up?'

Belligerent tone; his eyes bulging, devouring me.

'I didn't instruct her; I gave her a choice; the arrangement wasn't working. She talked only of you; it was wrecking her analysis; she had a weakness for womanisers.'

'Hah!' He laughs contemptuously. 'Womaniser! You can say that! You, with that grip of your patients' hand, before and after the session! More than one woman who'd experienced it said you were a psychic Don Juan. They felt your grip was like the clasp of the Stone Commander.'

I ignore his coarse simile, merely remarking: 'And from

221

what *she* said, you could only talk about *me*, since you knew there was a direct contact.'

'I *had* to talk about you – I could see you were all she thought about.'

'In that case, you're agreeing with me: it wasn't working, Victor.'

'*You* should have taken me. She was just a greenhorn.'

'But loyal. She didn't try to destroy me by taking her life.'

He is silent; his eyes as watery as the broad grey windows on which the spray dashes. I take pity on him; after all, we shall not meet again. I rest my hand on his. I can feel him, unlike my attempt to embrace Signorelli. I wonder if it means that ghosts may take centuries to become insubstantial.

'Perhaps you are right, Victor; perhaps I should have taken you instead of her. She bored me often, with her talk about babies' napkins and weaning. A couple of times I actually nodded off; my cigar fell to the floor.'

'Really?' A wan smile flickers.

'Yes! It was most embarrassing.'

'It's not quite so rough; would you care to go up on deck?'

We stand, make a grab for a rail, and pull ourselves up to face the blast. Tausk is right; the sea is merely choppy now and visibility has increased. We lean on the deck rail, breathing in the salty spume. It brings back to me the voyage to America: leaning on the rail with Jung and Ferenczi each side of me. We analysed each other's dreams. And then had that extraordinary séance. I haven't told you about that. I fear it's too late. Ah, well.

'I dreamt about Frau Deutsch last night,' I shout against the blast. 'I dreamt she had died.'

He nods; but I don't think he's heard me. I worry about Anna. A stroke. Why should I dream that?

He points. 'The white cliffs!' I look, and there they are, in a sudden patch of blue, the cliffs of Dover.

'Well, I forgive you,' he says, with a sigh that turns to a cough.

'Yet how many in your circle took their life! Federn, Silberer, Weininger, Stekel, Karin Stephen, Eugenia Sokolnicka, Tatiana Rosenthal, Schrötter, Meyer, Peck, Kahane, Honegger, Frau Kremzer, Weiss, Mausi your niece, myself, possibly Emanuel, possibly John . . .'

I smile grimly. 'Yes, but I survived all the assassination attempts.'

There is little more to say about my brief encounter with Tausk. I made it quite clear to him he would not be welcome to come to London with me. He was working, he told me, on the theme of the sadness of the Shekhinah. The Shekhinah is sad, in his view, because she strives to give life to as many creatures as possible; to give life 'more abundantly', in the Christian phrase. Yet even if she gives it to an infinity of beings, there is still an infinite number, potentially, deprived of it. He describes it as a logical extension of his early work on schizophrenia.

He was always an original thinker; but unfortunately of weak character. He loved too easily and it made him cruel. Distrust men with blond hair and blue eyes.

44

Doctor Tod has a formidable presence. She lives in a rambling Victorian house called The Three Caskets on the very edge of the white cliffs. She has a reputation for sorting people out. Anna thought I should see her: hoping, no doubt, that a lengthy analysis might arouse my interest and so postpone death.

I lie on her purple couch; she sits behind me. Far from allowing me to associate freely, she plunges in . . .

'Where were you before you were born?'

'I don't know.'

'Who were your parents?'

'I'm not sure.'

'Who is your wife?'

'I'm not sure about that either.'

'Well, Professor, your daughter sent me your unfinished memoir. I've read it with interest. It's full of lies and other defences, of course, but that's common, as you would know; and they can teach us more than the truths can. I would say you are a seething mass of irrationality; all your life you have been a prey to demons. As a result, you have tried to make your life appear orderly and rational, and you fooled everyone. Secretly however, unknown even to yourself, you wanted everyone to be drunk on sex and poetry and fabulous internal drama. Every man an Oedipus, and every woman an Elektra. Tormented by otherness, you want carnal knowledge of everyone in the world, everyone who has ever lived, in fact. But it's impossible, even for you.

'I liked your idea', she continues after a long pause, 'of life being a paraphrase of a few important dreams. Only it didn't go far enough. A whole century of history is just a fragment of a dream in the mind of the Shekhinah. I hope I've been helpful. That will be twenty guineas.'

I stammer – I was prone to it in childhood: 'Is that it?'

'Yes. I'm not a believer in long analysis. Goodbye.'

45

Envy!

I slap my forehead, appalled I didn't see it earlier. Not a stroke; Helene Deutsch always envied Anna; my daughter, sensitive to that, would not steal the limelight at her funeral. Of course!

This thought occurs in the train, crawling through the quiet hop-fields of Kent.

Another thought occurs to me: since I am experiencing the death-trauma at the start of a war, it is natural my mind should have run so much on my life-trauma in a previous war.

Or imagined it – if you prefer. Good Martha and evil Bauer wrestling for my soul.

My heart quickens in the final taxi ride. It will be good to see her again.

Anna embraces me and is happy. Commiserates with my blackened eye, which I attribute to a fall. She bathes it gently. Tired and weak, I am glad to have her put me to bed. When I am tucked up, and she has sponged my brow, she asks: 'And did you find your parents?'

'No. Well, I found my father; but stupidly I'd forgotten my mother wouldn't be there.'

She frowns. 'Not there? In Freiberg?'

'I went to Tysmenice.'

'Stupid!' She smiles indulgently.

Her image in my dreams is so strong still, I feel relieved to see her comparatively young again; though still she looks strained and tired. 'How have things been here?' I ask.

'All right. We missed you.'

'I missed you too. Of course. My trip wasn't completely wasted. My dream analysis continued. I'd like you to take it down.'

'I will.'

'My absence was a rehearsal for you, Anna,' I murmur. 'It can't be much longer.'

She flinches as if I've struck her. 'Well, yes, my unconscious has been preparing me. I've dreamt a lot too. About you. At first you seemed to be lost on a mountain-top, but of course it was I who was lost. In the very first dream I heard you say, "I've always longed for you so."'

'I have. I have.'

'I know that. And you've had me. Whenever I'm cast down, by any particular human folly or cruelty, I know you'll be with me; I'll hear your wise, true, consoling words.'

'I don't feel at all wise, Anna.'

She lies beside me in silence for a few minutes. She asks if I am in much pain.

'Not much.'

'Pur can come and give you an injection, if you like.'

'No. A clear head is best.' I take her hand. 'So here we are again! Anna-Antigone, Anna-Cordelia, Anna-Athene!'

'Always. For ever, Papa.'

'Anna-Gradiva.' Always the magical, gliding woman. Woman the dark continent – but how unforgettable, how matchless, her deep jungles, her sudden rushing waterfalls!

'I've been thinking about your fictional war diaries,' she murmurs. 'At first I didn't believe they were fiction, and you knew I didn't believe it. But now I know what you were doing.' She gazes at me with steady, shining eyes. 'You made them up – I imagine later, probably in Rome – certain I would read them one day, and would no longer idealise you so strongly and could be free to live my own life.'

'You've guessed it, Anna.'

'It was a wonderful thing to do, Papa – to pretend to be all-too-human: weak, manipulative, childish.'

She is running her hand up and down my bare arm.

'Oh, of course,' she adds, 'Mama and you did act kind of crazy when my brothers went off to fight.'

'Crazy? Then why – '

'– Why didn't you kiss the hot stove!' We chuckle and hug each other. 'But really, dearest, do you think Athene would have preferred to find out her real father was not Zeus but an Athenian street-cleaner?'

I have a choking coughing-fit and she says, 'Rest, Papa. Sleep . . .'

This time, a very short dream. In a place called Oregon, a man is tried in a court for raping his own wife.

When I wake, in Anna's work-room, she is not there. I lie, expecting her imminent return, and reflecting on the dream-fragment. A man cannot, by definition, rape his wife, since they are one flesh. Presumably if a wife has an ingrained and non-neurotic distaste for her husband's embraces she will take steps to become separated or divorced from him. If rape were possible within marriage, the state of matrimony would become meaningless. But one can just imagine a society in which sacraments had so yielded to 'rights' that such a law might be introduced. I should logically welcome it, yet it fills me with horror.

The early Christian theologian Origen, suggested by the name of an American state, wished to suppress his sexuality and therefore took the logical step of self-castration.

The dream is telling me that logic, reason, can be dangerous. But that is illogical. I am forced, therefore, to conclude that the dream belongs to that rare category of truly 'absurd' dreams, dreams without meaning.

My book of dreams contains a few examples.

I look down at the garden. Leaves are piled on the lawn. I have lingered too long.

Anna does not return. The light begins to fade. Eventually I go to her desk; I see a letter she has been writing in a quavery hand. It is to Sophie. It might be to the Sunday-child, her sister,

228

or a niece in America. I note that she has misdated the year as my age on departure from Vienna ('82); as though with this her clock stopped.

'My dear Sophie,' I read: 'Thank you so much for the beautiful silk knitting wools. Unfortunately I am not knitting these days. I have been in a depressed state. *Sehr schlecht.* Thoughts of the old times obsess me. I am distressed, among so many other things, to learn of the fate of Sabina Spielrein. I did not know her well, but met her a few times when father was attempting to rectify the damage done to her by Jung. I liked her. Father succeeded so well that she became, as I'm sure you know, a strikingly original analyst. All these years since her return to her native country she disappeared from view, apart from one or two letters to father. But now, at long last, we know what happened. We suspected her brothers had been killed in the Stalinist Terror, and that's been confirmed. But the horror doesn't end there – we learn that, during the Nazi occupation, she and her daughters, with hundreds of other Jews, were herded into a synagogue and then engulfed in flames.

'I think of so much wisdom and love, absorbed partly from my father (and Jung too in his dissolute, treacherous way), destroyed by evil, and I can't bear it. I need my father's stoical understanding of what Man can do.

'May she and her relatives rest in peace. Her daughters did not pass up such a wonderful bargain: even had they been able eventually to emigrate from their tragic homeland. I am sickened, as you must be, by what's occurred in Beirut. What a betrayal of Jewish dreams. And the West commits spiritual genocide; we may no longer have the Nazis, but there are other ways of killing the soul. For instance, with technology, economics and crude sociology (not your kind, that serves as an extension to psychoanalysis): all that we seem capable of worshipping. Much better the *honest* shit that Sabina was sexually preoccupied with.

'The children I have tried to help have been increasingly illiterate. They know they must not be caned by a schoolteacher, but nothing about their far more important right to be given the best of what has been thought and written. Everything that I value, all that dense culture I learned with my mother's milk (not that she breastfed me), or rather from my father, seems to have vanished. No one reads any more; not seriously, hungering for the riches passed down to us. The young are growing up with no knowledge of the Classics, none of the Authorised Version of the Bible; with the result that their imaginations will be forever impoverished. It cannot be made good. *Wer jetzt kein Haus hat, baut sich keines mehr . . .* "Who has no house now, long will so remain . . ." (Rilke).

'And yet the world thinks it is *freeing* its children from its dark places, its forests of illusion.

'I've become a *laudator temporis acti*, a sure sign it is time to go. Thank you again for your kindness. I still think of your visit. I am rather lonely.

Anna'

I walk slowly downstairs, but find no one in the living rooms. No Martha, no Minna, no Pauli. The house, though spotlessly clean, has a desolate, empty air. I shiver: the autumn, so fine earlier, has grown cold. I open the door to my study. I see Anna asleep, hunched over, curled up, in my chair. The sight of her shocks me; she has wrapped herself in my old woollen coat; she looks shrunken inside it: at once like a small schoolgirl and like the white-haired, frail old lady I have seen in the Dreamtime.

Tired after my exertion, I stretch out on the couch. When she wakes up I will ask her to talk me through some of my recent violent, sexual dreams. She will not be shocked; she has often enough heard people with the smell of festering lilies describe her Papa as disgusting.

As I gaze around at Buddha and vestal virgin, Isis and Gradiva, I am struck by the room's unusual cleanliness and order. It holds, suddenly, the chill of a museum.

Or of a pharaoh's tomb. And – if Anna is right, if her letter is not just a gloomy reaction to my approaching death – the tomb-robbers have already done their work.

I sit by Anna. I will tell her that fairy tale of our love. I describe for her that day in the mountains, one of so many. The sudden blaze of gentians. A cloud's shadow stealing across a green valley. The joyous sense of freedom; Anna laughing like the winged Victory, her hair tossed, her apron-skirt blown back, pressed against her thighs; one's leg muscles aching, the air like pure oxygen . . .

I stop; she is asleep still and can't hear me. Sadness for her overwhelms me. In her exhaustion from taking care of me she grants me a vision of how she will look in her last hours. Who will be left to mourn for Anna-Psyche herself when she descends into the shades?

A NOTE ON THE AUTHOR

D.M. Thomas is the author of many novels including *The White Hotel*, *Ararat*, *Flying in to Love* and most recently *Pictures at an Exhibition*. His selected poems, *The Puberty Tree*, were published in 1992.